Move Over, Scopes *and Other Writings*

JULIAN SILVA

Move Over, Scopes *and* Other Writings

TAGUS PRESS
UMass Dartmouth
2011

PORTUGUESE IN THE AMERICAS SERIES 15
CENTER FOR PORTUGUESE STUDIES AND CULTURE

General Editor: Frank F. Sousa
Editorial Manager: Gina M. Reis
Manuscript Editor: Richard J. Larschan
Copyeditor: Richard J. Larschan
Typesetter: Inês Sena

Distributed by University Press of New England
www.upne.com

For inquiries regarding the series, please contact:
University of Massachusetts Dartmouth
Center for Portuguese Studies and Culture
285 Old Westport Road
North Dartmouth, MA 02747-2300
Tel. 508-999-8255
Fax: 508-999-9272
Email: fsousa@umassd.edu
www.portstudies.umassd.edu

Library of Congress Cataloging-in-Publication Data
Silva, Julian, 1927–
Move over, Scopes and other writings / Julian Silva.
    p. cm.—(Portuguese in the Americas series; 15)
ISBN 978-1-933227-33-7 (alk. paper)
I. Title.
PS3569.I459M68 2011
813'.54—dc22
                                    2011009623

In Memory of
Thomas Sheldon

CONTENTS

Acknowledgments

Two men have earned my undying gratitude: Alex Blackburn, who as editor of the University of Colorado's *Writers' Forum* was responsible for publishing the majority of these stories and Frank Sousa, who has chosen to give them a second chance at life. *Brave Cossacks* first appeared in *Writers' Forum 7*, 1981; *A Man of Taste* first appeared under a different title in *Writers' Forum 10*, 1984; *Kimi* first appeared in the *San Francisco Chronicle*, March 3, 1985; *A Candle in the Wind*, first appeared in *Writers' Forum 13*, 1987; *My Jo* first appeared in *Kansas Quarterly*, vol. 23, 1992; *A Visit to Haworth* first appeared in *Writers' Forum 20*, 1994; *Coming to Terms with the Facts of Animal Life* and *The Woman in the Doorway* were originally published online by RTP.

MOVE OVER, SCOPES
a political memoir

CHAPTER ONE

OF GOD, THE APES AND GENESIS

At their first meeting Arab Ramos and Estelle Dobson were cast in the role of adversaries. Principles as well as personalities were involved, and in matters of principle, at least, neither was willing to compromise.

Prematurely gray at thirty-seven, Miss Dobson wore at all times that look of harried desperation peculiar to teachers about to initiate yet another onslaught against the forces of apathy. So dedicated to her profession was she that anyone who had been her student remained her student for life. Many were the clerks in Hayward—where she did her major shopping yearly, purchased her sturdily practical tweed skirts and her sensible, flat-heeled walking shoes, as well as San Oriel, where she purchased most of her perishables—who viewed her visits with far more trepidation than affection. Sweating under the discomfort of her withering scrutiny, the poor victim of her well-intentioned patronage would attempt to add up her account only to discover his memory of the multiplication tables gone suddenly and inexplicably blank. With foot-stomping impatience she would note the telltale drum of fingers on the countertop with a smile too resigned to imperfection to be malicious. Then unable to let the miserable creature find his own way out of the predicament, she must prod him with her guidance. "Never were much good at math, were you, Albert. Five," she would add, with her finger tapping the appropriate square of the invoice. "Then carry the three. There. And now ten percent off for cash. You do remember how to find percentage, I trust, after all the pains I was to drill that into your head. But," she would add with clinical objectivity as her keen eye remained fixed on the point of lead unsteadily tracing the disputed numbers, "always too keen you were to make poor Mary Silviera's life a torment to pay much attention to anything I had to say."

And poor Albert, already the father of a two-year-old son by that same Mary and the proprietor of the family haberdashery, would blush like the tongue-tied ten-year-old idiot she always made him feel as she guided him to the final reckoning. Then, with some sharply personal observation—"Still haven't learned to brush your nails when you wash your hands, I see"—she would strip away the few remaining shreds of his manhood before bestowing upon him her final blessing: "Always nice to see you, Albert. Remember me to Mary." And with one last, devastatingly unsentimental, tax-appraiser's scrutiny of his features, she would move on to the Five-and-Dime, where young Winona Pimental innocently waited behind the ribbon counter blissfully unaware that she too was about to be subjected to her periodical tutorial.

For whenever possible, Miss Dobson went out of her way, and sometimes far out of her way, to patronize her former charges. It was as close as she ever allowed herself to come to a sense of family. For these former students were in a way very much her children, and if she could not give them her affection, she could nevertheless be unstinting in her loyalty. Albert's failure to master mathematics or Winona's penchant for cheaply flashy makeup were simply the crosses any would-be mother must learn to accept with forbearance and hardly cause to take her business elsewhere, where the men might be more competent or the women more sedate.

It is spirit that makes a school, she was fond of saying, and, she was quick to add, that same spirit also makes the teacher. She was, therefore, by her own standards, a success; for if she had any virtue, spirit was it. Her energy was indefatigable, her loyalty unquestioned. And for those few who could ever get beyond the manner to the woman herself, she was not, in truth, unhandsome. Though she herself seemed determined to do everything in her power to disguise the fact, hiding her splendidly athletic body under the horse-blanket coarseness of her customary costume and neutralizing the sculptural features of her face by the fierceness of her gaze or the severity of her bob.

She prided herself on not having once failed to meet her classes in her thirteen years of teaching. So resolute was her dedication, she had even been known to carry on undaunted by a temperature of 102 rather than entrust her carefully disciplined charges to the disintegrating influence of some weak-willed substitute. If after every blow she was quickly back on her feet, it was not so much a matter of resilience as of her imperviousness to assault. She might occasionally be thrown off balance, but so unshakable were her own principles, so sterling her credentials, she had never yet been effectively challenged where it truly mattered. No one had ever before come close to threatening her integrity.

The pugilistic image is apt, for she thought of her role in terms of struggle and conflict. She saw herself as a warrior in the army of education whose commanding general was John Dewey. Already the veteran of numerous battles, but few defeats, she bore her scars proudly, her severe bob held down by a jaunty military beret festooned, like a French sailor's, with a red pom-pom. Nor was she insensible to the irony of her situation. That her brightest pupil should be her greatest problem was a matter of no small concern to her. That he had denied her his affection, she was quite prepared to accept. She was interested in minds, not hearts, and willingly sacrificed affection to respect. The latter, however, was essential. Yet perversely, he seemed every bit as determined to deny her that respect as she was determined to have it. And any goal she set her sight upon was virtually as good as won.

Here, at any rate, was a challenge she could meet with relish. To see this boy with such potential already snared by a trap of discredited medieval dogma stirred every last ember of the missionary fire that had been so decisive in the choice of her profession. Yet every one of her efforts to woo him to her side—which was simply to say, the side of enlightenment—seemed from the first doomed to failure.

*

Their very first clash some four years earlier was a political one. Not, where issues were crucial, given to the blatant hypocrisy of good manners, Arab Ramos (*né* Vasco) bore his heart upon his sleeve with all the flare of a falconer exhibiting his prize hunter. His features were symmetrical and, except for the eyes, conventionally pretty. The face, like his mother's, was an almost perfect oval; the lips were thin and perhaps too vividly red; the ears, larger than ideal, were nevertheless where they should be, close to the skull; and the nose was pertly tipped. But with their hooded lids buried under oriental folds, the eyes were anything but conventional. Compellingly intense, they burned with a fanatic's fire. Right was right, they said, and wrong was wrong. Nor did their dark and impenetrable depths allow for a hair's-breadth of compromise. And his chestnut hair was very fine. If his arrogance was sometimes

3

overweening, it was also the product of principles so touchingly virginal they had never been sullied by so much as a smudge of doubt.

His first day of school as a member of Miss Humphrey's kindergarten class took place shortly after Roosevelt's nomination but before the election that was to make him, for most of the nation's youth, a cross between Judge Hardy, that endearing image of wise and tolerant fatherhood, and Jehovah Himself, who made of the radio loudspeaker a burning bush, whose words seemed every bit as intimidating or reassuring as the times required. And the times had never more desperately required a leader. The Depression hung over the town like a perpetual cloud cover blocking one and all (with a few rare exceptions, his Grandfather Woods among them) from the sunshine of prosperity. For most it was the single great fact of life: the catch-all, blame-all phenomenon, the not-to-be-questioned cause of every deprivation, of every meatless meal, of every forfeited vacation, of every unpurchased outfit, as well as of every light bulb left unscrewed in the ceiling fixture, and no one living at the time was ever for an instant allowed to forget it. One's very cradle was rocked by the word "Depression."

To the five-year-old Arab Ramos, Roosevelt's appearance on the horizon had all the force of a Second Coming, the Redeemer returned to right all wrongs and transform every poor frog into a prince. The conflict between the two unequal giants was as simple and as clear-cut as the War between the Angels—with the hapless Hoover cast in the role of a pathetically blemished Lucifer. The election was, therefore, more than merely a question of politics; it was a question of Faith. Thus, the loud raspberries slobbered between chants of "Hoover, Hoover," which so offended Miss Dobson, who had been unfortunate enough to draw yard duty that recess, were—viewed from his own perspective, and no five year old recognizes any other—as almost a sacred ritual, a form of prayer.

Herself a woman of no firm political allegiance—she voted for the man, not the party, she was wont to say—Miss Dobson did not see the muddled political situation with quite the same clarity, and she found Arab Ramos's commentary upon the present incumbent of the White House as tasteless as it was passionate. The office, if not the man, demanded the respect of everyone who pretended to call himself an American. More so than ever in times of crisis. And these were indeed times of crisis.

Nor was the child's age an extenuating factor. She did not recognize any such distinction. If poor Albert, the haberdasher, was still treated like a ten year old, it was simply because she treated everyone, without exception, with the same unblinking honesty, with the same witheringly impartial recognition, of "facts," which had always to be "faced." If imperfections were ignored, even for the sake of politeness, they were only apt to grow, until, like some voracious cancer, they consumed the entire person. Children were merely people of a smaller growth. Their respect could be won, their characters formed, only by treating them as such, with the same unblinkingly objective appraisal of their shortcomings as well as their virtues. If one treated them like children and allowed them to behave as children then they would surely remain children. And the world's standards were, happily for the world, adult.

5

The force with which she grabbed the young boy's arm and dragged him unceremoniously back to Miss Humphrey's room had caused him in transit to drop the graham cracker for which he had paid a penny of the milk money securely tied in one corner of his handkerchief; and money, as even Miss Dobson must acknowledge, did not grow on trees—thanks partially to that very Hoover whose honor she seemed so indignantly called upon to defend.

*

Miss Humphrey was, happily, the most motherly of maidens, with oversized features, a large mouth filled with what seemed far too many teeth, and great soft breasts capable of cushioning any hurt and smothering all tears. She was also—besides being a registered Democrat—gifted with a sense of humor. With her aid the conflict was somehow brought to a peaceable conclusion without too great a sacrifice of principle by either contender, and the still irate Miss Dobson satisfied herself with a final snorting toss of her head and a defiantly self-righteous retreat.

From such small beginnings mighty animosities grow. Yet even this incident might have been forgotten had not Miss Dobson later compounded the insult by precipitately pulling Arab out of his assembly seat and sending him to the principal's office to apologize for what she considered an unnaturally loud hiccup far too well timed to be accidental, coming as it did during the principal's talk on sanity and respect during times of trouble. Since a hiccup was clearly a physiological phenomenon beyond human control, Arab felt, for justice's sake, compelled to withhold the demanded apology, and for the additional offense of obstinacy he was forced to sit the entire afternoon on a hard-back chair outside Mr. Larsen's office. No amount of cajoling by Miss Putnam, the secretary, or even by the principal himself could tempt him to bow to Miss Dobson's will. Right, he knew, was right. And he had the stuff of martyrs in him.

Thus a habit of enmity was established long before he found himself a reluctant—and having skipped the second half of the third grade, a premature—member of Miss Dobson's fourth-grade class.

*

There was nothing soft about Miss Dobson, nothing the least bit maternal. Her students did not hurl themselves into her open arms nor cling lovingly to her sturdy thighs. Nor did they wash ample breasts with their tears. She did not believe in utilizing the classroom as a substitute for a nonexistent nursery and teachers who did so—Miss Humphrey take note—she considered a very real blight upon the profession. She liked to think of herself as a thoroughly modern woman and above all such unwholesome nonsense. She longed to be a molder of minds, not a substitute mother for the emotionally starved, and in that respect she was far from frustrated.

While still a very young girl she had marched alongside her suffragette mother for women's right to vote and was just as ready today to devote her not inconsiderable energies to any cause, popular or unpopular, worthy of her support. There was at first glance, perhaps, a superficial inconsistency in her choice of sides. She had, for example, from the first championed the "positive poetry" of Darwin, but on the other hand she considered Freud a charlatan and, she feared, not a very nice man—which was just about as severe a criticism as she was apt to level against the opposite sex. Men who were not "nice" did unspeakable things it was best not even to think about, to innocent women they duped into the slavery of marriage. Or worse. Though she ranked Susan B. Anthony alongside Abraham Lincoln and George Washington in her private pantheon of national heroes and considered women rather superior than equal to men, at least where moral strength was called for, she would have gone to the stake rather than be caught in public wearing trousers, by whatever name one chose to call them.

Although she considered any politician who had opposed votes for women as deluded at the very least, when not positively venal, she had an otherwise touching trust in governmental institutions (what she venerated as The Law of the Land) and those who ran those institutions. Thus she had refused to join some of her more militant sister-marchers in opposing the executions of Sacco and Vanzetti, perfectly secure in her conviction that the courts and the law in league were so constituted as to protect the rights of the Little Man, and these particular little men, who had been properly convicted by a properly constituted jury of their peers, must therefore be properly guilty. Talk to the contrary she considered positively seditious. Thus she had at one time or another won both the admiration and the scorn of liberals and conservatives alike.

After thirteen years in the classroom, she was still a taut string vibrating to the music of the spheres. Like her young adversary, she also burned with the zeal of an early Christian, a Saint Paul among the heathen Gentiles. San Oriel was backward because its educational methods were backward. From the first she had been determined to change all that. She who responded to the poetry of the twentieth century—which was to say, the poetry of science, of new and ever-wider horizons—would open eyes to new vistas, ears to new rhythms, to the sounds and wonders of those truly enchanted isles, the Galapagos. With all the impatience of the idealist, she had leapt alone and armed only with the untested mettle of her mind and will to destroy single-handedly the dragon Ignorance.

With more fervor than discretion she had begun in her first year with a revision of the Social Studies hour. Begin at the beginning, she believed, for teaching was as much a matter of *un*teaching the positive errors of her less enlightened colleagues, of first sweeping the mind clean of all its false trappings and meretricious ornament, of preparing the field, as it were, as of planting the seeds of new truths.

Her voice trembling with reverberations of primordial thunder, she must first call into existence the pristine world in which all of Darwin's marvelous species originated. A cataclysmic explosion in the heavens and a spinning ball of fire, which, cooling, sprang to sudden life. Blue seas and green fields. Nowhere was there a mention of ancient mythologies, of an anthropomorphic, father-figure deity or the seven days. There was, she had never doubted, far more poetry in truth than in fiction. And her eyes watered at the beauty of beginnings.

For years the lesson had surprisingly gone unchallenged by any opposition more effective than indifference. That was until a young Benjamin appeared among them, and like Moliere's *Bourgeois Gentilhomme* surprised into the knowledge that he had, all his life been speaking prose, the townspeople, to their dismay, discovered that they had, all these years, without knowing it, been inadvertent Darwinians and therefore carriers of the deadly germ of Evolution.

Fired himself by the sweet voice of Sister Margherite, the itinerant nun from St. Elizabeth's in Fruitvale who conducted the Saturday catechism classes, Arab Ramos just as single-handedly set out to see that God was given His due. Not only did he not listen to Miss Dobson's heretical tirade, he made certain everyone *knew* he was not listening. Lounging with theatrical disdain, he hummed throughout the entire reading as his eyes scrutinized the starkly sinister spire of the Protestant church across the street. It was there his teacher took part in her evil rites, plotted with the Masons to murder the Pope and steal the Sacred Host. And before he himself was conscious of the metamorphosis, he was making his intrepid way across the Protestant barricades with dauntless courage, a small boy on a man's mission, to retrieve the purloined host. Somehow he must rescue it without touching it—an act forbidden to all but consecrated hands—and bearing it heroically back in splendid, crowd-cheering triumph, once again return it to the safety of the tabernacle. And the heavens themselves exploded in a confectioner's dream of candied angels cavorting in clouds of buttercream icing.

Not herself privy to these thrilling exploits, Miss Dobson found in the stubborn set of the thin, humming lips a challenge she could not ignore. With a look of scorn constituted to weaken the strongest of bladders and dilate the tear ducts of the most case-hardened of recalcitrants, she interrupted her reading, placing her hand over the open page of her book with all the authority of a judge about to pass sentence and calling upon God and the courtroom to bear witness to her impartiality.

"Do my ears deceive me, Master Ramos, or do I actually hear what I seem to be hearing?" The instant a student became "Master" he knew whatever offense he was about to be charged with was a capital one. "Be so kind, please, as to tell us all what it is you think you're up to?"

"Not listening," he responded, keeping a tight rein on both his bladder and his tear ducts, and obviously lusting after the martyr's palm.

"And just exactly *why* are you so noisily not listening?"

"Because it's not true," he shot back, for the first time fixing her with eyes so fierce with anathemas they were far too hot for tears, though he could not quell the throbbing in his throat.

"Not true! *Well!*" Her snort was wet with disdain as she surveyed her other charges, letting her glance wash over the class with all the subtlety of a tsunami. Surely they must all be equally astounded by their classmate's audacity, yet their solemn faces revealed not so much as a clue to their true feelings. Keenly aware that someone who did not have to scribble crib notes onto every available surface before every test and was therefore an acknowledged "brain" had had the temerity to challenge the teacher, not on a point of order, but on the veracity of her text; they were, one and all, indifferent to the issue involved. The outcome, on the other hand, interested them greatly. A challenge had been hurled and accepted, and though they were less than dimly curious about the truth or falsity of any story of the creation—for them it was quite enough that the world *was* and more than a waste of time to speculate as to why or how that might have come about—they could not help being viscerally involved in such crucial matters as defeat and victory. Being themselves young and American—thus obliged by tradition to root for the underdog—they were mostly hoping to witness their teacher's humiliating defeat. The fall of the mighty is invariably the stuff of popular tragedy.

"And on what learned authority, may I ask, do you base your judgment?"

She had decided to wither him with her scorn rather than demolish him with her anger.

"That isn't the way the Bible tells it," he responded with a split-second chasm between each word wide enough and deep enough for her to tumble to her doom.

"This happens to be the hour for Social Studies. Not a course in religion," she answered with deceptive calm. "You can get your own brand of that at Sunday school. And welcome to it. But since our Founding Fathers so wisely kept all matters of religion separate from matters of state, and education is clearly a matter of the state's, we can hardly be concerned with what the Bible does or does *not* say. Now can we?"

Though her voice remained as assured as ever, a heightening of her color might have indicated an incipient stage of panic. For so many years had she been spared the anticipated challenge that now it had actually

9

come, she found herself taken completely by surprise. Most of her well-reasoned arguments were, she discovered to her dismay, too deeply filed away in her memory to find their way to the surface with all the alacrity the situation called for.

"Nor does the Bible," she continued, grasping at straws, "pretend to be a scientific work. We are not concerned here with mythologies, but facts. Scientific facts. Not religious doctrine."

Had he been more familiar with the multiple and insidious ramifications of the word "mythology" he might then and there have rested his case and damned her out of her own mouth, but happily for her he was far too proud at such a public moment to give her a crucial advantage by asking for a definition of terms.

"You mean what the Bible says isn't true?"

"Indeed, I said no such thing. And I'll thank you, young man, not to put words into my mouth."

She looked about to make sure that on this most crucial of points, at least, she had the support of her class, and she was heartened to find a few encouraging smiles breaking through the stony wall of impassivity. For with the mention of the Bible the dispute had taken on a new aspect. No longer was it merely a question of a student's challenge of a teacher, but of religion. And all questions of religion were easily resolved in San Oriel on the single overriding issue of denomination. The Catholics knew that Arab was not only daring, but probably right, and they must not any longer be forced to listen to another word of the disputed text, while the previously indifferent Protestant minority immediately wanted the reading to resume. Dickie Aiken, who hated all teachers on principle and had only a moment before been gloating over Old Lady Dobson's acute embarrassment, suddenly discovered that he hated Catholics and Portagees (the two were virtually synonymous in his mind since he had seldom met one who was not also the other) even more and Arab Ramos most of all.

"Black Portagee," he mumbled too low for his teacher to catch.

"Fat Protestant," Arab quickly rejoined, not quite so discreetly.

"What was that!" shrieked Miss Dobson, suddenly losing all composure, but happily spared from any further discussion of the issue by so flagrant an outburst of insolence. "What did I hear you say? Am I to believe my ears?"

"I wasn't talking to you," Arab answered, lamely, then couldn't resist adding, "Anyway, you're not fat," lost the battle by sacrificing the unassailability of his position to the cheap laugh. For which he was at any rate well repaid by his classmates.

"I'll have you know I don't have to put up with such insolence from anyone. Even the son of a trustee. We'll finish this discussion in the principal's office, thank you. After school. In the meantime, both of you will be so kind as to remove yourselves from our presence and wait for me there."

No one was deceived by the terrible calm of her voice. It was, they knew from experience, only the controlled trickle from a dam about to burst. The catastrophe was merely postponed. But they, unfortunately, would now be denied any view of the ensuing mayhem.

If with that cowardly show of rank she terminated the present skirmish, she also prepared the field for those to come. War was declared. But from the first the struggle proved an unequal one. The big guns were all on one side.

*

"Miss Dobson says God didn't make the world."

The terrible accusation fell from his lips almost casually as he stared at his dinner plate, empty, except for a mound of cauliflower, which he could not brace himself to put into his mouth, let alone swallow. Since his grandfather raised this most despised of vegetables, there seemed to be no end to the supply.

"Nonsense," said his father. "You've obviously misunderstood her."

Pressured by Father Moriarity and the entire Sacred Heart Sodality to assume responsibilities that brought added burdens without a corresponding increase in income, Henry Ramos was a reluctant member of the San Oriel School Board and as one of its three trustees had yearly, since his election, approved Miss Dobson's contract. Though he was already in his mid-thirties and sported a mustache originally grown to add an air of age and distinction to a face altogether too boyish to command the respect of his first students, like so many who move directly from the classroom to the lecture platform, he retained an air of the collegian. There was about him something of the perpetual student, with his jaunty bow ties and clothes altogether more flashy than one might expect to find on a man of his age strolling the corridors of any of the

11

country's financial centers. One knew at a glance that he was not a banker or a businessman. As one knew by the easy authority with which he wore his difference—his lapel always flowered with a boutonniere in an age no longer given to elegance or flamboyance—that he was also a man to be reckoned with; one, in other words, who knew his business, whatever it was, and performed it with a certain panache as well as competence.

"Is this another one of your tricks to get out of eating your vegetable?"

Skeptical, but also more aroused than her husband, Louise Ramos, neé Woods, cast a warning glance in the direction of her son's plate.

As inimically opposed to cauliflower as his younger brother, the myopic Tony watched and waited for his chance.

"It's not a trick." With haughtily offended innocence, Arab shook his head. "She says it all happened when the sun exploded. The world was just a little chip." Then giving way to a sudden impulse to giddiness, he added, "A chip off the old block," and giggled uncontrollably at his own joke.

Premonition weighing his eyelids, Henry met the challenge of his wife's eyes. He was enough of an historian to spy the tiny seed of a mighty issue planted at his own dinner table. His wife's look was all he needed to tell him he would not, even if he wanted to, be allowed to ignore the issue, and he resigned himself to captaining a cause he less than half believed in.

In the distraction of the moment, Arab regained sufficient composure to spear a stem of cauliflower and feed it directly from his fork to the blond cocker spaniel that always sat next to him at table.

"Besides, she doesn't like Roosevelt," he added, as if that alone were sufficient proof of anyone's incompetence.

Proof or not, it was enough to transform the private duel into a public scandal. The woman was, everyone agreed, entitled to her own political and religious preferences. What she was not entitled to was the right to inflict those preferences upon her defenseless charges. Although in the light of what followed, their defenselessness proved more putative than actual.

*

Louise Ramos wore her black coat with the genuine astrakhan collar, and that in itself was sufficient to establish the importance of her visit. Her twenties' bob had only recently given way to a thirties' marcel, but the sloppy brim of her felt hat hid most of her head in Garbo-inspired shadows. Sitting far forward on the straight-back chair of the principal's office, she held her purse firmly in her lap, her black-gloved hands clamped over the tortoise-shell clasp.

Like her new opponent, she too, in her college days, had espoused unpopular causes, though of a consistently more liberal tint. She had even once leaned so far to the left as to intimate within the sanctuary of her most conservative family that White Russia might not have been quite so spotless as its name implied, nor Red Russia so bloody, and for such unabashedly radical pronouncements she had been precipitously removed from the University after only two years. The termination of her formal education merely exacerbated the conflict with her father, whose lifelong generosity and affection she further spurned by marrying against his express command and even under the rather grandiloquent threat of disinheritance. No one, not even Vince Woods, in whose hands the financial destinies of half the town rested, had ever been known to intimidate her into contravening the dictates of her conscience or her heart. She had been born a fighter and become a liberal by conviction, and she was quite prepared, if need be, to shed her blood upon the barricades in the defense of her principles.

Her liberalism, however, stopped short at the church door. In matters of religion she was the staunchest of conservatives.

The possessor of energies scarcely tapped by her household duties or her gardening, or even, for that matter, her husband, she was, moreover, a born organizer and thus a formidable opponent. So recognizably—and often infuriatingly—competent was she, so brusquely efficient in her manner, that she was sometimes, in the dazzling speed with which she carried out her directives, apt to offend; but also, and alas for her detractors, so invariably sound were the results of her ministrations that she was universally recognized as the true heir to her father's talents, if not his fortune. In her presence strong men had been known to quail, and Mr. Larsen, charming though he might be, was decidedly not a man of steel.

"Miss Dobson is, of course, entitled to her own views," she said, making no attempt to disguise what she herself thought of those views, "but—and on this point I will not budge—she has no right—none whatsoever—to indoctrinate her students with them."

Mr. Larsen fidgeted nervously with the glue-flap of an envelope, his blandly handsome face helmeted with a silver pompadour. He had many times before run head-on against Mrs. Ramos's will only to be

13

left stunned by the experience. She was decidedly not an adversary to be taken lightly.

"Now, Louise, I'm sure the child has exaggerated," he offered timidly as the blandest of oils cast on the most troubled of waters. "You know how these things are apt to get muddled in the re—"

"Exaggerated or not," she returned before he could complete his thought, "the very subject is out of her domain. The Creation, indeed! She should concern herself with the creation of our Founding Fathers and leave God's creation to God's own priests. Or ministers, as the case may be."

He dropped the envelope, and with the eyes of an experienced public relations man appealed to her for forbearance.

"I'll have a talk with her this afternoon and give Henry a ring tonight."

It was a coward's dodge, but it worked.

"I wish you would," she said, rising. "Otherwise we may be forced to take 'steps,'" she added, setting off the final word in the ominous shadow of quotation marks.

With an eager bound he beat her to the door, and with a perhaps too-gallant bow reminiscent of the music hall, opened it for her. Her smile was radiant. Her dark eyes grew soft, her figure lush. In an instant all the shadows cast by her terrifyingly masculine will were dissipated in sunny femininity.

"Remember me to Elizabeth," she said, and there was an echo of castanets in the click of her heels and the sheen of hibiscus in her hair.

Mr. Larsen was not for an instant fooled. Though he thrilled to the hidden promise it hinted at, he could see through the charm the iron skeleton of her determination. Still, he could not help being dazzled and he answered the flash of her dark eyes with an involuntary flicker of longing, a shiver of desire spiced with a tremor of unease. It was the least that Louise Ramos required from any man, and the most that she tolerated. She was obviously more woman than he had ever dared to tangle with outside the wildest flights of his adolescent fancy.

*

"A spoiled, willful child!"

Miss Dobson sat erect in the same straight-back chair. Though her charm was somewhat less than seductive, her will was quite as formidable as Mrs. Ramos's, and with her integrity worn like a chip on her shoulder, she revealed evidence of the same inflexibility. The immovable object encountering an irresistible force. Nor was she, Mr. Larsen knew, so apt to respond to his own considerable charms. There would be no seducing her to choose, even in the face of insurmountable odds, a graceful retreat. Voluntary surrender rather than enforced defeat.

"Caution," he warned.

"And I say, caution be damned!" She seemed for the nonce to exult in her daring. "Yes, Mr. Larsen, I will not mince words with you. Nor will I be placed in such a position that a mere student can tell me how I am to conduct my classes. I am a professional, Mr. Larsen. A trained and experienced professional. If this child is allowed to get away with this—why, I shudder to think what might become of this school. To say nothing of the boy himself. Are we all to be placed at the mercy of a nine year old? Just because his father happens to be a member of the Board?"

15

"Aren't you somewhat overstating the case, Miss Dobson?" Removing his glasses, he massaged the bridge of his nose ruminatively. "The boy seems to have gotten on well enough with his other teachers. Even something of a favorite, I've been led to believe."

"Which says a great deal more about the quality of my colleagues," she was quick to retort, "than it does about the boy himself. Silly for every pretty face. And blind to the consequences of their pampering. Slobbering does not build character, Mr. Larsen. Nor do we build leaders by giving in to their every childish whim."

"Oh, surely, Miss Dobson—"

He was clearly shocked now at the intemperance of her defense and longed, for his own sake as much as hers, to give her the respite of an evening's solitary reflection before she embroiled them all in a ruckus he was sure they would live to regret. But before he could so much as suggest a temporary postponement of their discussion, she had already initiated another charge.

"Truth is truth," she snapped. "Unpleasant though it may sometimes be."

"Yes, I quite agree." He placed his glasses back on their narrow ridge. "Truth is indeed truth. And at the moment one of these uncomfortable truths, like it or not, just so happens to be that Henry Ramos is a trustee."

Since his own principles were apt to guide him rather single-mindedly onto the path of least resistance, he was destined always to be intim-

idated by the more rigid principles of doctrinarians and he felt himself at
the moment being strong-armed into a position he was reluctant to take.

"And like the rest of us, an educated man subject to reason," she was
quick to reply.

"And a pillar of the Catholic Church," he was just as quick to counter.

"But surely, no one today takes Genesis literally. Not even the Catholics."

Mr. Larsen shrugged. "Who knows anymore what anyone believes?"

She was, he thought, with more awe than affection, like some highly
strung filly of impeccable breeding, undoubtedly handsome but too apt
to treat every trot around the track as if it were the Kentucky Derby
itself. Nor was he the man to feed her the bit. The most timid of lechers,
he was constantly stirred by the itch of lust but far too much the gentleman ever to be caught scratching. Such an unquestioned thoroughbred
would, he recognized with a sigh, take a jockey far more skilled than he.

"Darwin," Miss Dobson continued, blushing indignantly at the
obvious appraisal of her person, "is not the Antichrist, despite what Mrs.
Ramos may think, but an apostle of enlightenment. Nor are we living in
some southern bayou, I might add. This is the West Coast, Mr. Larsen.
And the twentieth century."

Mr. Larsen shook his head. It was, he feared, going to be much worse
than he had anticipated, and he could only hope that in dodging the
Scylla of Louise Ramos he was not going to be sucked into the Charyb-
dis of Estelle Dobson. Faced with such a dangerous course to steer, he
chose instead to cast anchor and remain himself absolutely neutral. He
was not the stuff out of which heroes are made. Whatever action must be
taken could be left safely to the discretion of the Board—which would
also, he was only too well aware, not long after the coming election, be
called upon to renew his own contract.

*

"Certainly no one any longer takes Genesis literally." Henry Ramos
smoothed the unruly edge of his mustache with thumb and forefinger
as with his other hand, he held the bell-shaped receiver to his ear. That's
not the point. The seven days could just as well have been seven million
years. All that matters, theologically speaking, is the initial act of creation. The unmoved mover."

Graced with a professorial title bestowed upon him as compensation
for a drastic cut in salary, he was the natural spokesman for the liberal

wing of the Catholic party. Though every bit as prepared for the barricades as his wife, he was, in matters of doctrine and liturgy at least, far less rigid than she. He even professed himself to be an anti-clerical Catholic, as much for the welfare of his Church as for the countries concerned. He would like to see all priests confined to their sacramental duties and kept clean out of politics. Separation of Church and State was a principle he, as an historian, felt the entire world might benefit from. As long as that "Church" encompassed temple, synagogue, and mosque as well.

His almost heretical views (even his wife found some of them too shocking to be aired before the children) in no way lessened his attachment to the Church-spiritual. Rather, they refined his faith, hewed it down to a fine rod, flexible enough to be bent without breaking.

They were at the moment, however, enough to cause him no end of embarrassment, for he had his own suspicions that Darwin, an unquestionably honorable man with more than a touch of genius, had, in fact, stumbled upon a great and disturbing truth. Thus Henry was as wary of the portentous revelations of the Galapagos as if they had indeed been enchanted islands.

17

"I think we can persuade Miss Dobson to stress that point." Mr. Larsen was more than ready to accept the distinction.

"I'm sorry, Al." Henry shook his head, though there was no one there to see him; for his wife, seated in the next room, her ears carefully attentive to the least crack in his resolve, had had the good taste to grant him the illusion of independent action by removing herself from his sight. Though there could be no question in ordinary matters as to whose was the stronger will, there was in their relationship an invisible line which she did not dare to cross. And not without cause. Though not easily riled, her husband could, she had learned very early in their marriage, when actually roused, be almost brutal in the force and suddenness of *his* resolve, whatever it might at the moment be. "I think the whole subject had best be dropped. How are you ever going to explain to nine year olds that both sides may be right? That truth isn't always a simple matter of two-plus-two equals four? No, I think she'd better stick to the prescribed curriculum and the standard texts. We don't, after all, want to turn them all into skeptics. Or worse, cynics."

"It's quite possible she may refuse." Mr. Larsen's voice rang with intimations of foreboding. "And I'm afraid she's developed something of a following."

"Nothing unprofessional, I trust?"

"Oh, no. It's all been quite spontaneous. Quite spontaneous."

*

The monthly meeting of Saint Anthony's Guild was held in the Ramos bungalow. The house had been a gift to the young couple from Vince Woods in one of his infrequent and typically unpredictable outbursts of generosity. Unfortunately the Woodses' gift had trapped the Ramoses in quarters best suited—in Henry's ungrateful phrase—to a couple of childless pygmies. Though we may take the remark as understandable hyperbole, grand the house was not. Nor was it, strictly speaking, even the Ramoses'. Though usually unpredictable, Vince Woods's generosity had never been foolhardy, and the deed to both the house and the land remained securely in his own name.

A white stucco, red-tile trimmed, low-ceilinged box modeled on the honeymoon cottages seen in countless auto courts throughout the state, it did not lend itself to entertaining on a large scale, and the four whist tables had to be spread throughout three rooms: two in the living room, one straddling the open archway between the living and dining rooms, and one before the open door of the guest bedroom.

Against her best instincts, Louise Ramos had formed the guild, not out of any love of cards and even less out of a love of feminine companionship, but solely in response to Father Moriarity's considerable pressure. It was her duty, he had finally persuaded her, because of her position in the parish as well as her superior education and privileges to exercise her natural talent for leadership by creating the group so that Saint Anthony's (that is to say, Father Moriarity himself) would always have at its (his) beck and call an army of militant mothers for just such emergencies as the present situation afforded.

Seated next to her hostess, Sarah Furtado, the Woodses' maid-of-all-services, was flushed with indignation, her great-warted jowls mottled, her pronounced mustache bejeweled with miniscule beads of sweat.

"All I know is *I* didn't come from any ape."

Mrs. Fogarty looked as if she did not find the large-featured and hirsute Sarah the best example to disprove Darwin.

"Happy I am to know Beth Anne's with the good sisters of Saint Elizabeth's," she said as she inspected a disappointing hand. Though she insisted upon pronouncing her name after the English fashion with a

18

strong stress on the second syllable, she always affected a brogue whenever speaking of matters pertaining to faith or morals.

Louise Ramos stiffened at the implication. "Well," she said, arranging her hand with emphatic precision, "if we want a Catholic on the Board, the very least we can do is send our own children to the school he runs. It's one of the sacrifices we've been forced to make. What chance would Henry have at the next election if none of his own children attended the school he's meant to administer?"

"To say nothing of the transportation."

Sarah blotted the beads of perspiration on her upper lip with a perfumed handkerchief of Madeira lace that Louise found suspiciously like one she had last Christmas given to her mother.

"Sad, but only too true." If Mrs. Fogarty had known she was to draw Sarah as partner, she would have given in to her impending headache and stayed at home. "Sex education will be next. And we certainly need someone to put a stop to *that*."

"We appreciate your sacrifice, dear." Though directed to her hostess, Sarah's words were clearly intended for other ears. "With Henry on the board I can sleep nights knowing Immaculata's safe. Because," she continued with an expansive smile that exposed equal amounts of good will and amalgam, "I'm not letting my girl spend two hours a day on public buses. No sirree. What with the world filled the way it is today with all kinds of sex maniacs roaming around."

Louise had not the heart to tell Sarah that her husband's authority did not extend to Hayward High School, where Immaculata was threatening to become a permanent fixture, still, after three years, a sophomore in precarious standing.

Molly Fogarty made no reply. Except when absolutely unavoidable, she never replied to Sarah Furtado, who, as a domestic, usually had the good sense to keep her place. Louise Ramos's embarrassed insistence alone had opened the doors of Saint Anthony's Guild to her. Pressured both by her mother's snide comments about "people who preach democracy but when it comes close to their own doorsteps don't practice it," and even more by Father Moriarity's sinister references to Christian charity whenever the name came up for admission, Louise had, against all her own instincts, finally become Sarah's sponsor. Although both of Sarah's champions could be accused of conflict of interest—for once a

19

week Sarah did all the church linens on Clara Woods's mangler, and after Father's initial refusal to intercede on her behalf, two altar cloths and a Sunday surplice had been irreparably scorched—their arguments nevertheless proved unassailable, and blushing at the exposed sophistry of her own objections, Louise had submitted. Right was right, distasteful though it might sometimes be. Once resigned to Sarah's right to membership, Louise would not rest until that right was acknowledged. From chief objector she became prime promoter, and few causes that Louise Ramos espoused ever became lost causes.

"Saint Elizabeth's," Mrs. Fogarty continued, ominously, "has dropped whist for auction bridge."

The threat implicit in Molly Fogarty's seemingly innocuous observation was not lost on Sarah. It was no secret that she did not play bridge. With such a liability she must broaden her support.

*

The ladies of the *Sociedade Portuguesa da Rainha Santa Isabel*—sparingly known as the S.P.R.S.I.—met on the third Thursday of every month in the *Irmandade do Divino Espirito Santo* hall. For want of any other building, the I.D.E.S., as it was universally known by Protestants and Catholics alike, served as a substitute town hall and housed everything from the annual Holy Ghost parade to traveling medicine shows. It also served as quarters for summer catechism classes, wedding receptions, and anniversary parties, its unwaxed, unstained spruce floors polished slick by countless dancing feet, old-timers shuffling through the *chamarita* or their offspring tripping over a more fashionable foxtrot blared from the hand-wound Victrola on the corner of the stage.

The long redwood tables in front of the side benches that lined the two side walls were covered with paper "cloths" on which sat great steaming earthenware bowls of *sopas,* mint- and garlic-flavored beef cooked in a thin soup and served over thick slices of sourdough bread. Since there was no heat in the building, the women ate with their hats and coats on, the skirts on some of the stouter forms pulled above the knees, exposing the tops of rolled stockings and ample expanses of white loin.

"Yes, sex education," Sarah Furtado said to Alverta Pimental. "I got it straight from Mrs. Fogarty. At the last Guild whist," she added, knowing full well Mrs. Pimental would never herself have presumed to storm the gates of young Mrs. Ramos's Guild. Though the senior Mrs. Ramos was a dues-paying member of the S.P.R.S., she never attended their meetings.

"But something must be done about it." Mrs. Pimentel lifted a *sopas*-soaked crust of sour bread from her plate with two wet but exceedingly dainty fingers, her large napkin tucked in at her neck and spread over the great expanse of bosom prepared to catch the excess, as bending over her plate, she took a large bite. "Certainly Henry won't allow it," she continued, speaking with her mouth full, and then punctuating her remark by dabbing the drooling corners of her mouth with her napkin.

"*If* he wins the election."

"But is there any question?"

"The Protestants are out to get him."

Confronted by a vision of dark hordes led by Lucifer himself, who in her unlearned mind had been responsible, not only for the rebellion of the angels, but also for the ninety-five theses nailed to the door at Wittenberg, Mrs. Pimentel shuddered.

The uproar became general.

"Stop them! Stop who?"

"Sex education, did you say?"

"Out to get Henry Ramos—the Protestants? Well, we must do something."

"Yes, but what?"

It was Sarah who first sounded the keynote—campaign.

The women, few of whom had ever been so presumptuous as to cast a ballot in any election, were stunned by the simplicity of the solution. Campaign? The word was explored, tentatively at first, as a solution almost too daring to contemplate. But then, why not? They, too, were Americans. Didn't the Stars and Stripes share the platform with the green-and-red emblem of their homeland? And the word was bandied about with ever more boldness—campaign. Resolution swelled, fervor conquered timidity, and what had begun as a diffident question soon became a fiery challenge. Campaign!

Almost as a body they turned to Sarah for leadership. She was not one to lose an opportunity. Already looking forward to next year's possible selection of Immaculata as queen of the Holy Ghost parade, Sarah, with all due humility, deferred to Madame President, Julia Freitas. Unable to think of any more appropriate beginning for what promised to become a Holy War, Madame President called out, "Rosaries, Ladies," and pushing forward her empty plate, she stumbled onto her knees. With her head bowed against the edge of the table, she then led her companions in the first of the five Glorious Mysteries. And the campaign of 1936 was off to an auspicious start.

CHAPTER TWO

Lucifer's Legions

"Academic freedom," said Miss Dobson.

"Big words for such small charges," said Henry Ramos.

"No bigger than the issue."

"Oh, come now, Miss Dobson."

She had to struggle to hold back the tears in this their first confrontation of the crisis. Fully aware nothing would be so apt to give her the prize as just such an abject surrender, she disdained any victory so shoddily won. Yet the very coolness of his composure seemed to intensify the stridency of her voice and thus throw the advantage to him. Nor could she altogether ignore the man's physical charm, which merely served to muddy an issue that should have been limpid in its clarity and further colored the passionate defense of her cause.

"I have principles too."

"No one is questioning that, but this is, after all, a grammar school. Not a university, Miss Dobson."

"I wasn't aware that the Constitutional guarantee of the Separation of Church and State was limited solely to universities."

"It's a question of family rights and has nothing whatever to do with Church and/or State. I no more want you proselytizing for the Catholic Church than I want you proselytizing for any other church, Christian or pagan."

"Truth is Truth, Mr. Ramos. And as you should know, it and it alone will keep us free."

"And what exactly is Truth, Miss Dobson?"

"Really, Mr. Ramos! I am no scoffing Pilate."

"Hardly. But then neither are you Jesus. So why not stick to the prescribed curriculum and save Truth for the university? It seems to me a mighty powerful weapon to put into the hands of fourth graders."

"But intellectual honesty?"

"There are plenty of honest facts to keep your class well occupied without concerning yourself with every fly-by-night theory that comes along."

"Shame! Mr. Ramos. Shame! Darwin was a great scientist, and you know that quite as well as I—or should, at any rate. And no fly-by-night."

Henry Ramos came as close as he ever came to blushing, which manifested itself in the slightest curl of his lips, acknowledging a point well taken.

"Yes, of course he was. But his theory is still a theory and the only theory you're paid to concern yourself with is that which led our Founding Fathers to write the Constitution you seem so determined to uphold."

"The very Constitution which guarantees me freedom of expression."

"Freedom, Miss Dobson. Not license. And freedom, as you well know—or should—carries with it certain responsibilities. And your primary responsibility, may I remind you—since you force me to—is to carry out the directives of the Board. As I'm sure you will. Just as you always have so splendidly done in the past."

And he concluded his speech with a smile of calculated charm.

By blatantly bypassing her intellect and attempting to disarm her with a direct appeal to her femininity, that smile scarcely seemed sporting, since she herself had eschewed the specious use of tears.

*

"I will not give in to tears, I will not!" Miss Dobson said, the tears streaming down her face.

"I understand, dear," said the elder Mrs. Aiken, patting Estelle's hand. "You needn't be ashamed. Tears are a perfectly normal, healthy release."

The two figures were virtually lost in the warm shadows of the over-furnished little room, the tan window shades, down to prevent the late-afternoon sun from fading the central carpet, already so worn that each seat was fronted with a patch of exposed weft, though the colors remained indeed fast. Adding to the darkness, walnut wainscoting rose two-thirds the height of the wall and was topped by a shelf upon which sat sundry pieces of earthen-colored pottery and tarnished copper. Yet the room was far from gloomy, its rich, honey-brown shadows embracing one in snug security. A camelback Seth Thomas clock centered the mantel over the tile fireplace and chimed the quarter hours with such a whimsically light-hearted melody it seemed to mock the very time it measured.

Upon the death of her husband, Madie Aiken had more than happily turned over the family home, along with the management of the family salt works, to her son, the fourth Robert to head the business. She had had more than enough of grandeur and was quite content to end her days in less pretentious and far less taxing surroundings. Her boarder, needless to say, was more companion than anything else and hardly evidence, as rumor might have it, that the Aiken fortune—not of course what it had once been in its glory days—was now more front than substance.

"To think that a child, a mere child—" Miss Dobson turned beseeching eyes upon the handsome, white-haired old woman—"that a mere child should be allowed to disrupt the entire school! The entire community. Where's the justice in that, I ask you? Where?"

Looking distractedly past her distraught boarder, Madie Aiken shook her head with a not altogether convincing show of sympathy. She found so much passion expended over so little more than distasteful. God and the apes and Genesis—it was all so remote. There were no apes in San Oriel, or hadn't been until grown men began making monkeys of themselves. And as for God—well, in that quarter she did not think it proper to delve too deeply. Religion in any of its multifarious forms had always made her vaguely uncomfortable. There were more immediate matters at hand. She rose to raise the shade on the front window, flooding the room with the safely muted light of dusk. Outside she could see the fallen delphiniums badly in need of staking calling to her in words she was far better equipped to answer.

"A powerful family," she said, distractedly, dropping the word "Catholic" from a silver-pronged voice as if it were one to be whispered in polite society.

"There's never been any question about *that*," Miss Dobson answered sharply, stinging the older woman with an implied lack of seriousness.

Mrs. Aiken sighed. Estelle, she feared, was much too intense for her own good. "They're organized," she said, her mind still romping among the fallen delphiniums. "That's where they always have the advantage."

Miss Dobson also sighed. Right, she would like to believe, was Might enough, and Truth the ultimate conqueror. But the world, alas, offered too many examples to the contrary for comfort.

"Well," she said, "if that's the way it's to be, then *we* must organize."

"Yes, dear, but how? Since we've no resident minister to rally the opposition."

Then spying a large snail brazenly turning one of her prize cannas into a green salad, Madie Aiken could no longer control herself, and mumbling something that Estelle Dobson failed to catch, she fled to the sanctuary of her garden before there was time to answer.

More and more, as she grew older, she found plants infinitely more appealing and far better company than people. What relief there was in a rose! What companionship in a dahlia! Whoever heard of hydrangeas organizing to keep the agapanthus in their place? The world was already too violent, she thought, as she lifted the offending snail off its leaf, and dropping it to the ground, stepped on it lightly enough to crack the shell without messing her shoe. The world was already far too violent for her to add to it. All of her desires, all of her passions, except this last one for her garden, had faded along with her hair and her sight and her hearing. She had only one longing left, for a tranquil end. To fade away without fuss, without any garish Maxfield Parrish display of false fire, like the light in her own garden, to sink quietly, and without any great pain—most of all, without pain—into the purple shadows, medicined by the perfume of a rose, pillowed on a bed of maidenhair.

*

"Are we to allow that impossible boy to determine the curriculum of our public schools?" Hazel Aiken asked the next evening at the dinner table. In every way more formidable than her mother-in-law, she was a staunch advocate of immediate and concerted action. Her figure encased in what her husband endearingly referred to as the Iron Maiden, she sat at the foot of the table like an armored tank guarding a strategic pass.

Her house too was formidable. The converted gas jets of the dining room chandelier dripped with crystals dulled by films of smoke and dust and glass lanterns blossomed with etched-glass flowers, each illuminated by a forty-watt bulb. The upholstered backs of the dining chairs were covered in a maroon cut-velvet, their tops soiled by years of greasy fingers, the sides facing the windows bleached to a dim mauve. The same material draped the windows in lushly extravagant, if faded, folds. The flocked paper had once, a generation earlier, been a rich emerald green, but was now bleached almost beige, and except where it had been rubbed thin by the furniture, the lovelier for it. Like the rest of the house, the room was seen at its best in artificial light, its splendor apt to turn tawdry in the brazen rays of the sun. It was easier and far more economical simply to keep the drapes drawn than to begin refurbishing; for once a single wall was painted or a single chair reupholstered, there would be no stopping. The fresh wall would simply expose the shabbiness of all the other walls, and the new fabric show up the dinginess of other worn-out arms and soiled backs. Though the Works were doing quite as well as ever, thank you, a national depression was scarcely the time for a showy and extravagant display of wealth. Good taste, if not straitened means, demanded some recognition of the present crisis. Parsimony had become a civic virtue and none need any longer be ashamed to practice it.

27

"Black Portagee," the rotund Dickie muttered as he eyed the silver tray of petits fours on the sideboard left over from his mother's afternoon bridge. Fat and freckled, his face was blatantly sensual. One could easily imagine him blithely licking away at an all-day sucker while witnessing the worst excesses of some inquisitorial torture chamber.

"That's quite enough from you," the younger Mrs. Aiken remonstrated, her pince-nez trembling on the sharp bridge of her nose, a fine platinum chain tucked into a thick, grizzled wave. Though reputedly still in her forties, she seemed, with her stoutly corseted figure, to be striving to achieve *grande dame* status and sat now with the rigid back of a dowager duchess receiving her annual tribute from the household staff.

"But Arab," she continued, turning once again to her regular Friday night guest. "What an odd name to give a child."

"That, of course, isn't his given name," Estelle Dobson elucidated. "Though no one seems to know him by any other. Vasco's his proper name."

"Proper?" Robert IV guffawed. "That odd appellation!" he fairly exploded then, leaning back in his chair, he curled his lips contentedly about a fat cigar. Though his once flame-red hair had, like his waistline, become part of the refuse of youth, the ruddy freckles that stippled the otherwise chalk-white skin gave him still the look of a firebrand—which always, after a few cocktails, glowed, as now, with incandescent glory.

He was a large man with thick, hairy fingers and a stout neck currently strangled by a collar at least a half size too small. All of his clothes were a half size smaller than they should have been, merely drawing atten-

tion to the expanding girth he himself staunchly refused to acknowledge. Though they did not flinch before any gaze, his watery gray eyes
revealed the sham bluster of a top sergeant rather than the sure authority
of a general. He was, as those who had known them both never tired of
declaring, not half the man his father had been. But then sons seldom
are. His wife's failure to bear him an heir—or of his to engender one—
had forced the middle-aged couple finally to adopt a son, upon whom
they now lavished every luxury and sweet within their still considerable
means to procure.

"He was a Portuguese hero," Miss Dobson said. "Vasco da Gama. An
explorer," she added, in response to Bob Aiken's scowl, as though apolo-
gizing, and then blushed at the denigration implied in her unadorned
aside and the need to play the pedagogue before her kindly and well-
intentioned hosts.

"And I say it's time they started thinking of themselves as Americans
for a change. Take a lesson from old Vince Woods. Worth more than the
whole damn lot of 'em put together," he added, not entirely disinterested, since Vince Woods, whose father had been born a Silva, was the
only man in town who could conceivably lay claim to being worth more
than Bob Aiken.

"It's an ugly language and an ugly people," Hazel Aiken said with a
lack of passion she herself mistook for objectivity, her blanket condemnation unencumbered by a single reservation, for she never thought of
Clara Woods, *née* Bettencourt, with whom she had spent other after-
noons playing bridge, as anything but one of themselves.

No, truth was truth. Miss Dobson would not allow her emotions to
cloud her judgment. "I've never thought of Mr. Ramos as particularly—
unattractive," she ventured timidly. "He has considerable charm, actually, though he does tend to employ it rather shamelessly at times. And
as for his wife—though I personally cannot abide the woman—she is far
from unhandsome."

"But there is something of the Semite about him, don't you think?" Hazel
asked with the open-faced sincerity of a seeker after truth. "That nose."

"Probably is part Jew," her husband concurred. "They seem to be
part everything else."

Miss Dobson sighed. The issue had an unfortunate propensity to be
sidetracked by irrelevancies. Certainly she did not, in any way, want to

blemish the purity of her cause with anything so ugly, so patently un-American, as racial prejudice.

"Black Portagee," Dickie reiterated as slipping from the table he stuffed a fistful of petits fours into his trouser pocket.

*

The first meeting of the San Oriel Improvement Club was held in the storage room of Elsie Grubb's Grocery. The walls were lined with cardboard cartons and shelves of canned goods, of soups and vegetables and scouring powders. A single, tin-shaded bulb hanging from the ceiling, its chain tasseled with a crocheted doll fixed with two sequins as eyes, lit the room.

Pleased at the quality, if not the actual numbers, of those who had taken the pains to answer her summons, Hazel Aiken put on a brave smile as she told the assembled ladies, "One good worker is worth a whole grandstand of cheerers." She did not want to waste her time and energy on anyone not willing to play an active role in the coming campaign by going out into the field to harvest votes.

Besides her glumly silent mother-in-law and Elsie Grubb herself, there were the Mesdames Marlin and Perkins, the wives of the two other Board members, who would, when their husbands were up for reelection in a few years, need Hazel Aikens's support and thought it best to take advantage of the opportunity now afforded them to get her properly into their debt. There was Miss Tutt, the librarian, looking as though she were fresh from campaigning for the first Roosevelt's first election, her blue-rinsed curls hidden by a large-plumed hat that might have been fashionable at the turn of the century but whose likes were most apt today to be found behind the glass of a museum display case. Mrs. Ferguson, the postmistress, was also there, her face as whitely powdered and mask-like as a geisha's, though considerably more wrinkled, with two fans of tiny mortar cracks opening from the corners of her mouth. Her hair was bottle-black and held in place by a net, the knot of which formed a kind of widow's peak. It was, appropriately, the focal point of her face; for as the widow of San Oriel's single casualty of the Great War she held that revered position bestowed in small towns upon the victims of authentic tragedies. Widowhood, one might say, was her true calling and she answered it with professional aplomb. Though she had long since forgotten the details of her husband's face and body and

29

had not for years taken a serious look at the photograph that sat in a tarnished silver frame upon her bedroom bureau, she still honored his memory by wearing nothing but black, enlivened occasionally with a trim of white. Professional ethics forbade Miss Dobson from making her appearance, though she was later filled in on the details by Hazel herself.

"I really don't understand," Miss Tutt said, her head shaking with the palsied rhythm of repressed laughter, a sure sign that she was about to give another display of her famous wit, "why it is we have to huddle together in this shabby little storeroom like a group of anarchists, sitting on cartons filled with articles so personal in nature we'd scarcely dare mention them in public, let alone display them, and usually have the good taste to keep hidden away in our cupboards. I do hope you're not going to propose we blow up a bank. Even though the practice has become so common of late it's virtually a national sport."

Though her conversation was sometimes considered archly racy for a maiden of her advanced years, she had read everything fit for a lady to read and no one ever took offense, least of all Elsie Grubb, who considered the librarian "a regular card."

"No, dear Miss Tutt," Hazel Aiken was quick to take up the challenge, "you may put your mind at rest. We are none of us going to rob any banks. At least I trust not. Nor are we a cell of Bolsheviks plotting to overthrow the government. We are simply a hard core of aroused patriots gathered together to protect their inalienable and now-threatened rights. Modern-day minutemen, one might say. Except, of course, we aren't men and don't, I might add, mean to apologize for the fact."

A hearty round of applause greeted her final remark. It was a splendid beginning and quite convinced any doubters among them that Hazel herself should be chosen chairman of the group by acclamation.

"Now," she continued, once the formality of an election was dispensed with, "if I may for just one moment, further elaborate on Miss Tutt's well-taken complaint. As you all undoubtedly know, the First Christian is available to us any time we want to use it, but I thought it best, considering the somewhat sensitive nature of the current crisis, that we keep ourselves as clean as we possibly can. Now you and I already know what manner of unprincipled charges we can expect to have hurled at us by the opposition—and we are quite prepared to answer them, I might add—but if we hold our meetings in the church hall, we will simply be furnishing ammunition for their guns. We are a public-spirited group interested in political action and in no way restricted to any one denomination. Citizens performing the duties of citizenship, that's all. A most American pastime, I might add. I'd even thought of asking Clara Woods to join us, but considering her close relationship to Henry Ramos, I thought it best not to embarrass her. She cannot, poor dear, very well openly oppose her own son-in-law without precipitating a terrible family row I'm sure we'd all like to spare her. But I think it not amiss to let you know she no more approves her daughter's strong-arm, pressure tactics than any of the rest of us."

"I should hope not," Mrs. Perkins huffed. The combination of beauty and a strong will she found particularly offensive. Any woman was entitled to one or the other, but to utilize both, as Louise Ramos so shamelessly did, seemed a breech of the most fundamental rules of the game.

A resolution endorsing Miss Dobson's stand and commending her courage was unanimously passed, after which, to no one's real surprise, Mr. Aiken was proposed as the candidate most likely to defeat Henry Ramos at the November elections. In his absence his wife accepted their endorsement for him. Though the added tasks would in no way add to their income, Duty was Duty and the need to set an example was, they must never forget, one of the concomitants of success.

Volunteers were called upon to ring doorbells. Miss Tutt pleaded age and Mrs. Ferguson her duties, though she would be happy enough to do any amount of telephoning. She also took the opportunity to draw attention to the deplorable condition of the Protestant cemetery, which had become a veritable blight upon the town. The recent appearance of a hard little knot no larger than a sparrow's egg on her left breast as well as the view from her post office window made the problem personally more pressing than it was for the others.

"Couldn't we get some volunteers to weed the place? Even pay them, if we must. It does seem a shame we don't care enough about our own dead to keep them properly housed. Stones toppled all over the place. And the iron gate—a pretty thing, really—rusting away for lack of paint. A disgrace, I say. A perfect disgrace."

Mrs. Aiken found the suggestion, under the present circumstances, and despite Mrs. Ferguson's undisputed right to chide them on their neglect of the dead, not merely ill-timed but rather tasteless. It was all

---

very well for one who had no living responsibilities to devote her own life to those already departed, but for others there was, if nothing else, a question of priorities.

"I think it best," she said, "not for a single instant to let ourselves be diverted from our main goal, which, need I remind you, is the defeat of Henry Ramos and the integrity of our schools. If, after the election is over, we wish to direct our attentions to other civic concerns, well, then, that's as it may be. But we must do everything in our power to keep our efforts focused upon a single objective and not let anyone or anything come between us and our goal. Our strength will be in our numbers and in our dedication. And we must not for a single instant forget that united we conquer, but divided we fall."

"Abraham Lincoln by way of John L. Lewis," Miss Tutt whispered to an appreciative Elsie Grubb. "For a minute there I thought she was going to tell us we had nothing to lose but our chains."

"Improvement Club!" Mrs. Ferguson was heard to mutter, somewhat ungraciously, Mrs. Marlin thought, as she repeated the remark to Velma Perkins. "All we're apt to improve is Bob Aiken's chances of replacing Vince Woods as director of the Bank of Italy."

Since the directorship had already been all-but-promised to her own husband, Mrs. Perkins said not a word, but the finger that had an instant before been itching to get at those doorbells became, upon the instant, singularly numb.

*

Miss Dobson was waiting for the two Mrs. Aikens in the brown shadows of the snug parlor. It was the senior Mrs. Aiken who first entered. Without so much as a word of greeting, she removed her hat and gloves, and placing them on the dining room table, with no more than the merest glance at her boarder, silently passed through the house and out the kitchen door to the solitary comfort of her garden.

It took Estelle, who rose to greet them, no more than that fleeting glimpse into those sad and lovely eyes to realize that she, who had a week before been treated as a surrogate daughter, had suddenly become the enemy. The destroyer of peace. The bearer of discord. It was a chilling discovery, for she was as fond of the dear old thing as she was of anyone, and she scarcely attended to Hazel's excited account of the proceedings. Her eyes were too intent upon the gentle old woman's dispirited ramble through her bed of dahlias to follow her daughter-in-law's words with half the attention they seemed to demand.

"Yes, yes, of course," she could hear herself saying. "That's the American way." But the words had a hollow ring to them. Perhaps it was ungracious of her, but she could not help noting that the main objective of her enthusiastic supporters was no longer the defense of academic freedom, but the election of Robert IV.

It was, of course, mad of her ever to think it might have been otherwise. And the first faint rumblings of panic stirred within her. Everything she had ever believed in would be turned about and twisted and stretched until it became so grotesquely contorted she would never be able to recognize herself or her ideals. They would all be free to use her now for their own purposes and all else be damned. Not one of them, she knew, truly cared about the great Darwin and a vision of the world as startling, as beautiful, and yes, ultimately, as tragically poetic as any since Shakespeare's. She was about to become a cause. But the wrong cause. And she suddenly longed to join her old friend in the late afternoon sun staking her dahlias. There was a cause, limited though it might be, that anyone could safely trust in.

33

*

"Old Dobson seems harmless enough."

"A shrieking hawk, if you ask me."

"Nothing a good man couldn't take care of."

"You volunteering?"

"Hell, no. Time for another beer?"

The San Oriel Improvement Club was not the only group in town to be preoccupied with Miss Dobson's cause. Situated at the crossroads of the town's two main thoroughfares, Costa's Corner was the natural forum of San Oriel. Its new respectability, however, demanded that Costa himself remain neutral, particularly now that his business had been threatened by the repeal of Prohibition, which had, overnight, transformed him from a necessary evil into a doubtful good. Even Elsie Grubb's Grocery offered nearly as great a selection of wines and spirits for those who chose to drink at home, as a good many did so choose, now that the spirited camaraderie inspired by an unpopular law had been brought to an end. Principles or no principles, the Costas could not now afford to alienate any segment of the population, large or small;

for as he pointed out to his wife, they did not make their money on her salami-and-sardine sandwiches, or even her famous Saturday pot of baked beans, all of which had as their primary purpose the provocation of thirst, and unless the bar was filled, their coffers would never be.

Not herself so ready to sacrifice principle to expediency, Minnie Costa felt no such compunctions as her husband and openly let it be known what *she* thought of any old-maid schoolteacher who set herself up as such an expert in sexual matters that she felt qualified to instruct the young. As if anyone needed instructions in such matters! Did a flower, she asked, her most unflower-like hands stacking the dirty dishes, have to be told how to bloom? Of course not! And anyone who thought otherwise was simply declaring her own ignorance. Or more to the point, her inability to net herself a proper man of her own.

34

"How'd sex get into it?" Her baffled customer asked, his stunted, primeval face pleading for enlightenment. "I thought it was a question of apes."

A Mona Lisa smile slinked across Minnie's ample face, as from a tilted head tied with a red bandanna she studied her customer as though seeing him for the first time, his heretofore hidden simplicity of mind suddenly revealed in all its shocking nakedness.

"So they've buffalo'd you, too," she said, and shaking her head sadly, bore her burden to the kitchen, glancing back as she shouldered open the swinging door for one last incredulous shake of her head, a shake which seemed to encompass the whole helplessly deluded sex.

*

"She might at least have mentioned God." Henry Ramos's hooded eyes were virtually hidden under heavy lids weighted with weariness. Except that it would now appear as a cowardly flight from the field of battle, he would not for an instant dream of running for re-election. "Or," he continued, his voice every bit as dispirited as his face, "indicated her theory did not, in any fundamental way, disprove Genesis."

They were meeting in the Board room opposite Mr. Larsen's office. It served also as school library, such as it was, as well as a faculty lunchroom.

"Separation of Church and State," Mr. Perkins said with all the flare of a magician who has just pulled a rabbit out of his hat, and smiled so broadly at his point the gold caps on his molars flashed from the shadows. He always wore the embarrassed look of a freshly plucked chicken with a neck so skinny it seemed denuded of its proper plumage.

"Nonsense," Mr. Ramos said. "In God we trust. It's on every dollar bill in the land."

"I think not." Mr. Perkins's smile continued unabated. Mr. Marlin had the flu and did not appear at the monthly meeting. "Dollars and education. Two different things altogether. Can't mix God in with science or we'd all be in a proper fix. With the sun still circling the earth. Soon find ourselves back in the Dark Ages. But with business the way it's been, we'd damn well better trust in God to protect the dollar, because the market certainly hasn't been doing much of a job. Not that the goddam government's given it any help. Passing out our tax dollars to every hard-luck Johnny in sight while the goddam Oakies are taking over the state. By the way," he continued, "what's your father-in-law think he's up to, anyway, planting cauliflower?"

Mr. Perkins saw no reason to let this little matter of Miss Dobson interfere with business.

"Why, is that so unusual?"

"With prices the way they were last year, everyone else planted corn."

"Then I suppose that's why he planted cauliflower."

". . . Oh!"

*

"You'll get no help from me. Not a penny nor a vote."

His tweed vest tightly buttoned across a belly bulging as plumply round as everyone in town assumed his wallet to be and richly crossed with gold chains and ornamental fobs—a tiny gold knife for cutting his Cuban cigars in a style befitting their cost dangling just outside his watch pocket—Vince Woods was adamant as he slouched in his gold plush chair.

A handsome, white-haired old sheik, he had built his empire out of whole cloth and once again proven the American Dream a viable reality, only to have his spirit broken finally by the knowledge that his only son and heir was an incorrigible, dissolute wastrel too worthless for the slightest hope of redemption. The Great Depression, which had fortuitously left his own fortune unscathed, had become for him something far more personal than a financial disaster, a great depression of the heart—that bitterest of resentments known best to those whose bravest dreams have been realized, only to see the world that supported them crushed under the very weight of their triumphs. So bitter was the disappointment of his son's failure that it tainted his relations with his

35

daughters as well, and in his moments of brooding self-pity he saw himself now as an old Lear, his unparalleled generosity repaid with the wintry curses of ingratitude.

"Well, I could hardly have expected you to support your own family." His daughter's tone was scathing. "That would have been too much
to hope for. But your Church as well! Or doesn't Almighty God mean
any more to you than the almighty dollar?"

Her father's smile was only superficially benign. "I trust the Church
will survive Bob Aiken's election." His white hair as rich and lustrous
as everything else about him—the glistening porcelains, the lavish bro-
cades, the carved mahogany—he lacked only a turban to transform him
to a lordly Ottoman pasha.

"It's not a question of survival, it's a question of principle," she
snapped, but her father refused to be riled. It was nothing more than
a tempest in a teapot and he would not allow himself to become upset
by so inconsequential a storm. Stung by the ruination of his own son,
why should he join in the triumph of anyone else's? Any successes his
sons-in-law might garner would only add insult to injury. He longed for
nothing less than the failure of an entire generation. The collapse of a
civilization. That alone would be sufficient to medicine his bitterness.

*

"I certainly hope you didn't ask your father for his support. Or did
you?" Henry's mustache bristled with indignation.

"Of course I did?" Louise's eyes flashed with righteousness.

"But can't you see, if it had to be asked for, I don't want it."

"Well, you haven't got it."

"And just as well."

Incipient tears welled in her eyes. "I wish you wouldn't talk like that,
Henry. After all, like it or not, he is my father."

"Yes, and I'm your husband! And where, I'd like to know, has that
gotten me but into one damn commitment after another? Lectures to
prepare, bluebooks to correct. And these goddam citizenship classes
every other night just to keep our heads above water. And on top of all
that, I'm expected now to help my own parents stave off financial ruin
against odds no gambler in the state would wager a wooden nickel on.
And you expect me to throw myself, body and soul, into small-town
politics with all the enthusiasm of Napoleon poised on the borders of

Russia, just because some damn fool schoolteacher thinks she's going to change the world and single-handedly lift us all out of the Dark Ages."

"And I suppose you think it's easy for me, trying to stretch your salary to keep the children properly fed and clothed. Well, you just try it sometime and see how far you get on your pittance, keeping the icebox full and shoes on their feet."

"Maybe your father was right, after all; maybe you should have married a doctor or a lawyer. Anyone raised in the kind of luxury you were used to—"

"There's no arguing with you, Henry. There's never any arguing with you. Because you're always right. And everything wrong with the world, from the Depression to your own inadequacies, can be laid at my father's feet."

"So I'm the one who's always right! Well, that's a hoot. I'm the one who's always right. Me. Louise Woods's poor put-upon husband is the one who's always right. Ha!"

Under the pressures of the campaign they seemed now to be constantly at each other, quarreling or loving, and both passionately clawing away at feelings and bodies with such abandon, taking out their frustrations with such reckless excess, with such a wild, careless disregard for any consequences more removed than the immediate healing of wounds they themselves had inflicted, staunching the flow of blood with their kisses, splintering shattered egos with their embraces, that long before the election was held, the most crucial result was a third and unplanned pregnancy.

*

"I do wish Louise would tend to her own family affairs and keep her nose clean out of politics."

Clara Woods stood in front of her hall mirror and removed the pins from her hat, gently laying the amber-tipped, lethal weapons upon the mantle. Her hats were quite the most splendid in town, as strikingly oversized as her face and figure, or the diamonds that adorned her fingers. Though it had only been an afternoon of bridge she had returned from, her costume would not have dishonored a royal garden party—as long as she herself could have played queen.

"It's no place for a woman," she continued, fixing her eyes upon her husband's reflection. "Poor Hazel had all she could do to keep from treading on my toes all afternoon, as if she could say anything unkind to anyone!"

Vince smiled. There was something about his daughter's ability to get the whole damn town riled up over nothing that did not altogether displease him. "Leave her alone, Clara. The girl's all right."

It was always easiest to defend his daughters when they were not around to get in his hair.

Clara shook her head, the pheasant feathers adorning her hat trembling in iridescent splendor. "Sometimes I don't understand you, Vince. Sometimes I simply don't understand you at all. What Louise's gadding about has to do with suddenly winning your admiration I fail to see. I suppose you know," she continued, laying her feathered hat on the mantle alongside the lethal pins and turning to confront her husband full-face. "It isn't only Bob Aiken she's out to defeat—she's also canvassing votes to keep *That Man* in the White House for another four years. How does that tickle your fancy?"

"Roosevelt!" The change was sudden and dramatic. There was not in the entire census of the world a name more apt to rile the old man to positive torrents of rage. The very voicing of it, like the first rumblings of a volcano, was an indication that an eruption was imminent. "You don't mean to stand there and tell me, after these last four years, she still intends to support him again?"

"Yes, Roosevelt."

The tiniest smile of triumph slid across her lips, but she did not indulge it. Her face always reacted with litmus-paper sensitivity to her husband's moods, and his anger now left no room for any other emotion. Though she longed for nothing so much as for peace within her own family, the welfare of the country, laboring as it was under the terrible threat of Socialism poorly disguised as a New Deal for the undeserving, surely took precedence. Fired by Hazel Aiken's sterling patriotism, how could she any longer fail to remember that she was an American as well as a mother!

"Well," he snorted, reaching into his tobacco cabinet for his third cigar of the afternoon and the fifth of the day, "we'll see about that!"

Though the doctor had expressly forbidden him more than two a day, she would not have dreamed of reminding him in his present mood for fear of provoking an attack of apoplexy. Nor could she truly believe that anything so apt to pacify him could also harm him. So she contented herself with a sigh, which he was free to interpret any way he chose to, as a comment upon the hazards of smoking or upon the ingratitude of daughters.

*

"Black Portagee," Dickie Aiken called across the baseball field as Arab Ramos headed for the Southern Pacific tracks and the forbidden shortcut home.

"Fat, pink-faced Protestant."

"Go kiss the Pope's bottom."

"It's cleaner than the Protestant Devil's."

"Your mother takes in wash, fish-eater."

"Your mother isn't even your mother."

"Dirty bastard!"

"You're the one who's the real bastard. Don't even know who your real mother is. Or father."

Dickie was much too stout to make more than a token effort to catch the lithe Arab, who, before his opponent was halfway across the baseball diamond, had already wiggled his way under the hole in the fence and was blithely skipping across the redwood ties, trumpeting the shame of Dickie's unknown antecedents to the entire world:

"Yaw, yaw, Dickie Aiken's adopted! Dickie Aiken's adopted!"

*

"Made up your mind who you gonna vote for?"

"Ramos, naturally."

"And for President?"

"Oh, Roosevelt, I suppose."

RAMOS and ROOSEVELT read the banner spread across the front of the I.D.E.S. Hall.

AIKEN and LANDON read the sign in the window of Elsie Grubb's Grocery.

Despite the supplications of his wife, who had been threatened with expulsion from the S.P.R.S.I., Costa resolutely remained neutral and banished all signs from the premises. His impartiality, however, did little to temper the violence of the arguments that raged within; for apes and sex, Ramos and Roosevelt had become the preoccupations of the season and few were they who could remain indifferent.

CHAPTER THREE

SUFFER THE LITTLE ONES

Arab could easily make out the silhouette of Father Moriarity's averted   *41*
face in the dark confessional, the head sunk heavily on a cupped hand,
the ear cocked in resigned boredom. As always, the young penitent tried
to keep his own face as far away from the screen as possible, and as an
added precaution, he held both hands in front of him with a spread
between two fingers acting as peephole. He tried to muffle his person-
ality in a harsh whisper clearly intended to disguise his identity as he
recounted his sins of commission and omission.

Despite Sister Margherite's lectures on the manifold graces of frequent confession, he invariably found the monthly chore an ordeal to be
gotten through as quickly as possible. It was, first of all, often a struggle
to gather enough material for a good showing, so that he was, and not
infrequently, reduced to fabrication, or at the very least, exaggeration,
for he couldn't very well begin, "Bless me, Father, for I have not sinned."
True though the claim might sometimes be, there was an arrogance in
it that not even he would willingly have been a party to, and though a
small but not easily repressed part of him longed to startle his pastor
awake with some truly shocking admission of depravity—that he had
set his grandfather's barn on fire, for example, or smashed his grandmother's precious collection of porcelain birds, or stolen the cash box
from Elsie Grubb's Grocery—there was a dismally monotonous simi-
larity to all these ventures into repentance that bored him as much as it
must bore his long-suffering pastor: he disobeyed his mother twice, he
forgot to say his morning prayers three times, he fought with his brother
more times than he could count on ten fingers and ten toes together,
and on a particularly warm night he slept without pajama bottoms.

Still it was never entirely satisfactory. There was something about the dark, tight box that induced a sense of shame, that made him feel like one about to be caught in a particularly revealing lie with devastating consequences. There was also something snidely insinuating about Father Moriarity's inevitable question: "Are you sure that's all?" As if he were about to uncover some secret, dirty corner of his soul too repulsive to contemplate even in the protective shadows of the confessional.

In the awful silence that followed the question, Arab decided once again not to mention the sip of communion wine he had sampled while helping Granny Mae decorate the altar. It had been such a small taste it could hardly be more than a venial sin easily erased with a simple Act of Contrition, and wherever a question of personal censure was concerned, he was a firm believer in simple solutions to simple problems. There was, moreover, despite the lure of additional graces, always the chance that Father Moriarity had recognized his voice, and even with the seal of confession at stake, priests were, it was best to remember, human.

"Yes, Father," he mumbled, his disguised voice unable to disguise his own sense of inadequacy. Or very much else, for that matter.

With the final blessing of the absolution, Arab rose to leave and perform his penance, the inevitable three Our Fathers and three Hail Marys, when the sharp stab of the priest's voice pinioned him to the confessional floor.

"One minute, Vasco." A sudden spotlight cast upon him squatting on the toilet seat, his trousers bunched about his ankles, could not have more shocked or shamed him, and despite the darkness of the confessional, he blushed to the tips of his ears.

"Is your Grandfather Woods going to be at Mass tomorrow?"

"I guess so," he stammered, dizzy with relief as he realized how close he had come to mentioning the wine, so sure had he been of the effectiveness of his disguise. Even the use of his real name, which both Father Moriarity and Sister Margherite, put off by the infidel overtones of Arab, insisted upon employing, added to his embarrassment. For some unfathomable reason he could never hear the strange sound without blushing.

"I want more than a guess. Tell him I especially requested he be there. So he doesn't find some excuse to sneak off to San Leandro to the neglect of his own parish. There'll be an announcement I particularly want him to hear."

Though the tone of censure in the priest's voice was directed against the Woodses, who made no pretense about resenting the length of Father Moriarity's sermons and often drove to the earlier Mass in far more fashionable San Leandro, under the pretext that Clara, with her notoriously delicate health, could not fast until the end of the 8:30 Mass at Saint Anthony's, which seldom let out before ten. It was their grandson who suffered from its sting, and he once again stammered a weak, guilt-ridden, "Yes, Father."

*

Clara Woods leaned forward to receive the homage of her grandson's kiss, as he dutifully pressed his lips against her cheek, while she herself seemed more intent upon a windblown curtain caught on the back of a chair. As his grandfather grunted his greeting with a not unfriendly, though typically ironic, smile, she rose to reorder the recalcitrant curtain panel.

43

Their house was as close as he had ever come to a palace. The sunshine streaming through the bay windows romped with joyful and unashamed abandon among the gloss of marble, the sheen of silk, and the sparkle of crystal, dazzling the eye. The fabrics were all luxuriously sleek or sumptuously soft and unmarred by head-stains or greasy palm marks; the rugs were as richly piled as freshly mown lawns; and every sofa and easy chair offered down hillocks to sink into, one's fall cushioned by the slow sighing release of air. The shabbiness of the times made the house seem all the grander, the temple of too-much when every other place he knew suffered from the stigma of not-enough. It was the single house he knew that could greet the brazen afternoon sun without blushing, that looked every bit as lovely in the daylight as it did by candlelight. But palaces are ruled over by royalty, and what he felt for this particular royal pair, though he had never taken the pains to analyze it, was closer to awe than affection. Even the names by which he addressed them were a measure of his reserve. They were Grandma and Grandpa Woods, while his other grandparents were a more familiar Grandpa Tom and Granny Mae.

"Father wants you to be sure to go to Mass tomorrow," he said, his eye suddenly caught by a new porcelain cockatoo perched upon a marble-top table in the corner bay, its pink and white wings preened for flight.

"Father?" His grandfather's dark eyes were alive with mischief. "What business is it of your father's what I do with my Sundays?"

"Oh, Grandpa." He smiled, turning from the cockatoo back to the handsome old man who held the entire town in thrall. "You know what I mean. Father Moriarity."

"But we go to Mass every Sunday." There was a querulous note to his grandmother's voice. "He knows that well as anyone. What's he trying to do, shame us in front of our own grandchildren? I don't like it, not for a minute, suggesting we miss Mass on Sundays. Like Easter Catholics."

"But he wants you to be sure to go here tomorrow. Saint Anthony's. He says he's got a 'nouncement he wants you to hear."

"What's the old charlatan up to, I wonder." Vince turned to Clara.

She shook her head. "Well, whatever it is, you can be sure of one thing. It'll cost us a pretty penny. It's the only time he's ever particularly interested in our salvation. Him with his camel eyes."

She had still not forgiven the man a remark he had made several years before in a moment of terrible crisis, when longing for his sympathy and his prayers, her son at death's door, she had been stung instead by a crudely ill-timed reference to camels passing through the eyes of needles.

"You any idea, Arab?" His grandfather queried him in the voice of one who enjoys riddles only when he himself holds the answer book.

Arab shook his head. He was shocked that anyone might call their pastor a charlatan, which he knew by his grandfather's tone—though he would have to look the word up as soon as he got home—was hardly meant as a compliment. But his grandfather, he also knew, was a law unto himself, free to use with absolute impunity words that would have earned him a slap across the mouth and even from his father a rebuke guaranteed to sting his ears.

"The cockatoo's new, isn't it?"

Flattery he had long ago learned was the quickest, surest path to his grandmother's heart. She received all tributes to any and all of her possessions as personal compliments. To tell her that a new purchase was lovely was to tell her that she was lovely; and she fattened on the sweet taste of praise.

"Why, yes, it is." For the first time she seemed truly alert to his presence. "Do you like it?" Her hand fell almost unconsciously to the top of his head and she idly ran her fingers through his soft mop of hair.

"Oh, yes. It's beautiful." His voice pulsed with sincerity as he felt the fine glaze with the tips of his fingers, a possessive glint in his eyes, a prepubescent but clearly discernible lust for luxury that, more than any-thing else, marked him as his grandmother's true descendant.

"Well, anyone can see you're going to have Grandma's eye. That's for sure." Her face was bathed in smiles. "It is beautiful, isn't it? From Dres-den. A beautiful city, Dresden. Your grandfather and I were there when you were just a tiny thing." And she lifted the bird to reveal its mark-ing of crossed blue swords as though he might have doubted her claim. "How would you like to stay and have dinner with us tonight? I'm sure there's enough to go round."

It was an idle qualification. At the Woodses' table there was always enough to go round.

"I'll have to call home first," he said, taking the long devious route to the telephone, through the kitchen to get the evening's full menu from Sarah before finally committing himself. He did not want to give up Saturday-night short ribs at home for anything so repugnant as cau-liflower or broccoli, but the sight of a dried-apricot tart and a bowl of cream ready for whipping were enough to convince him that his grand-parents' table was decidedly the better bargain, and humming happily to himself, he skipped to the telephone table on the first landing of the grand staircase, confident that his mother, only too happy to have one less plate to share their more scanty fare, would give her consent.

45

*

Saint Anthony's was a simple clapboard structure almost Protestant in the austerity of its design. Aside from the crypt, which was outside the church proper and popularly known as Olaf's Tomb, though Olaf himself lay buried in the unweeded Protestant cemetery alongside the post office, the most festive note was sounded by the circular stained-glass window of Christ in the Garden of Olives over the main altar. The altar itself, a simple wooden affair painted not very convincingly to simulate marble, was flanked by life-size polychrome plaster statues of Saint Anthony on the right and the Sacred Heart on the left. A mere lectern before the communion rail served as pulpit. At the rear of the church was a small choir loft with a pump organ. Here the visiting nuns sat with their young charges, each clutching a hymnal. The main floor was taken up with four rows of gray pews. Though there was nothing to distinguish one from the other except location, all the key pews had for years belonged to specific families who paid their annual rent and no one but a stranger would have dared to sit in one that tradition assigned to another, so that their pastors needed no more than a single glance, his eyes marking off the empty seats, to know who was or was not in church on any given Sunday. Since the Woodses occupied one of the side front pews, their presence today was not easily overlooked.

The morning promised to become one of those sweltering autumn days so typical of the Bay Area, hotter than any summer has to offer. The amber-glass windows were all tightly locked and the air was fetid with human odors, every ill-fitted armpit ringed with a wet bib. Lace hankies and colored bandannas blotted damp chins and foreheads and open prayer books acted as fans, but nothing seemed to help, the very movements made to ease one's discomfort adding to it. Not a breeze stirred the flames of the altar candles and even the roses in the brass vases, fresh only the day before, drooped disconsolately, their wilted petals almost touching the altar cloth.

Father Moriarity chose as his text: Suffer the little ones.

His smoke-gray hair, parted in the middle, was so coarsely thick that the resulting peaks, like the horns of prophesy, made him seem more than ever an angry Moses exhorting a gathering of passive Israelites submissive to their bondage. Though feared, he was not a popular pastor. Modeled on the seventeenth-century Bolognese school of which Guido Reni is the prime practitioner, his gestures were somewhat too grand for so rustic a church with its bucolic congregation. Such manifestly theatrical mannerisms seemed to cry out for marble pilasters and bronze baldachins, or at the very least, a ceiling of whipped-cream clouds filled to bursting with peach-bottomed putti rising heavenward in some saintly apotheosis, but the only remarkable aspect of Saint Anthony's ceiling was an accumulation of smoke and dust and cobwebs so thick that some local Michelangelo might have traced his own version of the Creation with no more than the tip of his finger.

The priest's extravagantly embroidered chasuble, his gilt-laden stole, and his alb of Brussels lace reaching all the way to the worn, faded carpet of the altar gave him the air of some disgraced queen cruelly consigned to the Tower and clearly made for a grander stage upon which to act out her role. It had for years been clear to all that he had Episcopal longings and looked upon his parishioners as yokels not quite worthy of his great talents. The swine before whom he was destined—

only Providence knew why and Providence was not telling—to cast his pearls. With a brother archbishop, another brother bishop—to say nothing of his cloistered sisters, one of whom was an abbess—he had within his own family come close to touching greatness. He was, moreover, and not without some cause, apt to speak of the Church as a family concern and of the Irish as the race especially designated by God to keep the faith of our fathers burning bright. It was an attitude scarcely constituted to endear him to the Portuguese, who comprised well over three-quarters of his parishioners and whom he sometimes treated like Indian converts whose barbaric practices had somehow to be tolerated for the Greater Good.

He spoke as usual without notes and with a truly supernal indifference to the heat, which seemed to assume a physical form in the flames that colored his ruddy cheeks, so that the mere sight of him added to everyone's already intense discomfort. With a cavalier disdain for the niceties of syntax and a penchant for ornately convoluted metaphors of Baroque splendor, he expounded upon the dark forces of irreligion rampant in the world, of the new Luthers that crushed the lily-pure flesh of the little ones beneath the cleated boots of heresy; he spoke of the Antichrist of science rising like a new Goliath against the David that was the Church; he spoke with only a few digressions into modern history of the crass materialism of the modern world that held captive the Christ-of-the-spirit and loosed the Barabbas-of-the-flesh. Needless to say, brevity was not one of the chief attributes of his considerable oratorical skills.

"The Church," he continued, "is a small candle in a dark world, a candle whose light must be held aloft from every mountain peak to shine into the valleys of iniquity, to reach into the jungles of materialism and illuminate the rankest corners of the fleshpots of our modern-day Babylons, drenched as they are in the stench of lust. "It is a torch," he added, his voice rising to a stirring climax, "handed down from generation to generation. Yea, even to the end of time. It is a beacon which we, growing old with the weight of years and care, must entrust to the arms of these very little ones now so gravely abused, so foully employed with heathenish doctrines; these same little ones whose arms must be made strong and sturdy, whose muscles must be toned with the grace of example until they are fit to bear the burdens we entrust to them. For the future of the Church lies in its youth. Your children."

47

The congregation stirred. The sigh was audible as with a single movement all leaned forward to rise for the *Credo*. Opening her missal, Sarah Furtado rose without so much as a glance at the altar, so sure was she that such a peak had been reached the priest would never dare attempt to top himself. A poor listener, she could not distinguish a breath-catching, sweat-mopping pause from a conclusion. Father Moriarity had merely scaled the foothills.

Flustered, Sarah plopped back onto her seat with such precipitate haste, a medley of holy pictures, litanies, special prayers, and memorial cards fell from her missal and scattered about her pew. Beside her, resplendent in a blue-lace dress with a shocking peek-a-boo bodice, her daughter Immaculata giggled. She alone seemed appropriately garbed for the heat, if not the service. Granted a glimpse of what she was prepared to swear before a host of angels was the rose-mole shadow of a nipple, Mrs. Fogarty whispered, "Well, I never!" Then leaning against her husband she shared her disdain. "Just look at that, will you! And in the very presence of the Blessed Sacrament!"

Too far over for a first-rate view, Mr. Fogarty picked up one of the fallen cards, and leaning far enough forward into the next pew to verify that the nubile Immaculata was indeed not wearing a brassiere or any other impediment under her lace halter, returned the card to a grateful Sarah. Mae Ramos, her blue eyes bleary with fatigue, blessed herself and offered her considerable discomfort to the poor souls in Purgatory, her customary morning flatulence calling up heroic reserves of self-control, while next to her her husband dosed contentedly, his multiple chins supporting his large head against his even larger chest.

Less altruistically inclined, Clara Woods bent to her husband's ear. "Camels, indeed!" she whispered. "That's what you'd have to be to get through the eye of one of his sermons." Happily she had remembered to bring her little palmetto fan from the Philippines, which acted as much as a nervous release as a cooling agent. "If someone doesn't open a window, we'll all soon perish," Louise Ramos said to her husband, who knew an order when he heard one. Taking advantage of the pause, he rushed from his central pew around the full length of the church to avoid passing between the priest and his congregation and opened all the lower windows, but the air outside seemed as still as the air inside and no breeze stirred. The open windows let in the noise of the street, but little else.

After blotting the sweat on his face and neck, Father Moriarity tucked his handkerchief back into the sleeve of his cassock and waited with an awful silence for absolute attention. Henry quickly resumed his seat, in his haste inadvertently stepping onto the edge of the kneeler, which rose and crashed to the floor with a resounding bang, rousing poor Mr. Pimental from his slumber with such a start that he leapt to his feet, the collection box thrust before him like a lance to stave off any charging dragons. The rest of the steaming congregation stirred, sighed, and resigned itself to another hour-and-a-half service.

"Verily, verily, I say unto you," the priest continued, his booming *basso profundo* intimidating even the flames of the beeswax candles burning on the altar, "'He that shall scandalize one of these little ones that believe in me, it were better that a millstone should be hanged about his neck, and that he should be drowned in the depths of the sea.' And so," he continued, leaning forward, his right arm extended as if he were about to smite the golden calf itself, "were it better that a millstone were hanged about your necks also, if you allow the devil to flourish in your own backyard, turning the very classrooms of your children into sties of filth and abomination."

He paused, and in a silence so complete the crackling of the candle wax could be heard as ominous as the voice from the burning bush, he clasped the front of the lectern with both hands. "Saint Anthony's," he resumed, his voice lowered almost to a whisper, "must have its own school. Yes," he continued, startling one and all with the sudden crescendo of his voice, "a parochial school!"

"Ah, I thought we were leading to something," Vince Woods murmured. "At last we get to the finances."

"I told you so, didn't I?" Clara admonished as though he had for an instant doubted her. "Why else would he have been so interested in having us here? Certainly not to save our souls."

"Finally," Mrs. Fogarty sighed.

Mrs. Pimental's stomach growled—she had been up since six fasting—while, slumped over the collection box, Mr. Pimental was once again snoring audibly.

"Another drive!" Henry Ramos's sigh was less triumphant than Molly Fogarty's, for he read the announcement as one more demand upon his time and resources, one more curtailment of his already pain-

49

fully restricted freedom. And for what? The man was clearly out of his mind, during a national depression, when food itself was not always a surety, if he expected his congregation to join enthusiastically in an ambitious building project. With the current level of salaries it would take a major miracle even to get the drive off the ground. But a sudden light illuminated the dark prospect, for the drive could not, he realized, be any concern of his. This time he had an airtight excuse, and one he fully intended to exploit for all it was worth. As a trustee of the local board of education, he could not certainly in any way allow himself to become involved in the collection of funds intended to subvert the very school he was himself in charge of. It was a question of ethics. Cut and dry. And the second sigh to escape his lips was far more sanguine. No, he thought, smoothing his mustache with thumb and forefinger as a sly smile of contentment stole across his face, they can't have it both ways—a Catholic on the Board and that same Catholic leading a drive to replace that very Board. He was for once quite safe. And fully reassured, he settled back to listen to the remainder of the sermon with equanimity, as buoyed on the wings of his own eloquence, Father Moriarity soared, virtually unattended, into the empyrean.

*

"Like it or not, I suppose we'll have to give something." Clara settled back against the mohair seats of their mud-gold La Salle, a monumental migraine threatening. For some inexplicable reason they always seemed to come on Sunday. "And I did so want to redo our bedroom before Christmas. But you know well as I do the kind of tricks he's apt to get up to. The man has no scruples, even if he is a priest. Sure as your life there'll be a framed scroll in the vestibule with every name in the parish on it and every penny donated listed. And if our name isn't at the top—well, just suppose Mamie Dutra, or worse, someone like Sal's widow takes it into her head to find out what we're giving and then top it with five dollars just to put us in our place? And get her name on top of ours."

From behind the wheel Vince seemed far less perturbed than his wife. And as for their bedroom, he thought it just fine the way it was. Though he had always been more than willing to indulge his wife's penchant for constant redecorating, he secretly longed for an end to all change, to freeze his world as it now was and forever forestall the future with its promised oblivion.

"Get Louise busy to find out what Mae and Tom are giving and we'll top it with the usual fifty."

"But Tom's virtually bankrupt. Ever since The Strike things have been going nowhere but downhill for them. You know well as I do, they can't be expected to give much."

Like The Crash and The Depression, The Strike, duly fitted out with ominous capitals, meant only one thing, the bloody longshoremen's strike of 1934.

"No reason for us to change. Serves him right for selling out to the goddam Reds."

"But Vince, suppose that awful little tramp married Sal starts putting on airs?"

"Don't fret, Clara." Vince's smile was so smug she could not help feeling reassured. "Sal's money was all tied up in land, and who's buying land right now? We'll do just like always. And nobody's going to top us."

*

"Will I be able to go to the new school?" Arab asked. "Or will I still have to go to public school?"

In the distance, past the row of walnut trees that lined the road in front of the church and over the hump of the Western Pacific tracks, the dusty eucalyptus groves were already wilting on the sun-bleached foothills. Nearer at hand, the picket fence along his paternal grandparents' property was bordered with naked ladies, amaryllis jutting their satin-slick and shamelessly pink heads from brown nests of dried foliage, their perfume ponderously sweet. Not unaware of his role in the sudden dramatic turn of events, he felt a good inch taller as a result of the sermon and walked along the gravel siding with a new spring to his step. At long last something different was about to happen and he had been at least partly responsible.

"There isn't any new school to go to, if you haven't noticed."

His mother had become of late more than customarily testy in her relations with him, her once teasingly affectionate glances now apt to scrutinize him as if she too were about to uncover some secret and dirty corner of his soul. Nor did he for an instant doubt it existed, unknown even to him, but there waiting, like all undiscovered countries, for its Columbus to come along.

"But when it's finished, I mean?"

"When that happens, we'll have plenty of time to think about it."

"But it'll be finished before I'm out of fourth grade, won't it?"

His father laughed. "Fourth year of college, more than likely. If then."

The boy looked dismayed. His parents were once again playing their customary grown-up games with him, clouding over simple facts, teasing him with half answers, confusing him with hints that led nowhere, saying everything but what they truly meant.

"But the way Father talked—"

"Talk's cheap," his mother snapped, almost angrily, though he could not for the world imagine why, unless it was the heat, "and schools aren't. The archbishop," she continued, speaking now to her husband, "isn't going to let him get away with this. Mark my words. At a time like this—why, it would be madness."

"As long as he doesn't expect my parents to donate the land." Henry's spirits took a precipitate plunge. "You don't imagine—?"

"Finally it dawns on you! Where else do you think he intends to build his school? In Hayward?"

"Oh, Lord! Family's given enough already. No reason, just because we own the land on all three aides, we should be expected to give more than our fair share. After all, we wouldn't be in that position if the Old Whaler hadn't donated the land for the church in the first place."

"Well, just see to it your father and mother don't get carried away with themselves, as they're only too apt to, and start giving away what little's left over from the wreck."

"They wouldn't dare. Not after all I've been through trying to put some order back into their affairs. They wouldn't even think of it."

"You know very well that's probably the very thing they are thinking. Why Father, or anyone else with a sweet tongue for that matter, could wrap the two of them around his little finger without half trying. And since there's nothing left any more to give *but* land—" She had not told him yet of her pregnancy and she did not mean to until after the election. He had enough on his mind without that to trouble him.

Something was indeed happening in San Oriel, but Arab knew from the scowls that troubled his parents' faces that he was not about to be thanked for his part in it and he wisely chose to remain silent. The spring gone from his step, he shuffled the rest of the way home, dragging a clipped amaryllis in the dust, his resentment expended upon the bruised blossoms, their slick petals shredded by the sharp gravel.

*

"I do wish you'd send him to Saint Elizabeth's."

The senior Mrs. Ramos was speaking to her daughter-in-law, both waist deep in chrysanthemums as they staked the favored buds destined for survival and November glory.

"If it's money holding you back, why we'd be more than willing to help."

"Now you are talking nonsense. Just what is it you think you'd use?"

"Oh, Louise, things aren't that bad yet."

"If you actually believe that, then your husband's been mighty hard pressed to keep you in the dark. Things are indeed *that* bad. And possibly even worse. But that's as it may be. You know very well we can't send him anywhere else as long as Henry's on the Board."

There was, as always when speaking to her mother-in-law, a certain sharpness in her tone, as though she were the elder speaking to a young child who persists in asking why and then fails to attend to the answer.

"Well, it seems to me the boy's soul comes first."

Louise stiffened at the implied rebuke.

"You do want a Catholic on the Board, don't you?"

"Yes, I suppose . . ."

But that was a lie. She was not truly interested in who was on the Board, or for that matter, what fate befell the public schools. They might all close down tomorrow, for all she cared. She was interested solely in the welfare of her grandchildren, which was to her of considerably more import than the welfare of the country.

"What's your father giving for the drive?"

"I haven't the faintest notion." It was the opening she had been waiting for. "But whatever he's giving, don't think for one minute it can any longer matter to you. Things aren't what they used to be and you'd best remember that. Whatever my father gives, he can well afford to give. And there's no reason in the world you should feel compelled to compete with him. Or anyone else, for that matter."

"Yes, Louise, I'm sure you're right . . . but I still wish you could find some way to send the boy to Saint Elizabeth's. I'd be happy to drive him to the bus stop. More than happy. And help with the tuition," she added, as if she had not truly attended to a word her daughter-in-law had said, but a single glance into Louise's eyes told her that her favorite grandson must continue to place his soul in jeopardy under that terrible Miss Dobson's tutelage.

*

"A touch of port, Father?"

"Why, yes, I don't mind if I do. You'll join us, won't you, Mrs. Woods?"

Determined to remain distantly polite, to avoid offense as much as cordiality, Clara nodded stiffly, her smile barely perceptible. "Just a drop, Vince," she added to dispel any impression that her own wine was to be offered to her in the guise of a gift.

Vince poured two glasses of port, then returning to the liquor cabinet, he poured himself a glass of Napoleon brandy, swirling the golden liquor in the palm-sized glass with sybaritic delight, as with a pixie smile he drank in the envious gleam in the priest's eyes, a perfume every bit as heady as the brandy's.

"Strangely, never cared much for port myself. Keep it for the wife," he added maliciously. "Your health, Father."

With a brave show of indifference, Father Moriarity lifted his glass to both his host and his hostess before sipping. Having learned early in his ministry that nothing is so apt to intimidate a man as the sight of another man in skirts—that was why, he was convinced, the Scots were such renowned fighters—he had come wearing his cassock rather than his suit, trusting in its persuasive powers to win him more than mere words alone could.

"I suppose you've guessed why I'm here," he began, caressing the rim of his glass ruminatively as though he were reading in the ruby liquid the bright outcome of his hopes.

"Well, we didn't imagine it was to bring us the comfort of your blessings, Father. Did we, Clara?"

Vince winked at his wife, who for politeness sake kept her own smile under firm control.

"Yes, well, I'll lay my cards on the table right at the very beginning. As you may already have suspected, it's about the school drive. The archbishop has given us an ultimatum. Forty thousand pledged over the next ten years to cover the cost of four rooms and a house for the nuns.

And, of course, operating costs. The rest to be carried on a twenty-year mortgage by the diocese itself. Or no school."

Vince let out a low whistle. "That is dollars you're speaking of, I trust?"

The priest nodded.

The old man's eyes twinkled, his pixie smile more than usually mischievous. "Forty thousand dollars! I'll wager you could draw a whole caravan of camels through the needle's eye with that amount, eh, Father?" And he patted his wife on the knee. Clara did not smile. She did not need to. Her look of injured injury spoke eloquently about the ability of ancient wounds to resist the healing powers of time.

"I hardly think this a matter for levity." The fine network of veins stood out in relief on the priest's ruddy cheeks.

"No," Vince agreed. "You're quite right. There's nothing very funny about forty thousand dollars, is there?" He spoke with all the authority of a man who has learned his respect for such vast sums from firsthand experience. "And just exactly what part of that forty thousand were you planning on wheedling out of me?"

"From each according to his ability," the priest responded, raising the index finger of his right hand.

Vince's smiled broadened, the light fairly dancing in his eyes. One might have thought he was actually enjoying himself. "Well, if the devil can quote Scripture, I see no reason a priest can't quote Marx. Though I would say offhand—in the simplicity of my nature, you understand," and he nodded, to the priest, "he's no more apt to win over a rich man by such tactics than, shall we say, a discussion of camels."

Pink flames fired the priest's cheeks. So familiar was the swing of the words and so apt their message, he had thought he was quoting the Bible and had almost prefaced the speech with his customary, "Verily, verily I say unto you."

"You're a hard man, Mr. Woods. A hard man." He could only with great difficulty ever bring himself to call the old man by his first name. "Yet the message fits, even if it does come from the devil's own mouth."

Vince's smile continued unabated. "Yes, I'm a hard man, and that's precisely why you're here, isn't it, Father? If I hadn't been a hard man all my life and seen to it that no one ever got the best of Vince Woods, you wouldn't be here right now, would you?"

"But the scales, Vince, must be balanced sometime. And it is my duty as your pastor," the priest continued, puffed now with offended dignity, "to remind you that you aren't going to take any of it with you. Every one of those earthly blessings is going to have to be paid for in one way or another. And with interest added."

The smile disappeared, the voice grew cool, if not positively cold. "I wasn't at the moment planning on going anywhere."

"But how long, Vince? Ten years? Fifteen at the most. And that's considerably more than the just man's three score and ten—which I believe isn't far off, by God's grace. And you know how fast the years fly. Over almost before you've had a chance to catch your breath," the priest persisted, taking full advantage of the opening he had so brutally torn in the old man's pride. "And who's going to be praying for the repose of your soul then? Cutting down those interest rates? Even the best of us are going to need all the prayers we can get. It's only common sense—good business sense—to prepare ahead for the crash. A crash, need I add, that is going to be far worse and more permanent than any Black Thursday. And the Depression that follows that final crash—is that going to be permanent too? Now if you were to come through with—" He paused, just for a second, wondering how much he dare ask for without frightening off his prey entirely, "say, a good half. Or more," he was quick to add, "why we might even see what we could do about naming the school after your own patron saint, Saint Vincent's. How does that strike you? With prayers every morning for the repose of your soul. And there are no prayers heaven is so apt to listen to as those that come from the mouths of the little ones. Every morning calling down God's mercy upon the soul of Vincent Woods."

"Ah, Clara, they're circling already—the buzzards. Can't even wait for the body to grow cold. All anxious to get their claws on a piece of the pie."

He might have been coaxed out of more than he had intended to give, he might have been flattered, he might even have been teased, but he was not a man who could be threatened, even with death and damnation, out of anything. "Well," he continued, "I'm not done with it yet. The soul of Vincent Woods is right here at the moment and he means to hold onto whatever it is the government lets him keep as his own until he's done with it."

"Please, Mr. Woods, remember who it is you're speaking to." The priest placed his glass on the table top, his back rigid with dignity, his jowls trembling. "I'm here in Christ's name on Christ's own business and I will not be compared to—a buzzard." And the booming *basso profundo* that never had the least trouble filling every nook and cranny of Saint Anthony's seemed cramped now in the Woodses' parlor, spacious as it was. "It's not charity I'm asking for, but what is rightfully the Church's. I am here, not as a beggar, but a bill collector. You render unto Caesar what is rightfully his or you risk prison. If you don't also render unto God what is His, how can you expect to escape a similar punishment? The Bible says a tenth of each man's earnings, and I fear, if my records are anywhere near accurate, Mr. Woods, you fall sadly short of that. Sadly short. You are, of course, free to risk your own soul's salvation, but the souls of your grandchildren are also at stake. And those of their children. Are you willing to risk those as well?"

"The school they're attending was good enough for me and good enough for my children. I see no reason why it isn't also good enough for my grandchildren."

"But you and your children were spared the contamination of Evolution."

"It's not Evolution I'm worried about, Father, it's Revolution." A smile once again broke through the old man's gloom. "But all right, I'll tell you what I'll do. I'll give you a check. For ten thousand dollars."

The priest released an audible sigh, his jowls visibly deflated. Though less than he had hoped far, it was still, frankly, far more than he had expected. Even Clara was taken back, catching hold of her pearls as she gasped for breath.

"On one condition," the old man added, as soon as his listeners had regained their equilibrium.

"Yes?" The priest waited, the sudden flight of his hopes braced for a crash. "And that is?"

"The defeat of Roosevelt."

It was Clara's turn to sigh and she accompanied that sigh with the slightest of smiles. She never ceased to thrill at her husband's ability to manipulate people and affairs to his own advantage.

"But surely," the priest protested, his fiery jowls once again distended, "you can't be serious."

"On the contrary. I have never been more serious. The day Roosevelt leaves office, by whatever means, foul or fair, I'll give you my personal check for ten thousand dollars. You have my word and my wife as witness."

"But that's madness. Why should this matter be linked in any way with the election—which, even if I wanted to, I'm hardly in a position to influence."

The pixie smile was back on Vince's face. "Ah, but Father, you forget: the power of prayer. You keep telling us about it. Well, now, here's your chance to give us a little demonstration of that power. No one's going to arrest you if you sneak a few prayers for Landon into your daily mass. Work 'em up in Latin, if you have to. No one around here understands that. I don't care how you go about it. That's your business. Mine, as you well know, is making money."

Father Moriarity vacated his chair, standing well over six feet, the horns of his kinky grizzled hair bristling ominously.

"Mr. Woods, I am a priest. Your pastor. Not a witch doctor."

"And the power of prayer? All those little ones who are going to pray me right into heaven when you can't even pray a man into the White House?" Vince Woods also rose, shorter than his pastor, but hardly less impressive. "Surely, Father, you haven't been playing with me? Toying with an old man's natural fear of death?"

"Betray the party that nominated Al Smith?" He was speaking now as an Irishman as well as a priest.

"You have your answer." The smile was gone. All sense of triumph vanished. He was a banker now abiding by the letter of the mortgage: payment or forfeiture. "Defeat Roosevelt and you'll have your school. Elect him and you'll have nothing. Not a penny."

"You're a hard man, Mr. Woods. A hard man."

"Yes, we've already agreed that's why you're here. And now, if you don't mind, I've work to do. My affairs do not take care of themselves. Good afternoon, Father. My wife will see you to the door."

*

"Stuff and nonsense," Vince huffed from the gold velvet depths of his easy chair. "The boy needs a good spanking, that's all."

"I'll be the one to decide when he needs a spanking or not." His daughter stiffened defensively.

"Then why let him get away with murder? All this whoop-de-do over nothing. It's gone too far. Getting the whole town worked up, and for what? A schoolboy's squabble with his teacher."

"How anyone who made such a mess out of his own son thinks he has a right to tell me how I should raise mine is more than I can see."

It was a cruel blow and he staggered beneath it.

"I have no son," the old man answered, visibly shrinking into his scowl.

"Then why are you subsidizing his affair with that—that creature?"

"Subsidizing his affair! What affair? Clara, what's she talking about?" Hurt gave way to anger, his scowl an anxious query. "I'm not subsidizing anything, you understand? Not a penny. Not a single penny has he had out of me in the last five years."

"Well, someone certainly is." Louise turned to her mother, whose thick and richly ringed fingers fumbled clumsily with the tangled threads of her needlepoint tapestry. "Though no one seems particularly interested in supporting his child. Or his wife."

"If they needed my support they could have stayed. No one drove them out of the house."

"Your son did."

"And her husband," he retorted with telling accuracy. "She took him, for better or for worse, didn't she? No one forced her. No one twisted her arm. Wrong as he may have been—and I'm not defending him, you understand, not to you or to anyone—you have to admit she was the one who deserted him."

"A technicality no judge in the world would recognize."

"Don't tell me a good Catholic like you approves of her divorce?"

"How else could she get a job to support your granddaughter? Who's hiring married women when there aren't enough jobs to go around for the men? Did you expect her to starve waiting for one of his checks to arrive? She at least hasn't remarried. Or taken on a lover no self-respecting person would be caught talking to."

"I thought we were discussing the election," Clara interjected, preferring even Roosevelt to her son as a topic of conversation. "I don't see why Henry's name has to be linked with That Man's. It's bad enough as it is, having him running against one of our dearest friends, without dragging Roosevelt into it."

59

She could never say the name without wincing as if she had just dropped something foul from her lips.

"Your mother's right." Vince was just as relieved as his wife to shift his resentment from his worthless son to a far worthier target. "And if you care to see why, you're free to come take a look at my books. Anytime you like. To see how That Man's already robbed me. Anytime. Why, another four years and there won't be anything left for anyone to fight over when I'm dead and gone. And that'll be soon enough, the way you all peck away at me like a bunch of hungry buzzards before I'm even cold."

He was still fuming from the priest's visit earlier in the afternoon, but his daughter, ignorant of his allusion, ignored the blatant plea for pity.

"Oh, Daddy, you don't really think the poor should be taxed as much as the rich, and you know it."

"I think the poor should work as hard as the rich, that's what I think. Then maybe they'd become a little richer themselves."

"Then give them the jobs. I'm sure they'd be happy to prove you right. And a living wage."

"Give, give, give—that's all you and your damn socialist friends can think about. Rob from the rich and give to the poor. A fancy bunch of Robin Hoods you all are. Well, let me tell you, nobody ever gave me anything. Nobody." He shook his head as if her smile challenged his veracity, his voice rising in both pitch and volume. "Nobody left me a single penny. Not a single penny, do you understand. Anything your grandfather had before he died, he had from me. Not the other way round. And just because you think someday you'll be entitled to something you didn't have to work for yourself, the way I did for mine, every penny of it—well, I promise you this, young lady," he continued, already too carried away by the sheer momentum of the scene to stop it, "if Roosevelt's elected for a second term, you'll be scratched from my will. And I mean it. Yessiree, young lady, I mean it."

"Oh, Daddy." Her smile grew heavy with sadness, her face broodingly beautiful. "You're much too old to be playing that game with me. Much too old to still think you can buy love and respect." She rose from her seat, towering over him. "No one wants your money."

"I'll show you how old I am, I'll show you."

He lifted himself on the arms of his chair, hovered for a moment undecided whether or not to rise and challenge the authority of her commanding position, then with a heavy grunt, he sank back into the down cushions.

"And I'll show you—once again—my allegiance can't be bought. Even by my own father."

And unwilling to leave him with her angry words still trembling on her lips, she leaned forward to kiss him on his still fiercely unyielding cheek.

There were tears in his eyes before Clara had time to cast aside her tapestry and rush to him.

"Ungrateful girl," she said, taking his hand between her two hands and petting it. For the first time her husband seemed to be truly an old man, and the tears rose in her own eyes. "Ungrateful girl," she repeated. "Ungrateful girl."

But her husband proved himself yet capable of surprising her.

"If only she'd been our son—oh, Clara!" His hand limp in hers, he shook his head. "What a pair we would have made, the two of us. What a pair!"

CHAPTER FOUR

The Pope's Legions

Shaded from the early October sun, Arab sat on the cement bench
beneath the pepper tree. The sound of a bell broke the late morning
stillness. He shuddered. It was like a distant cry of pain echoing from
some unknown glade. It came, he knew, from the bleak spire of the
church without a cross. A breeze shook the dry peppers in their pale
red rattles. The sound of scurrying witches answering the brazen call to
dark rites. And he listened with no less horror than the good citizens of
Salem harkening to the Sabbath call.

*

"What's come over Estelle lately? After everything we've done for her."
Since they were just family, Hazel Aiken had eschewed the rigors of the
Iron Maiden so that she as well as the meal had a tendency to sprawl.
"What's the real reason, I'd like to know, she couldn't make it to dinner?"

Busy planning the next day's gardening, Madie Aiken was so intent
upon pruning the old hydrangea blossoms to hang upside down in the
garage for drying, she did not realize she was expected to say something
until her daughter-in-law called her up sharply:

"Mother Aiken!"

"Yes, my dear?" The pleasantly bland smile with which she ordinarily confronted the world, even those closest to her, fell, and she seemed
for an instant almost frightened, not sure precisely where she was or
why. Family, she had long since come to the conclusion, were simply
people somehow sanctified by habit and custom into making more and
greater demands upon one's time and attention than courtesy would
otherwise have allowed, and she was not altogether sure she wouldn't be
willing to sacrifice any one of them for a truly splendid rhododendron.

"What is it so important Estelle couldn't take time out to eat?"

"Oh, didn't I tell you? She's moving."

"Moving!" The effect was electric. "No, you certainly did not tell us. What's the matter? Is the room no longer grand enough now she's become a local celebrity?"

"She said something about people wanting to exploit her situation." The dowager Mrs. Aiken looked troubled. "But I don't think she meant us, exactly. I'm almost sure not. She seemed afraid people might think, since she was living with me, she was somehow involving herself unprofessionally in the campaign."

"Stuff and nonsense!" Mr. Aiken said. "Everyone's entitled to vote. Teachers as well as anyone else."

"She means well, dear," his mother replied. "She's been brooding lately, poor thing. I fear it's all been a bit much for her. She was carrying on last night so I couldn't make heads nor tails out of what she was saying. Something about being turned into a living cliché. Would you like some more dried hydrangeas this year, my dear?" she added, speaking now directly to Hazel with stunning inconsequence. "Or should I dry just enough for myself?"

"Why, yes, I suppose so. A bunch on the piano might be nice. But whatever could she be talking about? A living cliché?"

"More stuff and nonsense. One of those expressions the over-educated are always using to put the rest of us in our place," her husband opined. "Don't see why she can't speak English like everyone else."

"At her age," Hazel continued, "I suppose it's still far too early for The Change. But with that gray hair one never knows. It may not be quite so premature as she claims. And to tell the truth, I've never been altogether convinced she hasn't been fudging on her figures. Not that it isn't every woman's right."

The smile with which the elder Mrs. Aiken responded to the word "age" seemed almost wise as she slipped safely back through the garden gate. She liked them best—hydrangeas—when she could catch them with just enough autumnal red so that they dried a dusty rose rather than mauve.

*

"Grandpa's out front."

Alert to the dramatic possibilities of his grandfather's strange behavior, Arab rushed into the house. At the sink his mother, rinsing the breakfast dishes, spoke above the rush of water.

"Well, tell him to come in."

"He says he won't. We have to go out there. If we wanna see him."

"What do you mean he won't come in?" She turned the water off, and wiping her hands on her apron, she quizzed her son with her eyes as well as her words. "Is something the matter? Is he sick?"

Not even the driveway. He says he won't step foot in our yard, and if we wanna see him we have to go out here." So breathless with excitement was he, his words all came without pause into a single sentence.

At the front gate, in the shade of the hawthorn tree, Clara sat behind the wheel of her La Salle, her husband beside her, his face set, stonily gray and fiercely unyielding. A royal personage awaiting the homage of duty before the fall of the ax from one already condemned of treason.

"What's the matter? Are you ill?" Clutching the apron in her hands, Louise peered anxiously through the rolled window.

"Ill? Why should I be ill?" His voice was querulous; his eyes, focused on some invisible point directly in line with the chrome radiator cap, refused to meet hers. "Do you think the old are fit for nothing but sickness and death? I've a long time yet. A long time."

"Then what's all this nonsense? Certainly you're not—"

"Is that all you have to say to your father?" Clara called from the driver's seat, her own face every bit as fiercely unforgiving as her husband's. "If so, we'll leave. Right this instant." And she switched on the ignition key. "I'd hoped you were ready at last to apologize."

"To apologize!" The flood of tears that washed Louise's eyes did not extinguish their fire. "Apologize for what? Following my own conscience?"

"There's no talking to you, is there?" The tight, lavender-tinted curls that fringed the older woman's round face trembled like so many coiled springs. "You're always right. Always right. Even as a young girl there was never any talking to you. Incapable of ever seeing any side but your own. Never!"

"If that's true," Louise retorted, unwisely, but too sharply stung not to release a little venom of her own, "some of the blame must be yours, since it was you raised me."

"More sass," the old man grumbled above the engine's roar and they were off in a cloud of dust as golden as their La Salle.

65

"But why won't Grandpa come into the yard anymore?"

Trotting to keep up with his mother, Arab studied her face. Her cheeks were blotched with hot marks, her eyes were wet with tears. She was crying. Granted, it was a mild form of the phenomenon. There were no convulsions shaking her, no sobs racking her body—yet she was indisputably crying and the sight both confused and frightened him. His mother, the mistress of all situations, the terror of all salesmen, the invincible champion of all causes was, by her tears, now admitting her own vulnerability. She who by sheer force of will could intimidate his father, or any other man he had ever known, to any action she deemed fit was now demonstrating her own weakness. Had the very earth beneath him trembled he could not have felt a greater sense of panic. True, there were times when his mother's strength shamed him—shame was not too strong a word—if only because it so glaringly exposed his own shameful weaknesses; times when he longed to let the sorry victim of her displeasure know that she could be soft as well as shrill, a warm, loving refuge, a bank of sympathy, a fount of affection. More often he secretly thrilled at her ability to sweep all before her, to vanquish every foe and right every wrong. The only unconquerable Ramos. "No one ever gets the best of Louise Ramos" was an article of faith for the entire town to live by, and because he had himself so fervently believed in it, he had known from the first that, once his mother entered the fray, Miss Dobson did not have a chance. Now the sight of her tears revealed that even she was mortal, and the very foundation of his world was rent by a fault as potentially dangerous as that which undermined the town itself.

"But why won't Grandpa come in our yard anymore?"

"Because your grandfather's a very stubborn man."

"But he still goes to Aunt Lorraine's. I saw him."

"Sometimes, when people get old, they get childish again and there's no longer any reasoning with them. He's not a young man anymore," she added and her tears were as much for his dying as his rejection. "He's nothing left to cling to but his pride. And that's strong enough to outlive us all," she concluded, her tears suddenly dried in the heat of her resentment.

*

Despite the absence of Minnie Costa's customary pot of baked beans, the Saturday afternoon crowd at Costa's Corner was larger and

noisier than usual. Though it was raising havoc with Costa's marriage, the election was proving a boon for his business.

"Hear the Pope's gonna excommunicate all Catholics who don't vote for Ramos."

"The old man got nothin' better to do?"

"What better than get control of the government? Next thing you know, he'll be marching in with his legions."

"Doesn't have any anymore. Just a buncha fancy-dress guards."

"Don'cha believe it. He could muster a million. Overnight."

"Mussolini'd never let 'em outta the Vatican."

"They wouldn't have to be Italian. Ever heard of the radio? He's got spies in every capital."

"Well, San Oriel's no capital."

"Yeah, but it's a beginning."

*

With the parish list in her hands, Louise Ramos waited at Sarah Furtado's back door. Except on the most formal of occasions—a christening party, a wedding reception, a post-funeral gathering—no one in San Oriel ever knocked on anyone's front door.

There was nothing resembling a garden. A few herbs—rosemary and mint and parsley— seemed to flourish of their own volition against the house and within the wet range of a dripping faucet. Chickens roamed the gravel yard, the V-shaped lot pressed so snugly against the Western Pacific tracks that every passing train seemed to pass through the bedrooms whose rattling windows looked out upon them. Rabbit hutches, piled one on top the other, leaned against the tank house and a salted pelt tacked to one wall dried in the sun. Not a fleck of paint marred the bare boards of the house.

Wiping her hands on a soiled apron, a beaming Sarah opened the screen door and Louise stepped inside, surprised to discover that she who had for years kept the Woodses' mansion in such pristine order lived herself in a state of litter that amounted to squalor. The furniture Louise recognized as rejected pieces from her own childhood home, covered still in their original fabrics, tawdry and worn. Except for a church calendar, there were no pictures on the walls. The only carpet she could spy through the door opened to the front parlor was one that once covered the floor of her own bedroom when she was a girl. A chair hid what she knew was a black stain left by a bottle of India ink tumbled in a fight with her brother and for an instant so discommoded her she blushed. And the blush only intensified when she considered what pittance her parents must be paying the poor woman after years of virtual slavery.

Sarah herself seemed unembarrassed by her own surroundings, oblivious to her cluttered sink, her unswept floor, or her shabbily soiled person.

"Come in, come in," she kept repeating long after her visitor had already entered, Sarah's sweaty, crinkled face shining like crushed foil with smiles that contrived to be at once both warm and deferential, her hands clutched together beneath her monumental breasts as though she were waiting for instructions.

"I was just out ringing doorbells," Louise began, "and I thought—a hunch, you understand—but you are registered, aren't you?"

"Registered?" The smile on Sarah's face dimmed to dismay.

"Yes, registered to vote? Today's the last day."

There was an edge of panic in the young campaigner's voice.

Sarah shook her head.

"But surely you've voted before?" Louise was momentarily incredulous.

"Me?" Sarah laughed, her good humor restored. It was a sound that was to her almost as natural as breathing. What've the likes of me to do with running a country the size a this one? Why, if it wasn't for Henry—"

"But you can't vote for Henry or anyone else unless you're registered. Your friends—the other ladies—do you think they're registered?"

Again Sarah shook her head, amused at the absurdity of the very notion.

"Well, then, get your coat on." Challenged by a crisis to demonstrate her true mettle, Louise was in an instant a model of efficiency. "We haven't a minute to lose. I'll drive you in my car and we'll collect as many ladies as we can. You'll have to point out where some of them live. I don't suppose you'd have a list of members?"

"No, but Julia Freitas has."

"Then we start with Julia Freitas."

*

The post office, outside of which Louise Ramos dropped as many of Sarah's friends as they had managed to round up, was a tiny box of a building across from the Protestant cemetery and topped with an American flag almost as large as the building itself. Faded by many summers of relentless sun, the colors were now closer to orange, cream, and lavender, than the

original red, white, and blue. No details had been overlooked and each of
the ladies crowding into the tight little lobby clutched a copy of her bap-
tismal certificate as proof of citizenship. Shielded from the crushing crowd
by a brass grate and a wall of iron-framed, glass-fronted cubicles stuffed
with letters and circulars, Mrs. Ferguson sat in horrified state.

"What party?" she asked, two tiny, darkly disapproving eyes peering
through a mask of white powder, her coal-black hair revealing roots of
gray, held down by its customary widow's-peak net, her brilliant crimson
lipstick bleeding into a whole network of fissures and cracks about the
delta of her mouth.

"Party?" For the second time that day Sarah was dismayed.

"Political party."

"Oh, at Mrs. Ramos's," she promptly answered, nodding good-
naturedly as she studied the ghostly apparition before her with the barefaced curiosity of someone at a carnival sideshow who has paid for her
admission and means to get full value for her quarter. Never having had
cause to mail or receive a letter, Sarah had never before been inside the
post office, which was not in her part of town, and though she knew
of Mrs. Ferguson by reputation as the town's virtual monument to the
World War, she had never before seen her and like most public monuments, Mrs. Ferguson took some getting used to.

"I'm afraid that's not yet a recognized party." Always coolly proper,
the postmistress's voice dripped icicles, her stare glacial. "Republican or
Democrat?"

Sarah turned to Alverta Pimental who, if possible, was even more baffled.

"Maybe she means the New Deal," someone from the back of the
room called out. "Which is the New Deal party?"

Unwilling to take advantage of such invincible ignorance, Mrs. Ferguson, who had somehow survived Hoover's defeat, possibly because
most of the town's Democrats assumed the post, like the building itself,
was her birthright, if not her husband's deathright, readily registered the
ladies as Democrats. As they left, she sighed sadly, once again confirmed
in the wisdom of her own political choice, but fearful for the future of
the country her husband had sacrificed his life to defend.

*

Back in Costa's Corner the battle raged on. The wit bubbled like
froth on the new beer which had blessedly replaced the old two-per-

69

cent mouthwash that had masqueraded under the name throughout the long, dark years of Prohibition.

"Hear Roosevelt's gonna become a Catholic."

"No, don't say?"

"Yeah. Got Al Smith and Father Coughlin both working on him from opposite directions."

"Well, wha'd'you know."

"Won't be announced till after the election. Gonna send Eleanor off to Rome as ambassador to the Pope."

"Christ, what's amatter with the woman? Can't she ever stay at home and tend to her own business? Like everyone else."

"Hell, if your wife looked like that, would you want her hanging around the house?"

"You got a point there. Time for another beer?"

*

The grammar school auditorium was fast filling up. Since it served also as a rainy-weather gym, it was staked with iron posts for volleyball nets and basketball rings, fringed now with orange and black crepe paper in preparation for Halloween, which was even more extensively celebrated on every wall, by cutouts of witches, black cats, and pumpkins. The lettered motto—TIME AND TIDE WAIT FOR NO MAN—stretched across the top of the stage to warn those, most of whom had never seen the tide and all of whom were far too young to know the meaning of time, what the future held in store for them.

Mae and Tom Ramos entered in a splendor intended to belie the ruin of their fortune. Tom Ramos was stouter than ever since his wife seemed determined to cure his recent ulcer with kindness, overfeeding it with a rich variety of custards and desserts in the hope, one presumes, of smothering it with calories. The bluff manner and the jolly-friar face seemed, at first, little changed, but anyone who took the pains to look closely enough at the laughing eyes could see behind their superficial gaiety the terror of a man under sentence of death. And he moved to his front-row seat trailing a burden of memories like an iron ball on an iron chain. Neither he nor his wife had ever missed a single one of their son's public appearances from the time he had first stepped onto the stage as a gauze-winged angel in a Christmas pageant the year of the Great Quake.

Not quite such a staunch admirer of his father's hortatory talents, their grandson Arab squirmed. Although he relished the honor implicit in front-row seats—and his family always took the front seats at all public affairs—they did present certain drawbacks. Since the real show, as far as he was concerned, would not be on the stage, but in the auditorium, his was actually the worst seat in the house. Straining to see who had come in, he attempted to measure his father's prospects, but no sooner did he get anywhere near a fair estimate than someone new entered and threw off his count.

Across the aisle, also in front-row seats, sat the two Mrs. Aikens. The junior Mrs. Aiken wore her mink coat, which did not go over well with most of the other ladies present. Clara Woods, the only other woman in town who might have topped her with sables, had another of her famous migraines and did not make an appearance. Sarah Furtado wore a white crocheted badge with Ramos cleverly worked in blue. She and her friends formed a claque in the rear of the auditorium determined to drown out the opposition jeers, should there be any, with their cheers. A modest round of applause greeted the entrance of Miss Dobson, dressed in her customary plain tweed suit, beret, and flat-heeled walking shoes, the ends of her bobbed hair pointed up like the curved blade of a pitting knife. So severe had her lack of adornment become of late it amounted almost to a form of ostentation. Arab's restrained boo was quickly stifled by the claw-clutch of his mother's hand about his upper arm, which virtually lifted him off his seat. Estelle flinched without smiling at the applause and then with a determinedly polite smile as tight as a rubber band stretched for snapping, she nodded to the Ramos party. Arab longed to stick out his tongue but contented himself with a darkly sinister glare. Mae Ramos, who could not have been more offended had the devil himself greeted her, turned away with a toss of her chin. Tom Ramos seemed not to know or care who she was and continued to smile to the world at large as if the lines of his face had been fixed in plaster. Only Louise personally returned the smile with one of her own, though considerably warmer, almost lush, her dark eyes sparkling with the odds-on favorite's condescending magnanimity. Except for four folding chairs and the speaker's rostrum, the stage was bare.

Accompanied by Mr. Perkins and Mr. Marlin, the two candidates made their entrance simultaneously. They were greeted by a hearty

71

round of applause interspersed with a few cheers. Looking more than ever like a freshly plucked chicken under the glare of the stage lights, Mr. Perkins made the introductions.

Wearing a discreet Roosevelt button on one lapel and a miniature pink rosebud on the other, Henry Ramos, as incumbent, was the first to speak.

"The issues are clear-cut," he began, without notes and in his best public-speaking baritone, his natty polka-dot bow tie adding an incongruously frivolous note to the seriousness of his words. "It is simply a question of the rights of the family versus the rights of the state. Are we to follow the example set by Germany and Italy into the totalitarian state," he continued with all the polished ease of the experienced public speaker who knows that he has already won, not only the subjugation of his supporters, but the envy of the opposition, "or are we, like true Americans, to take our cue from Thomas Jefferson and uphold the right of the individual against the corporate, of conscience against dictation?"

He did not mention religion.

"Such a lovely voice," Sarah Furtado said.

"Such a handsome man," Alverta Pimental said.

"Skirted the issue," Hazel Aiken said.

"All he needs is a banjo to complete that ensemble," the Widow Ferguson said. "Never did trust a man with a mustache."

"Hrmphff," Mr. Aiken said and took his place at the rostrum.

His suit was tighter and his complexion ruddier than usual. A single deep breath and every seam might have burst. The veins at his temples bulged with the same precarious distention, threatening a disaster more fatal to his cause than any laughter induced by the burst seams of his trousers. He was all too apparently not at his ease, his back as rigid as the top sergeant he so resembled, his scowl as fierce as a samurai charging into battle and hoping to intimidate into submission an enemy he knows he is otherwise incapable of subduing. He wore a Landon button on one lapel and a white carnation on the other. The unquestionably less enthusiastic reception could be discounted if one took into consideration the natural exuberance of Latins.

"The issues are clear-cut," he began, his less experienced voice tremulous with unease. "It is simply a question of progress versus reaction," he continued, not once lifting his eyes from his typed script, each word issuing forth democratically with precisely the same emphasis as that bestowed upon its predecessor. "Are we going to step forward into the twentieth century lit by the torch of science or forever stumble unaided through the dark tunnel of ignorance? It was Lincoln who freed the slaves. Today it is the scientists who must free our minds."

He also did not mention religion, Darwin, or Dobson.

"Not much of a speaker," Sarah Furtado said.

"Can't hold a candle to our Henry," Alverta Pimental said.

"That'll put them in their places," Hazel Aiken said and then patted her mother-in-law on the thigh. "I hope you're properly proud of your son, Mother Aiken."

Mother Aiken, who had just been wondering if next year she might not have zinnias against the back fence instead of asters, smiled enigmatically. At her age, planning for the future was a luxury far sweeter even than motherhood.

"Prose as purple as his face," huffed the Widow Ferguson, sure she had detected the guiding hand of Estelle Dobson in the unimaginative Bob Aiken's apotheosis of science. Still disgruntled over the still unweeded cemetery, she wasn't sure that she might not, party regular though she was, just show them all and let her own vote ride.

"Hrmphff," Henry Ramos said, then pinning on a smile as perky as his boutonniere, he rose to shake his opponent's hand. It was a gesture that won the approval of Miss Dobson and so befuddled Bob Aiken that his face grew redder than ever, his lips and throat conspiring to cough up a few indecipherable sounds.

As with most such exercises in democracy, everyone had come with his mind already made up. There were no obvious conversions to either side and the crowd filed out much as it had filed in, though fired now with new purpose, new and renewed zeal.

*

The afternoon was as gray as Henry Ramos's mood.

"Yes, Miss Dobson? What can I do for you?"

"Good afternoon, Mr. Ramos." Estelle rose awkwardly, coming from behind her desk to greet her visitor. "I do appreciate your coming. I know it's an imposition, but I had to speak to you. And a telephone call simply would not have done."

"Well, I won't pretend that it isn't an imposition until I've heard you out." He looked about for a seat, but not tempted to try one of the miniature desks, he remained standing. "I'm sure you're as aware as anyone of the drain of the classroom upon one's emotional resources. By mid-afternoon my wells of sympathy and understanding run a little dry, I fear."

He made no attempt to temper his words with graciousness.

"Indeed I am. Oh, indeed I am," she responded, clutching a large envelope before her with both hands, as if it might, if she let go, fly away. "But what I have to say must be said now. Before the election. I wouldn't want you," she continued, her eyes watering with intensity, "to think I'd acted out of pique. Or resentment. Like a poor loser."

"Yes?" Suddenly more curious, he studied her.

"I want to hand you my resignation," she blurted out, furious at her inability to temper her blush as she thrust the letter stiffly before her.

"Oh, dear Miss Dobson!" He sank into the single chair alongside her desk as she remained standing, still clutching her letter, which he made no effort to accept. "Aren't you over-reacting somewhat? No one has ever challenged your abilities as a teacher. I least of all."

"Ah, but I have. And that's what counts most."

"I'm sorry, I don't understand." She had quite taken his breath away.

For the first time he could see beneath the forbidding manner, the austere cut of her hair and the eminently sensible garb how splendidly handsome she was. Not, like his wife, the least bit lush, but taut and angular, even muscular. She was like a woman of the frontier, one, he imagined, who would be equally at home behind a plow or a stove, yet at the same time undeniably a woman.

Acutely aware of his scrutiny, which, though far from hostile, even flattering, was so bold as to be almost rude, she continued to blush.

"There are, I've discovered, more traps for a woman than matrimony. And I fear that's what the classroom has become for me. A trap," she added with another blush.

"Oh, do please, Miss Dobson, take a seat." He waved his hand before the empty chair behind her desk though his eyes remained fixed on her. "I'm not here to judge you, but to help. Though I'm not sure how I can except to warn you of the seriousness of your step."

"Of that I'm already aware." She resumed her seat. Their faces were close now, their hands even closer, each suddenly—and disconcertingly—conscious of a strong undercurrent of sensuality.

"I hope my son hasn't been responsible for your decision." It was his turn to blush.

"Oh, dear me, no." Her laugh, though genuine, was not easy. "I will admit one of the chief factors was the sudden realization—and maybe I do have him to thank for it—that I don't really like children very much. Nothing truly personal you understand," she continued as he shook his head sympathetically. "Arab has more spunk than most and far, far more brains. But I'm a grown woman. Thirty-seven, Mr. Ramos," she added with a defiant lift of her chin, as if she fully meant to stun him with so outrageous an admission. "And here I am reduced to quarreling with a nine-year-old boy. Having my life shaped by a roomful of other people's children with their runny noses and their unsightly scabs, and—oh, Lord help us!—their sleepy little minds mired already—and irrevocably, I fear—in apathy. Well, I've simply had it. Had all I can take."

75

"Your daring, my dear Miss Dobson, dazzles me."

He sat for a moment looking at her with such frank admiration he quite lost his voice. Then suddenly aware that if he did not move, his hand, in another minute, would be on top of hers, he rose and walked to the window. "I suppose I should warn you—it seems to be standard in such proceedings—there is a depression on and perhaps you should take time to mull over your decision. Jobs aren't going to be had for the asking out there."

"But that's just what I don't want to do, I'm afraid. If I think too long and seriously about it, I'll lose my courage. Naturally nothing's going to be had for the mere asking. But a faint heart, as you must know, ne'er won fair maid. Nor anything else worth winning. And in this regard, I did want to ask a special favor of you."

"Please." He was now all affability, his charm, though flagrant, for once completely uncalculated.

"I realize my contract binds me to teach through June—and I certainly don't intend to leave you in the lurch—but if it were at all possible to find a suitable replacement, I'd like—with your permission, of course—to leave at the mid-semester break."

"I'm sure that can be arranged. I'm constantly being besieged with applications from well-qualified people desperate for any position. But only reluctantly, you understand. At your own insistence."

"And I do insist."

"What are your plans?" Their business completed, he seemed reluctant now to leave her.

"To go to New York. Isn't that what they always do in the movies? When the spinster schoolteacher, I mean, takes off her glasses and everyone suddenly realizes she isn't quite the old dragon they'd all imagined. She runs off to the Big Town to win fame and fortune." Her smile now was quite confident, with that special sense of power and elation that always comes from the sudden discovery that someone finds us sexually attractive. "And why not extend the cliché? Let it run its course. It'll be too far away to tempt me to fall back on anyone here. And as good a place as any to let whatever's going to happen happen. And if I make a fool of myself—well, who'll be there to notice?"

"I'm sure you won't do that."

She nodded, standing also now and moving away from the security of her desk.

"I am, you know, quite envious," he said. "All my life I've been fascinated by explorers—da Gama, Magellan, Cabrillo—and their great sea voyage. Yet the only ships I'll ever board, I know only too well, are the models I build myself. Unless you want to count the San Francisco ferry," he added with a sardonic chuckle. "I've taken that often enough. You'll be the voyager now, discovering new worlds. While I remain here. Mired in small-town politics." He shook his head, marveling still with such frank admiration, she basked in the warmth of his gaze, glowing. "I'd ask you to join me for a celebratory drink at Costa's, if I weren't so sure the shock waves would be more than the town could withstand."

"Oh, dear, that would cause a seismic rumble." Her laugh mingled with his. "But I'll accept the suggestion for the act." And laughing still, she could already feel the exhilarating play of the wind in her hair and the spray of the sea in her face, as she handed him her letter.

*

The line formed early outside the small, white-clapboard building next door to Costa's Corner that served as town library. It was for Sarah Furtado and most of the ladies of the S.P.R.S. a first venture into politics and they meant to make the most of it. Before the eight o'clock opening of the polls, the ladies, decked in full ceremonial regalia, white suits and gilt-fringed green-and-red sashes, and bearing their lodge banners, formed a cordon about the door. To pass the time while they waited, Mamie Serpa's drill team performed a few tricky numbers to the delight of curious bystanders and passing students laden with satchels and lunch pails. Promptly at five minutes to eight, Miss Tutt arrived in the town's only electric car still in use. It was almost as anachronistic and every bit as well preserved as she herself. Tightly corseted, her neck encased in a lace choker, her hair topped with a nest of blue-rinsed curls and looking for all the world like the ghost of the Dowager Queen Alexandra, Miss Tutt entered, armed only with her formidable presence to protect her books from the milling riffraff. She too saw herself as a missionary bringing culture to the natives and kept a chest full of prizes as eclectic and dated as the musty volumes that filled her shelves, everything from chipped crystal vases to glass-eyed porcelain kewpie dolls, to lure the town's young to the wonders of Camelot and Illium. As they had for every election within memory, Mrs. Ferguson and the senior Mrs. Aiken joined her.

There was not, Sarah was quick to point out, a Port, or even a Catholic, for that matter, in their number. It would not be a fair election. Sarah's suspicions were further confirmed when Mrs. Ferguson, her hair and costume as determinedly black as ever, her face its usual white mask, came out to order all banners removed at least one hundred feet from the polls. No one challenged calling the representation of the Holy Ghost an electioneering device and Sarah paced off precisely one hundred feet, then leaving Mrs. Pimental to guard all campaign materials, the Holy Ghost banners among them, she led the other ladies into the post office to cast their ballots.

A short time later, the ladies were once again in formation. Led by Immaculata resplendent in a cut-down version of her confirmation dress, noticeably too tight across the burgeoning breasts that were still unabashedly free from any restraining halter, and twirling a shiny new baton, they marched to the I.D.E.S. Hall to string the colored paper lanterns, tack the red-white-and-blue bunting and curl the crepe paper streamers for the victory supper of *sopas* and new wine.

*

Neither Arab Ramos nor Dickie Aiken was so fortunate as Immaculata. Despite vociferous protests, both were compelled to attend class, Arab wearing a large Roosevelt button and Dickie an even larger

Landon button.

The entire school seemed swept up in electoral fever. Miss Humphrey had tried to bring home the election's significance to her young charges by helping them construct a donkey and an elephant out of chicken wire and *papier mâché*, a project scorned by Miss Dobson as frivolous. But then Miss Dobson was apt to cast scorn upon all projects initiated by Miss Humphrey, whose classes were a perfect beehive of noisy, buzzing activity filled more often with the sound of laughter than the productive drone of intellectual exertion. Miss Emery, the eighth-grade teacher, had set up her own election booth and passed out stenciled copies of the local ballot, but since she herself was registered to vote in Hayward and not San Oriel, her own impartiality excused what for any other member of the faculty would have been foolhardy. It was a teaching device much admired by Miss Dobson, but with sons of both candidates in her class, one she herself did not dare employ. She decided instead to devote her own Social Studies hour to the state propositions and was almost immediately diverted from the discussion of the financial intricacies involved by Dickie Aiken's challenging question.

"Who *you* thinks gonna win?"

It was not, under the circumstances, a question she could easily ignore. Though the boy was putting up a brave front, she thought it wise to prepare him for the eventuality of defeat.

"We must all remember, in the long run, Dickie—and everyone else," she was quick to add, sweeping the class with her eyes, "and Manuel, stop picking your nose—it's not whether you win or lose that matters so much as how you fight the fight." And with a look that might have corroded iron, she fixed her eyes upon the smirking Arab.

Already galvanized by the cocky certainty of vindication, he remained unaffected by the stare.

"How come it's always the losing side makes that speech?" he asked, cheered on by Manuel, who was now busy licking clean the finger he had previously used for probing.

Though consoled by the still-secret knowledge that her days of classroom drudgery were blessedly numbered, she could not tolerate such barefaced insolence and long keep what remained of her self-respect.

"You are a perfect example of what I was just trying to get across to the class—the necessity for good sportsmanship. I fear no matter what the results of today's election may prove to be, you, Arab Ramos, have already won the prize for bad manners. And to see that you are properly rewarded, you will remain in your seat after the bell rings, please, and reap your harvest."

Foolhardy, Dickie guffawed in triumph. "Black Portagee," he snarled.

"Fat, pink-faced Protestant," Arab was quick to retort, his own snarl every bit as venomous.

In a display of almost superhuman neutrality, Miss Dobson kept both boys after school to write, "All men are brothers," three hundred times, and as the cramped, hurried fingers rushing through the final row of "brothers" grew ever stiffer, each boy, conscious that the world's first brothers were, after all, Cain and Abel, became more than ever confirmed in the justness of his own enmity.

79

*

As the day wore tediously on and the ladies, their decorations completed, their iron pots steaming, grew ever more restless, Sarah became ever more convinced that the election would not be a fair one, particularly with the opposing candidate's own mother officiating, a conflict of interest no one else seemed prepared to challenge. Suddenly, almost out of nowhere, talk of insurrection was rife. As chairman of the political action committee, Sarah was prepared, if called upon, to assume the armor of Saint Joan and herself lead the *coup d'etat* that would place Henry Ramos in the chair that rightfully belonged to him. By seven, when the polls closed, the crowd outside the library was already large and growing uglier by the minute.

"What's taking the old witches so long?" an anonymous voice inquired.

"They've only got ten fingers apiece," some wit responded. "You want they should take off their shoes too?"

"Besides," someone else added, "it takes a lotta time filling out all those unused ballots before they destroy the real ones."

"You don't imagine they'd actually do such a thing, do you?"

"With those old biddies I could imagine anything."

Fearful of any ill-timed precipitate action, Julia Freitas resumed her rightful position as Madame President, taking back the authority that Sarah Furtado seemed only too ready to usurp, and while the counting was still going on, she once again led her impatient ladies in an orderly recitation of the rosary. The Protestants grumbled at such unscrupulous tactics, made all the more offensive by the strange foreign tongue with its singsong sibilants which had all the force of an incantation. But they were clearly outnumbered. Somehow peace was maintained and bloodshed miraculously prevented.

By 8:15, after three careful recounts that in no way affected the outcome, the results were tacked on the library door and Miss Tutt barely escaped back inside before being mobbed by the impatient crowd.

Aiken 58 Landon 58

Ramos 197 Roosevelt 196

When the cheering subsided, the ladies, led once again by the triumphant Sarah performing an arm-waving, hip-swinging war dance, spontaneously burst into a rousing rendition of "Faith of Our Fathers Living Still."

*

Multicolored Chinese paper lanterns resurrected from Mae Ramos's party closet hung from strings of outdoor Christmas lights strung across the stage and entrance to the I.D.E.S. Hall. At stage center pom-pom chrysanthemums formed a single large golden R, economically serving double duty for both Roosevelt and Ramos. The barbecue tables that lined the two side walls were a clutter of used paper plates and napkins, of crumbled bread crusts and discarded bones. A blend of mint and garlic hovered in the air like a strong aftertaste to be washed down with liberal quantities of new wine. Seated on the stage, two saxophonists and an accordionist led a handful of reeling dancers through the last stages of the *chamarita*. The victor himself did not dance. His wife was not feeling well—and with some cause.

These ethnic celebrations always left her slightly embarrassed. Though her blood was as "pure" as that of anyone else in the hall and considerably purer than some, she could not help feeling herself a stranger in their midst, one to whom the language and the music were both foreign. She did not feel particularly Portuguese, and conscious that her reaction was undoubtedly a manifestation of class, since the only Portuguese spoken in her parents' home had been to servants and workmen, she was even more acutely embarrassed by her own embarrassment. She herself had never known any country but America or any language but English. She was, moreover, too deeply wedded to common sense to romanticize, as her husband was apt to, a world their ancestors had clearly found inadequate, if not intolerable.

She was also preoccupied with a more personal problem. Now that the election was over, she could not for much longer postpone telling her husband of the impending addition to their household, which she was confident he would welcome with all the enthusiasm of an extra bank loan as one more strain upon a salary already stretched to the limit. But whatever else happened, she was determined that she would not, under any circumstances short of imminent starvation—and that prospect seemed as yet happily remote—appeal to her father for a loan. For the election results had announced considerably more than her husband's victory. They had also measured the true depths of her parents' alienation. Though the one-vote discrepancy in the Roosevelt column remained somewhat baffling, it was only too clear that everyone who had voted for Landon had also voted for Aiken—which could mean only one thing. The Woodses, who might, for family's sake, if nothing else, have taken advantage of the secret ballot to leave that section unmarked, had chosen instead to cast their votes against their own son-in-law. And that knowledge soured the sweet taste of victory.

*

The initial adversaries whose vindication and defeat were being at least indirectly celebrated were both themselves missing from the festivities. Neither surprised nor upset by the results, since she was convinced that in both cases the better man had won, Miss Dobson was at home philosophically "curled up with a good book," as she told a commiserating Hazel Aiken, and one can be confident that the "good" was as much a comment on the moral as upon the aesthetic character of her reading. Nor did she really need consoling. She had always been in love with the beauty of beginnings, and now her own life was to have a new beginning. She was about to embark on a great voyage of discovery. There was a new and as yet unknown world out there awaiting her and she could scarcely wait to lift anchor. Two months at most with a two-week Christmas breather to break the tedium and plan her getaway. Though she had cause enough to celebrate, her own personal victory was still too private for public sharing, and it would be greatly overstating the case to say that she in any way regretted her absence from the election-night festivities.

The same cannot be said of her chief opponent. His vindication had proved less than the triumph he had anticipated. It would be a long, long time before he would be prepared to forgive his mother for denying him permission to attend. Not that he had expected to be borne like some Olympic victor on the shoulders of the crowd—though he would have been the last to resist such a move on the part of a grateful constituency. It was first of all that he could not, in these lean years, bear to miss *any* party, let alone one he felt himself responsible for. Secondly, he longed for some public confirmation that his parents did not, as he had secretly come to suspect by their refusal in any way to commend him in their condemnation of his teacher, hold his own role in the affair, for some inexplicable reason, against him, but were finally prepared to indulge him with praise and affection in quantities sufficient to compensate him for the indignities he had been forced to suffer on their behalf.

Denied access to the party, he was struck anew by the unreality of the last three months. After all the fuss and the turmoil, after all the shouting and the running about, nothing had actually happened. He and San Oriel were just where they had always been, both lost under the immensity of the open sky. The dull, interminable procession of days would continue their monotonous pace so sluggishly all motion must seem mere illusion. He was trapped, and forever, he feared, in this backwater of a great city that was at once both tantalizingly close and impossibly distant. True, his father had been elected trustee, but then he had already been trustee before and his re-election generally taken for granted. True, again, his own position in the conflict had been vindicated by an aroused electorate and the terrible Miss Dobson had per force curtailed her readings from the heretical book, but she was still his teacher and he her pupil and there was to his knowledge little chance their ill-mated alliance might soon be severed.

Nor had anything more been heard of Saint Anthony's new parochial school. Not a penny had yet been collected, not a stone laid. It was widely rumored that the archbishop's building committee had already vetoed Father Moriarity's application as untimely, grounding the drive before it had taken off. Thus the young of San Oriel were doomed, like their parents before them, for at least another decade, to hazard their souls in the godless environment of a public school. But with Henry Ramos now guaranteed four more years to maintain a vigilant watch over their welfare, most seemed reconciled to the prospect.

The greatest change was in the fortunes and the character of Sarah Furtado. Her venture into the world of public affairs had left her dazzled and not a little shaken. Already her name was being bandied about as the obvious replacement for Julia Freitas, whose term as Madame President was due to expire the following spring, and Immaculata's selection as Queen of the Holy Ghost Parade seemed now a virtual certainty. To make that certainty a reality, the young lady, wearing cork wedgies and a ruffled skirt made out of Clara Woods's old kitchen curtains, her head topped with a monumental mound of wax fruit, was at the very moment giving a very convincing imitation of Carmen Miranda singing "Ma-ma-mamma eu quero."

Sarah alone seemed—and so uncharacteristically—indifferent to her daughter's lively talents. Nothing for that matter, not the music or the dancing or the wine, could rouse her from her terrible lethargy. Her heavy, pleasantly homely features sagged disconsolately and her eyes shied from all contact. For after a second and more careful reading of the election results, she was doomed to spend the remainder of the evening nursing a dark and terrible secret.

In her understandable impatience to carry Henry Ramos to victory, she had failed to stamp her X after Roosevelt's name, and nothing could now convince her that she would not, the next morning, wake to the terrible knowledge that he had lost the election by a single vote, and she would ever after have to bear the awesome responsibility for having single-handedly changed the course of history.

She was flying west. In Joyce, she recalled, that meant toward death. And there could no longer be any denying, although Christmas remained the ostensible excuse for her visit, it was death that awaited her at her journey's end. And how happily she would have changed roles, taken her precious Nikita's place and herself moved willing westward into the setting sun.

But expressed thus, the image proved almost offensively trite, and for all the great innovator's claim to originality, as old, certainly, as literature itself.

She had met Joyce once. In Paris. Sometime between the wars. A party on the Seine, she remembered. Stravinsky had taken them. After the ballet it had been. Diaghilev's Ballets Russes. Joyce had been there. A funny, myopic little man with the thickest glasses she's ever seen, and despite his scandalous reputation, rather more seedy than heroic. And too drunk by far to say anything at all memorable. About setting suns and westward movements. Or anything else, for that matter. Years later, someone—or had she merely read about it?—told her Proust also had been there. An historic occasion. While for her it had been only another party in a continual round of parties, life itself a party for anyone so young, so beautiful, and so rich. The fame she had left to her husband and his friends. They were all, it seemed, famous. Or about to be. And all, sadly, dead now. Taken their own westward journeys.

The riches, at least, she had held onto, like a young lioness defending her cubs—even against her daughter's extravagances. Which had become of late so intemperate that Nadia at times actually questioned Nina's sanity. Which made her, now that the end of their ordeal was fast approaching, more determined than ever to harden her heart and once again tighten her defenses, if only for the sake of her remaining grandchildren. No longer would she allow thoughtless and irresponsible onslaughts upon a fortune already nurtured through an inflation that made a mockery of millions—no number of which, they had all too sadly come to learn, could halt the spread of her grandson's cancer or buy him one more hour of suffering life than they had already bought him. A cruel extension to which he—poor darling—clung so fiercely that her own agony was tempered with pride. At his undaunted spirit, the deceptively slender young boy forged on the fire of her Cossack blood into splendid steel. Against such odds to have kept death at bay so long! Oh, what a man he would have made! Worth a thousand of his father. A thousand Harrys. But then she had never been able to understand her daughter's taste in men. They were chosen, she sometimes suspected, more with an eye as to how thoroughly they might shock or disappoint her mother, rather than satisfy her own peculiar passions.

86

"Hebraic Cossacks?" she could hear the taunting Nina, ready to sneer at anything or everything her own mother said or did. "I'm sure the closest our ancestors ever came to a Cossack was the long touch of his whip across their backs."

But why, Nadia had wondered, her answering smile more sly than offended, that so telling "Hebraic," when, if her daughter had meant to stun her with a blunt instrument, a plain, straightforward "Jewish" would far better have served her purposes? For all her arrogant "honesty"—though "vulgarity" was too often, and sadly, the precise word—Nina had herself taken to calling Nikki her "brave little Cossack," whenever recounting one of the sardonic comments that had made the frail thirteen-year-old a legend of western pediatric wards and the terror of every trembling, whey-faced intern bumbling in his first attempt to get an intravenous needle clean into one of the long-since depleted veins on his first try:

"Have you ever considered joining the scavenger's union, because you sure as hell make a lousy doctor?"

Yes, without a doubt, Nikki had the soul of a Cossack.

And hadn't Stravinsky himself—and who should know better?—once called her a perfect type of Russian beauty? A beauty that was now so little more than a pale reflection of its former self, that death, her own death, had already lost most of its sting, could be greeted now in her dotage (and though there was no one nigh to spy upon her thoughts, she raised a well-ringed hand to still the polite denials) almost as an old friend. Little more than a long forgetting. No longer to have to remember anyone's name! The day of the week, the month of the year—anything at all. Which was not at all like her, for she had always prided herself on keeping up to date, familiarizing herself with the latest twist of the constantly spiraling world of fashion. Not that she for an instant intended to follow it, to substitute her sun-drenched Matisses for an entire gallery of Warhols. But not to know Warhol and his work, despise it as she might, would, she was convinced, lessen the value of those same Matisses.

But how remote that world seemed from thirty thousand feet! Poor Nikki! Although she had promised faithfully she would not in his sight or hearing, by so much as a gesture or an inflection, manifest pity, alone with her thoughts, the seat beside her in the first-class cabin blessedly empty, she let it now wash over her. The tears welled. But in a trice she bit her lip and, arching her back, mastered her emotion. No, she too would be a brave little Cossack. Until the very end, she would not succumb to grief. Not until she was once again winging her way east would she allow her heart to overflow and, safely alone, confront the rising sun with the full weight of her agony.

*

In the cavernous hall Nadia sat alone. Dusk was fast turning to dark, but the panel of switches alongside the front door was so formidably complex she did not dare touch anything. She was lucky to be indoors at all, the taxi having deposited her at the front gate just as the maid was leaving. A simple-minded Central American. Colombian? Nicaraguan? She could never remember which, not that it mattered. The poor thing next to useless. Not a word of English and the brain of a not particularly well-endowed five-year-old. But muscle enough to lug the two heavy suitcases up the three sets of stairs and the long walk to the front door of this miniature Versailles overlooking San Francisco Bay. Why her daughter had ever bought it she would never understand; but there was so much about Nina she would never understand. Her positive penchant for losers, for one. The down and out as well as the downright disreputable. Stray people as well as stray dogs. These pathetic, illiterate immigrants with their dirty habits and dirty nails contaminating every dish. Yet who else would put up with such a household? The five dogs, none of them properly housebroken, the drooling, rheumy-eyed Saint Bernard with her weak bladder and slobbering jowls the least of them. The constant chaos of missed appointments and late meals and clutter, clutter, clutter. Children—love them as she did—who dropped whatever they were playing with wherever they happened to be the instant they lost interest in it and never once made to pick up after themselves. Or to make their own beds or get anywhere at all even approximately on time. Caleb as bad as poor Nikita, and Elena, though she alone showed at least some evidence of anything so practical as common sense, all miserably undisciplined. Like the dogs and Nina herself. An irresponsible, self-indulgent lawlessness that the children, she knew in her bones, would one day grow up to hurl back in their mother's face.

But this time she would hold her tongue. This time, Nadia had promised herself, she would say not a word. This time she would be a well of pity and comfort. And love. Poor Nikki! Poor Nina! How her heart must be breaking!

But why, she could not help wondering, had no one bothered to call? They had all, she gathered from the maid, a few hours before her arrival rushed off to the hospital. A new doctor? A new treatment? A new crisis? She could make so little sense out of the woman's tearful babbling. An unwanted sympathy that merely steeled Nadia's resolve to keep her own emotions well under control. Fortunately she had decided to ignore the myth of California and come fully prepared for winter, which seeped through the large picture window behind her, a damp chill more insidious than ice. Outside, the misty bay, the hills of Marin black against a foreboding sky, the flashing yellow lights marking the towers of the bridge, formed a suitably melancholy scene, but too theatrical by far for her own tastes. What painter worth his salt would dare pit his genius against anything so spectacularly suited to a glossy, king-size postcard?

With smug disdain she turned her back upon the view and, wrapping her sables about her, buried her hand in her pockets. Her daughter, she knew, would sneer at the coat's pretensions, and her grandchildren ridicule her for wearing what they persisted in calling dead-animal skins—as if the very shoes they themselves wore were not also fashioned from the skins of dead animals. Though she was sure they had an answer for that as they had for everything else. She was too old to try to change. Or even to understand. The coat kept her warm. Luxuriously warm. And she would not even pretend she did not revel in its touch.

She found it, moreover, not just a little comic that someone who chose to live with such ostentation could sneer at anyone else's pretensions. But Nina, the same willful child she had always been, was never disconcerted by the inconsistencies of her own character.

*

The man who came charging through the front door was quite as startled as he was startling. "Charles," he said, quickly identifying himself, and Nadia immediately recognized the reassuringly mellow baritone. One of those handsome, sexually ambiguous, and now middle-aged retainers her daughter always seemed to gather about her person, like moths around a porchlight, though this one seemed rather more durable and less brittle than most, having for some twenty years or more been content to play walk-on parts in the continuing drama of Nina's life. A not unsympathetic Prufrock, she thought, as he groped his way through the shadows to kiss her proffered cheek. With Charles, at least, unlike most of her daughter's acquaintances, one could always be sure that his dress would be proper, his accent cultivated, his understanding broad enough to catch all but the most arcane of her allusions, and his own means, at the same time, so touchingly limited as to be positively reassuring.

"Nina said she'd been calling for hours."

"Well, I've been sitting right here, patiently waiting. Since well before four o'clock. Have you seen Nikita?"

"I just stopped by the hospital to get the keys. Nina was afraid you'd missed Faviola and were sitting outside on the front porch. Hasn't the phone rung?"

"No. And you haven't answered my question."

"No, I didn't see him. He doesn't like anyone but the staff in his room when he's being treated. Except Nina, of course. He can't bear to have anyone else see him without his wig on."

"Does vanity then outlive hope?" The smile that punctuated her question was filled with wry pride.

"Apparently," he answered his own face too deeply shaded to be interpreted. "But can't we get some light here?"

"I wouldn't dare tackle that panel. I'd be sure to set off the panic button and look up to find half the local police force massed out on the front terrace. Do you have any idea what's happening?" she persisted while Charles fidgeted with a barrage of switches.

"No. I never ask anymore." He kept his back to her. "Ah, that's better," he added as he dimmed the sudden glare of the spots with the rheostat.

"Is it so bad then?" She studied his face, now fully visible and, she thought, softly vulnerable, as if it too had been stretched beyond its limits and had settled itself into a mask of benign pity.

"Even Nina seems, for the first time, to have given up. After a year and a half of believing the two of them together could achieve the impossible. And they very nearly did," he added, almost defiantly as he met her eyes head on. "This summer I really believed he'd made it."

"We all did." She bit her lip to still the flow of tears. "Our brave little Cossack. That's what makes it doubly hard."

"Come," he said, taking her by the arm with practiced gentility. "There's no reason to hide in the hallway." Then opening the double sliding doors onto the main salon, he bared a dazzling display of Kazaks glowing from the spacious floor with all the splendor of a light-bejeweled medieval transept. "It isn't much, but your daughter calls it home."

She detected enough malice in his smile to invite conspiracy—an invitation she did not intend to pass by. For if she could not altogether win him to her side—and "sides" there always were whenever she and her daughter were concerned—she might at least enlist him as a kind of double agent. Middle-aged men of limited means and delicate sensibilities were always, she found, subject to bribery, as long as the bribe was presented with sufficient tact to make its acceptance appear as a kindness to the giver. And she was famous enough for her tact to head a vast number of charities.

"I don't understand," she said, settling back into a Louis XIV fruitwood chair, one of four, stripped and upholstered in a buff suede, "why she ever settled upon this place. It gives me the heebie-jeebies."

He smiled at the antique phrase. "Its sense of scale, perhaps, appealed to her."

"But I always feel as if I'm waiting for a train. Don't you?" She fixed her eyes upon him, her charm palpable. Insistent.

And ready to be charmed, he smiled. "I'll admit it isn't conducive to intimacy."

"Just look." She ran her hand over the arm of her chair. "Would you believe, the dogs have already been gnawing at it. Criminal! Absolutely

90

criminal! If one wants beautiful things, then one has to assume the responsibility to care for them. Really," she rose to check the damage to the matching three chairs, indignation shaking her. "Nina should be forced to choose. If she keeps the dogs, she simply should not be allowed proprietorship over such treasures."

"Ah, the dogs," he answered, as if the sigh were sufficient unto itself.

She would not, however, let him off so easily. "But certainly you agree it's criminal?"

He shrugged. "Where animals are concerned, you should know better than anyone, your daughter simply is not rational. But listen! What's that?"

Perplexed, she shook her head. "I don't hear a thing."

"It must be the telephone. Nina said she'd call." And he ran into the hall, but the phone was missing from its usual station, the muffled ring issuing from the guest toilet, where the phone had, for some reason or other, been locked away. When he tried to open the door, he found the way blocked by two pony-sized dogs noisily hurling themselves toward the narrow opening. Quickly he closed the door and descended the stairs to the kitchen. Nadia followed, catching her breath as Charles nearly lost his balance on a pool of urine at the bottom. Dodging past yet another dog, which could easily have been half Saint Bernard and half stallion, he finally reached the sideboard telephone.

Nadia, luckily, had not removed her rubber boots, and stepping gingerly around the outer edges of the puddle, she headed for the phone, her hand extended, like one groping through the dark.

"Hello, darling, how is he?"

"Oh, Mummy, I don't know—" Nina's voice seemed not so much to break off as to disintegrate.

"Do you want me at the hospital with you?"

"No, no." The response seemed almost a reflex, the fragments too quickly reassembled. "You'd only frighten him."

"Well, of course, I don't want to be in the way." She could already feel herself hardening against the exclusion, her voice prim with reproach.

"No, Mummy, please! No silly misunderstandings this time. Please. I can't take them. Nikki is so looking forward to seeing you. But he wants to see you at home. The whole family together. And if there's the least chance—any chance—we'll bring him home tonight. As soon as we can. Even if—oh, Mummy, if he dies, I want to go with him. I won't be able to bear it without him. I won't."

"Nina!" In an instant, personal hurt gave way to pity. "You mustn't even think such things. You have two other beautiful children who need you every bit as much as he does. And you mustn't ever let them hear you say a thing like that. Or even suspect you look on them as leftovers. Ever. Do you hear me? Now get a hold of yourself. For their sakes. And if there's anything I can do, I'll be right here waiting to hear from you. Right here. For as long as you need me."

As she hung up, she leaned far forward, both hands upon the counter, her elbows rigid, and breathing deeply, steeled herself with a shaft of air.

"Can I fix you some tea or coffee?" Charles's voice was gently solicitous.

"No. No, Charles." She looked up, surprised to find herself observed. "Thank you, but I couldn't swallow a thing. But you have something. You haven't eaten, I suppose?"

"No, but that can wait."

"The other children—I assume they're with her? I didn't even think to ask."

"She never takes Nikki to the hospital without them. It's been a family affair from the first."

"I'm not sure I approve, but that's her affair. And Harry? Still here?"

"Yes, thank God. He was supposed to return this morning, but stayed over."

She became suddenly the *grande dame*. "I'm not sure I'm prepared to thank God or anyone else for that honor. I can," she continued, interrupting the attempted demur with both hands, palms out, cupped about a globe of air, "forgive Harry for almost everything except taking the children to court. Forcing poor Nikita, as the oldest, to act as peacemaker. And for what? To reduce the child support he wasn't paying anyway to a sum so ludicrously inadequate it wouldn't have kept them in shoes. And don't tell me those constant legal battles didn't wear the poor boy down, until—"

"I agree. Taking the children to court was inexcusable. But someone has to be there now to help her bear the burden. It is his, as well. And he's cool, if he's anything."

"Cold, I think, would be more accurate. Do you really believe he cares for the children—except as a means of getting back at Nina?"

Again he shrugged. "I'm beyond making judgments. About any-one's feelings. But don't let's stay down here. Fond as I am of your daughter, I do draw the line at cleaning up after her dogs."

"Let me take your bags upstairs," he said, once again in the entrance hall, where two scuffed but elegant Louis Vuitton bags sat at the foot of the grand staircase.

"But where am I to stay? Harry, I suppose, has my usual room. Last time it was a colored man." She made no effort to disguise the bitter-ness of her resentment. "Would you believe, I wasn't even allowed to step foot on the third floor?"

"Ah, Salim—or so he chooses to call himself. His real name's Roger Tatum. At any rate, that's the name on his Princeton degree."

"He's actually got a degree?"

93

"Oh, yes. Quite legitimate. Though I think that's just about all that's legitimate about him. Claims to be a Sephardic Jew."

"Well, if he is, he's got quite a spectacular suntan. And why should a Jew—of any kind—choose a Muslim name?"

"I imagine he fashions himself in flowing burnoose with a jeweled sword jutting from a silken cummerbund. And you must admit, he would make quite a stunning picture. Straight out of the nineteenth century academy. Pure Gérôme. The Jew part throws me. Unless he hoped to give Nina some small means of identification. I find the 'Se-phardic' part touching, don't you?"

"I simply can't understand my daughter's penchant for colored men," she continued, ignoring his question. "I think, sometimes, like a little girl, she simply delights in shocking. To get even with me. Or perhaps I misjudge her and it's merely the world she's out to get even with. For something. Lord knows what, she's had everything."

"Maybe that's the problem. If you've had everything, doesn't it pretty much add up to the same thing as having nothing? But he isn't her lover. Of that I'm almost certain. She hasn't had time for a lover. Time for anyone or anything but Nikita. Salim's just a fancy con art-ist who's wheedled his way in with a patently phony story about los-ing the apartment he'd made a down payment on when the landlord discovered he was black. And next to stray dogs, Nina's a sucker for mistreated Blacks."

"Only if they're young, male, and good-looking, I presume you've noticed. He isn't the first. I suppose you know that, too. There was that other one. The actor in New York who was, as she finally had to admit, though at the time she denied it vehemently, accusing *me* of prejudice for my all too-accurate suspicions, trafficking in heroin. In her very own house, mind you, with the children right there, ready to get caught in the crossfire. But," she raised her hand to forestall any defense he might attempt to make, though he seemed quite content to listen in silence. "I've promised myself: this time I would hold my tongue. No reproaches. About anything. Money or men. Or anything else. This time I would save all my emotion for poor Nikita. They aren't, I hope," she confronted him with a face of tragic concern, "still torturing the poor dear with chemotherapy? At this late stage."

"As I've already told you, I no longer ask any questions. I don't want to know. Or become involved in any of the decisions. My only concern now is to be here when she needs me. Because when it does finally happen, she's going to—"

He broke off to answer the telephone, rescued with some difficulty from its pony-sized guardians.

"Speaking of the devil," he said as he rejoined her in the salon. "That was Salim. From Princeton. He's supposedly getting married this weekend. To some model, naturally. He sent invitations to the entire faculty at Town School, I understand, but none to Nina. He told *her* he was going to visit his grandmother."

"And what did *he* want?"

"Your guess is as good as mine. I told him Nina was at the hospital and in no state to talk to anyone right now."

"He has moved out, then?"

"Well, not altogether. *He's* gone, but his car's still in the garage and his things are all upstairs. So I wouldn't raise my hopes too high. But do let's get your own bags upstairs before I go. I'll put them in Nina's room and you can sort out the sleeping arrangements later."

"Here's my number." He handed her a card before he left. "And please, if you need anything, don't hesitate to call. I'm only four blocks down the hill."

"Thank you, Charles. You've already been an immense help." She offered her cheek to be kissed.

"And do be gentle with her," he added, catching hold of both hands so that she could not avoid looking at him. "You know how she adores the boy."

"But we *all* adore him."

"Ah, but she won't allow that—that anyone else's love can even begin to touch what she feels."

"Yes. They have been close. Too close, I sometimes think. More like conspiring siblings than mother and child. Building their own little bastion against reality. It hasn't been a healthy relationship."

"Cancer's not conducive to health of any kind. We all know Nina's impossibly extravagant and sometimes infuriatingly impractical, but you can be thankful her virtues are so much larger than her vices. So do be kind to her. She's going to need all the kindness she can get."

*

95

What an extraordinary thing for him to say! She could forget neither the words nor the look with which he had fixed her. As if she had not already been more than kind! What stories, she wondered, had Nina fed him that he should so much as think her capable of unkindness at such a time?

Her collar up, she was still wearing her sables, now wrapped around her nightgown, and her bunny slippers (a habit formed in the thirties as the byproduct of one of her husband's jokes, but by now far too comfortable ever to relinquish), adding an incongruously homely touch. Too restless to sleep, she roamed the empty house. It was filled with ghostly rattles and wheezes and groans, the wind sucking into empty chimneys or leaning heavily against plate glass. She did not believe in ghosts, but the place did indeed seem haunted, Nikita's room so filled with his still-living presence she could scarcely believe it possible a spirit so palpably present was at this very instant, perhaps, departing forever. And with a pang that gripped her heart like a cruel foreboding of her own impending death, she stooped to pick up an artist's tablet, the small, colored-pencil drawing touchingly precise, but when one considered the artist's age, there was just enough flare to hint at genius: the fallen lead soldier with its broken rifle forming the diagonal axis, the vanishing point precisely where the heart would be. Was it intentional, she wondered, or merely an accident? But what did it matter—*what might have been!* And where art was concerned she had long since ceased to believe in such happy accidents. No, in anybody's book he had been quite, quite exceptional. Too fine, perhaps, for so cruel a world. And aware suddenly that he had already become in her mind, companion to those other ghosts of her memory, of the past, she quickly fled.

Caleb's room, like Caleb himself, was far more robust. A mad scientist's laboratory cluttered with small armies of plastic spacemen, planetary monsters, and electronic robots, with here and there the battle-strewn remains of stuffed animals bleeding kapok. Toys on top of toys, like some ancient geological excavation, a modern Troy with all its years laid bare, layer upon layer. Nothing was ever thrown away, no toy, no matter how decrepit, ever discarded. In another few years, she feared, one would be hard put to wade through the debris.

She had never, alas, managed to hammer home to her daughter the lesson that life was a matter of selection, that one could not hold on to *every*thing. That one must choose the best and cling to that. And not like some spoiled, greedy child hold fast to the last minute while already reaching out for the next. She had, for that matter, never been able to teach her daughter anything. And suddenly with an ache stronger even than her grief she longed for it all to be over: to have what must be, be and have an end to it.

*

The telephone that woke her the next morning found her still in her sables, a wool afghan thrown over her feet, her head against a bank of pillows on top of Nina's bed. She held her hand upon the receiver before lifting it to allow herself a moment to still the sudden panic and brace herself for the inevitable—which proved, instead, to be neighbors complaining about the dogs. And the animals were, she could hear, now that she was fully awake, indeed making a fearful racket. But the poor things had not been fed and were scarcely to blame. She apologized—profusely, for her sympathy, treasonous though it might be, lay with the neighbors. One by one, she knew, they had all come to learn, as everyone who had ever tried must, that Nina was not an easy person to live with or near.

Alone as she was, she promised, she would do what she could to quiet them. But what, she wondered, as she hung up, for she was not, by herself, about to brave a charge of hungry animals the size of buffaloes. Charles's card tucked under the corner of the telephone offered an easy out. People who allowed themselves to be used, she had long since come to the conclusion, more often than not wanted to be used, if only to add a touch of color to their own drab lives. And Nina, certainly, even under the worst of conditions, offered color and drama enough to brighten any number of gray lives.

Before he arrived bearing a bagful of bones large enough to keep all five dogs occupied for most of the morning, she had already received two more phone calls, one from the water department and the other from the gas and electric company, both threatening to terminate all services if payment were not received by noon the following Monday. In cash. The bills were already three and four months past due, so Nina could hardly blame their neglect upon the current crisis. In the best of times she was apt to conduct her financial affairs as a series of critical confrontations to stave off last-minute disasters—court orders, foreclosures, repossessions, and terminations of one service or another, so why should she now, in the worst of times, have been expected to change? Yet there was in their very pettiness sufficient cause for annoyance: like some disturbance in the balcony during Hamlet's death scene, they dulled the sharp edge of tragedy, so that even in this supreme moment of her daughter's life the farcical maskers would be dancing in the wings.

Thus when the fatal call did finally come, the shock was at first blunted by the defenses raised to head off the importunities of yet another anxious creditor, and hanging up, she had to bite her hand to control the sobs she had not been prepared for, Charles there offering his chest as a momentary ballast.

"No, no," she said, as he seemed prepared to engulf her in his embrace. "I'm all right. Quite in control now. Quite in control." And she lifted her head like some haughty Clytemnestra schooled in grief, the patina of age adding new luster to an old beauty. "It's Nina we must look after. Nina who needs us now."

She would show him how kind she could be.

*

And poor Nina, she thought, not many minutes later, her daughter limp against her breasts, seemed more stunned than grieved, her cheeks hollow, the ghostly pallor of her complexion made all the more starkly white by the black brows, the always startling green eyes immense, but tearless, unable to settle for more than an instant upon a single object or person, her wildly prodigal hair transforming what might have been the face of tragedy into a pre-Raphaelite Medusa. A baggy, homespun

Irish sweater, the sleeves pushed up, covered her torso to mid-hip, from which a full gypsy skirt fell almost to her ankles, buckled with a scruffy pair of wedgies: for all the world, her mother could not help thinking, even at such a moment, like some orphan blown in from the storm. Poor Nina!

With maternal cooings, more sound than meaning, since there were for such an event no words remotely adequate, she passed her daughter from her arms to Charles's, and submitting a somber cheek to Harry's chill kiss, she shivered, not from the touch of his lips, but the grimly inappropriate plastic Santa Claus mask that adorned the closed door onto the room where Nikita's body lay. Through the window onto the playroom, she could see her two surviving grandchildren making a concerted effort to keep their eyes averted from the adult drama unfolding outside.

"The children," she said, answering Harry's kiss without meeting his eyes. Nina seemed almost anxious to be rid of her visitors, guiding them with her hands out of the corridor so that she might herself return to the closed door, alone, except for Harry's blandly somber presence. His most ordinary face unduly wary, as if he were expecting at any moment some obscenity ruder even than death to confront him with the need to act and wring from his customary passivity a reluctant decision. *Monsieur Moyen* was Nadia's pet name for him. Mr. Everybody and Mr. Nobody. It was a face that she could never recall from one meeting to the next, the sheep's mask that disguised the wolf she knew him to be, whose voracious appetite for luxury poor Nina had once mistaken for a passion more personal.

But for all his prosaic features and his moral deficiencies he had given her three beautiful grandchildren—reduced now to two, Nadia corrected with a sudden pang so sharp she had to steady herself on the playroom door, the lost Nikita, for all her attempts at impartiality, so far more precious than these sturdy survivors that her guilt transformed a very real affection into a parody of itself.

The solemn Elena, whose full-featured face might someday outshine them all with a lush, Titianesque beauty, though her figure, her grandmother feared, would always be that of a thick-waisted peasant, sat determinedly dry-eyed. Submitting to rather than answering the affection foisted upon her, she seemed more bored than moved, like one who has sat too long at a seemingly interminable service that demands an exhibition of her very best manners but does not for an instant touch her understanding. Having for the past year and a half had every free moment of her young life restricted by the cruel exigencies of her brother's illness, *her* every wish deferred to his needs, she would indeed be an exceptional child if she did not, in some secret part of her soul, rejoice now at her release—the chance at last to be someone other than Nikita's sister. But how was one to tell her, poor dear, that she must not ever be made to feel guilty for so natural a reaction, that they had all, Nikki included, been in a sense liberated at long last from the tyranny of his cancer?

As stout as a miniature sumo wrestler, his always sturdy body gone to fat from so many hours of idle waiting in hospital corridors with little to ward off boredom except soft drinks and rich pastries, Caleb seemed prepared to sit out the day. Or his life, if need be. Except for his somber mien, a caricature of unfelt grief, he seemed the very picture of contented lethargy, the face itself not so much saddened as weighted with the terrible knowledge that he now, at nine, must play the "man of the house," just one more excuse to retard action.

"Did you children already have breakfast?" Nadia could never look at Caleb's plump Buddha face without automatically thinking of food. "Here in the hospital?" she continued in response to the two silent nods. "And dinner last night—did you have that also in the hospital?"

"No, we went out," Elena volunteered.

"To Ciao," Caleb added, anxious once the sound barrier had been broken by his sister, to join in.

"To a restaurant? Did your father take you?"

"No, Mommy."

"Then who stayed with Nikki?" The name, she knew, must never become a sacred taboo, so best bring it quickly out into the open.

"He went with us," Elena answered, her expression so matter-of-fact it merely increased her grandmother's incredulity.

"Nikita went to dinner with you last night? In his condition?"

"It's his favorite restaurant," Caleb offered the information as if it should solve all difficulties. "Granny," he continued, his chubby hand upon her arm to hold her attention, "they have this great tagliarini with basil and—"

"But how?" she interrupted, ignoring the tug at her arm and looking to Charles for enlightenment, but receiving none, for he was quite

99

as mystified as she. "Certainly he couldn't have walked."

"Oh, no. We carry him in his wheelchair." Now that he had started talking, Caleb seemed unwilling to stop, his words tumbling forth in a mad scramble for release, his pauses determined, not by the claims of syntax, but the shortness of his breath, "We've been there / every night this week they have/ this really great *tagliarini* I was trying / to tell you about it's green / and they use this pesto sauce / with a whole lot of garlic / and gobs and gobs of butter and—"

Her eyes even more skittish, but ominously tearless, Nina entered and Caleb grew instantly silent.

"The children tell me you took Nikki to a restaurant last night."

"Yes." Her eyes, focused far above her mother's head, explored the view outside, the air washed from the evening's rain; the city sparkling in the winter sunlight though a dark line on the horizon portended yet another storm before nightfall. "He insisted we go out. He's simply amazing that way." She paused, her face momentarily troubled, as if she were trying to recall something. "You don't know what courage—"

"But why, then—" her mother began, but left her question unfinished, for she had promised herself there would be none of their usual recriminations, no word from her to add a featherweight to her daughter's already immense share of grief, and she meant to abide by that promise—yet she could not help feeling cruelly hurt that she had not also been included in that grim little dinner party and given one last chance to see her precious darling alive.

In the ensuing silence Charles rose. "Would you like me to take the children out for a walk?" he asked. "There must be so many decisions to make."

"No," Nina answered, her voice faintly censorious, "I'm sure the children don't want to go out." Her eyes for an instant met his with a flash of—hostility?

It was thus Nadia interpreted the look with a sudden flash of intuition: Nina would be now as jealous of her grief as she had always been of her son's love—a relationship that had in its excess bordered on the embarrassing. And as if to confirm her intuition, she noticed for the first time Nikita's ring, an antique Roman intaglio, already fitted onto the third finger of his mother's left hand.

"Then, if there's nothing more I can do, I think I'll take my leave. These are family matters." And like the perfect courtier, his ear finely attuned to the subtlest hint of dismissal, Charles made his departure—but not before Nadia had countered Nina's cool indifference with the warmest of handclasps and a silently soulful look intended to reassure him that if some people had already forgotten his immense kindnesses, she at least had not.

"Elena," Nina now turned to her daughter, "wouldn't you like to go with us to make the arrangements for Nikki?"

"I don't care." The voice was scarcely audible, the young girl's eyes intent upon a styrofoam cup whose lip she was neatly scalloping.

"I can't hear you."

"She says she doesn't care to," Nadia answered, despite her resolve, and unable to disguise her disapproval.

"I think, Mummy, Elena is quite capable of answering for herself." The voice bristled. "Well? Do you or do you not want to help make the arrangements for your brother?"

Without lifting her face or altering her expression, Elena repeated her answer.

"You see," Nina's voice continued churlish, "you heard what you wanted to hear. Not what she said. It's an all too familiar habit of yours."

"But Nina, darling, aren't you, perhaps, letting the poor girl in for more than she may be able to handle?"

"What's this?" His unshaven face creased with fatigue, Harry entered the room, a steaming cup of coffee clutched in his hands.

"Nina wants to take the children to the undertaker's."

"Well, she's doing no such thing." It was the well-known voice of quiet determination that had never before intimidated Nina and was not about to intimidate her now.

"They can sit in the car and wait for us, if they must. But they're going." Rising to the challenge the voice grew sharper, though the hysteria remained momentarily contained. "We've done everything together up to now. And we're not about to change just because—"

The silence was so sudden, so total, and at the same time so pregnant with the unspoken, it cried out to be shattered.

"What about the child's eyes?" Nadia began, her voice softly tentative. "Did you—?"

"The child?" Nina fixed her mother with a mad-Medusa look that fairly turned the latter to stone. "What child? His name is Nikita. Not

'The Child'! Please remember that. And he's keeping his eyes. I will not—Oh, my God! I need some coffee," she continued as she moved swiftly from the room. "Some very black coffee."

"Oh, dear," Nadia sighed. "Oh, dear, dear, dear."

Harry's laconic smile offered little comfort.

"It might," she added, compelled to defend herself, "have given some small measure of meaning to his suffering; to know that his—his death—gave some other child the gift of sight, just might, later, help to make the unbearable bearable."

"You're preaching to the converted," Harry answered, his voice, like his whole person, limply weary. "I was quite prepared to sign them away. But your daughter won't even allow an autopsy. Tomorrow she'll be bleeding—metaphorically, of course—for all of suffering humanity. But given the chance today to help the next poor devil of a child who's going to die from the same—"

"Harry, please. Not now. In front of the children."

"Oh, yes, the children. Well, she's determined not to spare them anything. Then why should they be spared the knowledge of their mother's monumental selfishness? I'm sure they've never been spared full knowledge of any of my faults. And they've got to realize that what's in there, in that room, isn't any longer their brother. With or without his eyes. *He* took off this morning for outer space."

"Harry!"

He chuckled joylessly, a sardonic grunt that was clearly not directed at her but at his own troubled memories. Both of his children now looked at him for the first time since he had entered the room, their somber masks giving way to flagrant curiosity.

"It's Nikki's own explanation of what took place in there. He actually used the expression. Said he was being sent into outer space for some mission or other." He paused a moment before continuing. "'I hate to leave you guys,' he said. A not half bad imitation of Humphrey Bogart. But I don't think he was just being plucky. Trying to shore us up. He seemed truly convinced he'd been chosen and the whole ordeal had been some kind of test to prove his mettle."

Caleb and Elena linked eyes, their smiles conspiratorial.

"Well," their father continued, "if it was a test, he certainly passed it. All colors flying."

"A brave little Cossack," Nadia added, trying to master her tears. "And," she continued, turning first to Caleb and then to Elena, "we must honor him now by showing that we too can be brave little Cossacks."

*

The promised storm broke well before dark, and though the house with its four floors and its numerous rooms should have proved large enough to allow them all ample space to seek out their own form of solace in comfortable privacy, they might just as well have been snowbound in some New England farmhouse with a single fire about which to huddle, so constantly did they come together to lash out at each other, as though the only way to heal one hurt were to inflict another. In the comparatively intimate upstairs sitting room with its tiny, elegant, but poorly stocked bar (a plethora of polished brass, marble, and mirror, but a mere scatter of half-empty bottles, most of which seemed to have been chosen for the beauty of their labels or the peculiarity of their shapes rather than for their content), Nadia, Nina, and Harry seemed destined to gather. In the adjoining room, Caleb and Elena found their own solace in front of the television, the drone of which blended with the torrential gusts of rain whipping the windows that overlooked the bay.

"He's the one who first taught me how to love," Nina offered at one point, and though Nadia knew the attack was aimed not at her but at Harry, she too was forced to flinch. "I didn't know what the word meant before he was born." And with a single phrase she dismissed, not merely her one-time husband but both parents and an overly indulgent grandmother whose loving generosity made possible this very house with all its treasures. "I suppose," she continued, after a melodramatic swig from the lip of the brandy bottle clutched in her right hand, "it's a talent as rare as any other. Loving." And she studied her interlocutors as if they, poor things, had been born defective, forever denied knowledge of that mystical bond that had linked her with her Nikita. Her hair had been twisted into a haphazard bun at the back so that she looked now less like a wild-eyed Medusa than a wan Aphrodite, her skin as white as Carrara and her green eyes, resplendent beneath her full brows, as softly vulnerable as a field of spring moss. "Maybe it is true, as I've been told," she added, "that a mother and her first-born son, particularly when he's premature, share a psychic understanding. We don't even need words to know what the other is thinking."

It was not merely the subject that Nadia found so distasteful but the persistent—almost defiant—use of the present tense. Her attempt to distract Nina, however, merely deflected her daughter's barbs from Harry to herself.

"Oh, Nina, darling, I almost forgot. While you were at the hospital, the water company called. And the gas and electric. They're all to be turned off if they're not paid—in cash—by noon Monday."

Nina's laugh, like the bottle clutched in her hand, seemed more histrionic than hysterical.

"Good. Let them turn everything off. What should I care now about a few lights more or less?"

"*The Dark is Light Enough*—eh? Sounds like the title of a very sensitive off-Broadway production." Slouched in the single remotely comfortable chair in the room, Harry watched his former wife with bemused cynicism. "Personally, I'd just as soon not have to grope my way around this gloomy ole manse in the dark, as romantic as the idea may appear to you."

"Then why don't *you* pay the bills? It's about time you paid for something. Because I've certainly had no time to worry about anything so monumentally inconsequential as household bills."

"They are," Nadia ventured, her eyes fixed with tragic concern upon the brandy bottle, "already three months past due. And not altogether inconsequential either, if we're to spend Christmas without water as well as lights. You can hardly expect a public utility company—"

"Oh, Mummy, how like you! How so very like!" Nina's voice was sharpened to a cutting edge. "All day you've been pestering me, as if I were some kind of invalid incapable of lifting my own hands, if you couldn't do something to help. Any little thing at all to make matters easier for me. Well, if you'd truly wanted to help, it seems to me you might simply have asked what the amounts were and sent off a check yourself. It would hardly have bankrupted you."

The shaft hit its mark, but Nadia quickly dressed the wound with the regality of her bearing. "My dear Nina, I'm sorry, I'd promised myself there'd be no arguments about money this time. But you have a habit of treating me more like your banker than your mother. I have, and you well know it—despite the lack of love you so loudly bewail—been more than generous. Rescued you time and time again from one ill-advised extravagance after another. For all the credit you've ever given me. Why, I even persuaded your father, against his express wishes, to leave the income of his estate to you rather than to me."

"The income, yes, but not controlling interest. That you were most careful to keep for yourself."

"Because, my dear, if I hadn't, it would all long ago have been thrown away on some folly or other. Why, if I had treated my money the way you've treated yours, we'd all long since have been condemned to the poorhouse, living at public expense."

"Oh, Mummy! Mummy! Mummy! You are too funny for words! Since I was a child that poorhouse of yours has been the family bogeyman. Why, I can remember, every time Daddy wanted to order a steak, how you and Granny, all wrapped up so snug and warm in your sables, content with nothing more for yourselves than a fruit salad and a dab of cottage cheese, would make the poor man feel his appetite for a thick, juicy filet might send us all cold and naked out into the streets. Oh, yes, I know, you always eventually let him have his steak. But never once was he allowed to enjoy it unless it came swimming in a sauce of guilt. But that's where Daddy and I differ. What really annoys you about me is not my extravagance but my refusal to feel guilty about it. About anything, for that matter, including this," she added, lifting the brandy bottle with a malicious flourish, "no matter how much you screw up your face."

"You might at least let the rest of us share it since there doesn't seem to be anything quite so prosaic as a bottle of whisky around." Harry rose and, getting two glasses from the bar, allowed Nina to pour. Nadia refused hers with an imperious lift of her hand. "Oh, well, then, I suppose I'll have to force myself to down both of them." He resumed his seat, lounging against a bank of tapestry pillows. "It promises to be a long night anyway. Well, cheers, everyone," he added and with a sardonic smile raised his glass.

He might have been talking to himself for all the attention he was granted.

"You seem to think, my dear," Nadia resumed, her regal manner somewhat relaxed but the scepter kept within easy reach, "you're the only one who's suffered a loss. The only one who's entitled to sympathy. Or indulgence. I am, after all, his grandmother. And if I hadn't been so worried sick over the poor darling, I just might have had the presence of mind to do what you suggested. But here you left me all alone in this Frankenstein's villa without a soul to share my anxiety. Anyone even to let me know what was happening, so that every time the telephone rang, my heart simply leapt into my throat. While you were all out having dinner at some fancy restaurant where, it seems to me, my presence might have been interpreted as a simple matter of courtesy, and not in any way so unusual as to frighten Nikki. Or anyone else."

"Well, now it's finally out! You've been holding that one in reserve all day, haven't you? I knew there was something eating away at you, some little bit of stored-up malice to offer me when it best suited your purposes."

"Now, Nina, darling, please don't talk like that. Malice? What malice? I was simply hurt, that's all, that, after flying these thousands of miles, I wasn't given one last chance to see him." And she punctuated her final sentence with a sob.

"Oh, do stop blubbering! You weren't asked because you would have suffocated him with your pity. That's why. As you very nearly did on your last visit. 'Poor darling little Nikki,'" she mimicked, "'our brave little Cossack. Is it so terribly painful?' Why do you think he was so cruel to you, when he's usually kindness itself, attacking you the way he did?"

"His attack—if that's what you choose to call it—was for never having taught *you* how to judge other people's characters. Always being taken in by every handsome face or sweet tongue." The sobs well under control, the voice now as sharp as polished steel. "If you remember, the contretemps was sparked by his black tutor—Salim, or whatever he chooses to call himself—whom you, to everyone's dismay, including Nikki's, had allowed to move in, bag and baggage. And though he never seemed to be around when it was time to help Nikki with his studies, he was always within calling distance whenever a meal or a drink was about to be served. Which reminds me, he *also* called. From Princeton. Where, Charles tells me, he's being married this weekend."

"And what would you have me do? Show him the door? No, I will not stoop to that. The only real power such people have to hurt you is to make you become like them."

"I think," Harry said, rising with the second glass of brandy, "the children have the right idea, after all. So, if you'll excuse me." And with a courtly bow he left the room to join Elena and Caleb beneath the elaborately carved teak canopy of an antique opium bed.

"Isn't it," Nadia asked with a glance at her watch, "time the children were in bed?"

"I'm not so far gone I can't make that decision for myself, Mummy. Though I think it is well after time *you* were in bed. Don't forget, your system's still on New York time, and tomorrow's going to be an exhausting day. For all of us."

*

The loud report that woke her seemed far too spectacularly catastrophic for anything so prosaic as thunder, and all senses primed, Nadia waited for the house to crumble in response to the explosion that had catapulted her bolt upright in her bed. The subsequent silence was enigmatic rather than reassuring. Somewhere in the distance a siren wailed, more plaintive than frantic. It was, she noted, 3:15. Nina's bed was empty; it had not been slept in. Nadia herself had fallen almost immediately, and so uncharacteristically, into a profound sleep. One moment she had closed her eyes and the next been startled awake by an entire squadron of planes breaking the sound barrier, and she wondered for one panic-filled instant if that long-dreaded moment had not at last arrived and the-war-to-end-all begun in earnest.

She rose, put on her bunny slippers, and gathering one of Nina's robes, made her way up the stairway landing. The rain had stopped, but the skies over the Pacific remained darkly menacing. Through a break in the clouds the moon spotlighted the bay and lit her passage up the stairs. For she knew in her blood where she would find her daughter.

Silhouetted in front of the open window of Nikita's darkened room, Nina stood, seeming more shadow than substance, and Nadia, remembering the precipitous drop from the tiny balcony, froze, sure that her daughter was about to leap and with a single spectacular gesture shatter forever the barrier that now separated her from her son. It was a terrible and strangely beautiful moment. Nadia's defenses melted. On the instant she became all love and pity, prepared, even anxious, to offer herself as a whipping post to divert her daughter from her own pain. Far better to flail out at the living than to face the void alone, the deep emptiness of forever. There was, in the end, only now; it was all any of us ever had, and that we must cling to it with every fiber of our being was the sole dogma of her faith.

"Nina, darling," she called, and to her surprise, the tear-streaked face that confronted her was not that of a grieving Niobe but a Dionysian bacchante.

"He answered me!" she cried. "He answered me! I just made him a solemn promise," she continued, her clenched fist in the traditional revolutionary's salute, as if she had intended to assault the heavens themselves had they not submitted to her demands, "and suddenly the entire sky turned white. And he answered me!"

Nadia's reaction was threefold: there was, first, that chill of unease she always felt in the presence of the inexplicable, a sense that the earth we stand on is not nearly so firm as we trust and that all matter is held together by the grace of some power which might, upon the instant, be withdrawn. But before it had had time to run its course, the chill evolved into a shudder of—distaste? contempt? revulsion? she wasn't sure which—for the egotism of those who read God's personal message in the heavens and without so much as a demur of modest doubt convince themselves that something so insignificant as a single human will can command the elements. Which led to the inescapable conclusion that Nina was one of the world's true innocents, for her naïveté was so great it could not be moved by logic, law, or common sense. Nikita had been right to attack his grandmother. Not only had she not taught her daughter how to judge others, she had not really taught her daughter anything at all.

"Yes, dear, I heard." It was a coward's answer, but she was powerless to snatch so frail a straw from her drowning daughter. Anything was always better than nothing.

"You heard him, too!" It was not a question but a cry of exaltation.

"I'm sure it woke the entire household, if not the whole city," Nadia answered, her conscience taking refuge in the impersonal pronoun. "But, dear, you simply must get some sleep. We've a long day ahead of us."

To her surprise—and relief—Nina submitted and without so much as a murmur of protest, her face transfigured, her eyes alight with glory, she allowed herself to be led to her room, undressed, and bedded, and all emotion spent, she fell soon to sleep.

*

Nadia fared not so well. Slightly above and just behind her left eye a tiny seed of pain heralded the onset of a migraine that would, if she did not act immediately, leave her virtually debilitated for days. Without a moment's hesitation, she downed a Fiorinal and lying on her back, arms at her sides, palms down, fingers spread, she indulged the flowering pain. The burning tendrils reached ever deeper into her consciousness until the drug's slow absorption began to work its magic; the growth was blunted; slowly the outermost tendrils withered, then one by one the flaming petals fell, and with a sense of true euphoria, she submitted to the dreams that invariably followed.

She and Nina, both near-contemporaries (for she was, strangely, never old in her dreams), were alone in a house that seemed to be the composite of all the homes they had ever shared. From room to room they wandered, Nina just ahead, dropping here a blouse, there the manuscript page of an unfinished poem. Noiselessly the items fell from her hands, paintbrushes light as feathers, books that seemed buoyed by their own weightlessness, flowers and clothes and recordings, each whenever and wherever it was no longer needed or wanted. And Nadia followed after. Stooping to pick up each castaway, she hurried to restore order, pausing here to right a chair that had been knocked over, there to rearrange some bibelot carelessly moved to mar the flawless composition of a tabletop still life. Ceaselessly and patiently she toiled to redeem the chaos left in her daughter's wake, and thus she might have continued, content, for she did not mind the labor, felt, even, a sense of fulfillment in the harmony she created, had not Nina, stepping suddenly and inexplicably through the doors of the French Academy (where mother, but not daughter, who had never set foot in the place, had spent her final year of finishing school), so triumphantly sung her own praises, like some exultant Mary, thundering down that great cataract of stairs to overwhelm a defenseless Nadia seated like some startled Martha in the Piazza di Spagna below (it was the only story in the entire Christian canon that she had ever connected with) the nuns in the background, their white caps bobbing like so many sails in some holy regatta, chanting away of brilliant, creative Marys and dull plodding Marthas and the world's need for both—though God and the world both well knew which was the worthier.

Although fully conscious it had been no more than a dream, and that Nina, disciplined by a succession of dour governesses, had never, unlike her dream self and her own children, been allowed to leave so much as a dropped hanky for someone else to pick up, Nadia could not shed her sense of burning resentment.

*

The rain returned with the dawn, its windswept fury almost tropical in its excess. But the storm's very insistence, since it demanded so much of everyone's attention, proved, ultimately, a blessing, and the burial was far less traumatic than expected. A slightly macabre family outing, but still a family outing.

And as so many before, it too began in acrimony. Nina's insistence upon taking the two largest dogs met head-on with Harry's refusal to attend at all if the animals were allowed, in such inclement weather and on such a dismal journey, to add yet another strain upon everyone's already overwrought nerves. They did not so much argue as use each other as sounding boards to bounce off resentments, one against the other, each listening only to his own. An exercise in futility, for as usual Nina got her way: both the dogs *and* Harry went.

The necessary detours, first to the gas and electric and finally to the water company (with Nadia, for all the thanks she knew she was not about to receive, paying at both offices, peeling off hundred-dollar bills, so deftly secreted in her purse that no one was able to glimpse the size of the rolls it harbored) made them considerably more than an hour late, Harry's sardonic comment that since Nikita, like his mother, had never in his entire life been on time for anything, it seemed only fitting he be late for his funeral as well was met with surprisingly good humor. Both Caleb and Elena giggled. Even Nadia, already the victim of more lost hours than she cared to count, smiled. While Nina herself seemed preoccupied with questioning everyone who crossed her path, from meter maids to morticians, about the early morning thunder. With every fresh assurance that the previous night's display had truly been exceptional, if not possibly unique, in the local annals of heavenly pyrotechnics, she confided her own version of the blast's origins, her eyes moist, her voice insistently pleading for confirmation that here indeed was demonstrable proof that life did not end with death. No one dared deny her. And since Nikita was already busy fighting new battles in galaxies unknown, the present rites, maimed as they were, seemed almost superfluous, and she bore herself throughout with a stoicism her mother and her former husband found both reassuring and commendable.

*

Her newfound serenity, however, did not last out the day. Doubt crept in with the evening shadows, and once again brandishing her bottle, she roamed the house. It seemed not to matter what the bottle contained—brandy, vodka, or liqueur—for she was, her mother noted, not nearly so interested in the contents as in the effect she was creating. Seldom was the bottle lifted to her lips. And because Nadia could not for a minute doubt the reality of her daughter's pain, she was all the more baffled by the theatricality of its expression. Like a poorly trained actress, Nina seemed intent upon stressing the obvious with gestures so broad they transformed tragedy to farce.

Partly to bring the exhibition to an end—for she herself was certainly not hungry—Nadia suggested some thought be given to dinner. Since the rain continued unabated, no one wanted to venture out again. Faviola had the night off and no one else seemed prepared to cook. Nina resolved the dilemma. Initially reluctant to use the phone at all, she seemed, once she got on it, even more reluctant to relinquish it, and the friendly proprietor of a local Middle Eastern restaurant proved only too happy to have dinner delivered—but not before he was first subjected to a detailed account of the last three days, including the tale of her midnight wanderings, her solemn promise, and the answering thunder.

It was not until the dinner itself arrived that some hint as to the nature of that promise was revealed.

"That has never been your seat in this house." In a voice every bit as imperious as her mother's best, Nina forestalled Harry from taking his seat at the head of the table. "It's one you long ago forfeited."

"And just who then is it set for?"

His challenge gave those who had not already done so the opportunity to juxtapose the five people present with the six places set.

"You know very well whose seat it is."

"Nina, you're absolutely shameless." Harry's laconic tone perfectly suited his hangdog face. "So it's to be the Queen Victoria gambit, is it? Well I, for one, will not be party to any of your self-indulgently morbid games. Nikki is dead. Like it or not, we've all got to face the fact. He's dead. Gone. And whatever form his spirit may have assumed, it is not one that needs a real chair and a real plate for him to join us at the dinner table."

"Are you quite finished?"

"No, I am not. Either I sit here. Or I sit nowhere."

"Then it's nowhere, I fear."

"Nina, darling, it's Christmas Eve." Nadia's dislike of the turn her daughter's grief was taking proved greater even than her dislike of Harry.

"You stay out of this, Mummy. When I want your advice, I'll ask for it. This is between Harry and me. It's my house and my table and if he chooses to eat with us, he will sit at the place set for him. And none other."

The only eyes directed at him were Nina's. All others studied the empty plates before them with an intensity the plates themselves scarcely warranted. Harry shrugged, shook his head, and without another word, left the room.

It was Nina who broke the oppressive silence that followed upon his exit. "Nikki can hardly take offense at his father's callousness. He only puts up with him so we won't all be dragged into court again."

No one attempted to answer, nor did a single eye turn in the direction of the empty plates. With cherubic inscrutability, Elena played with her food, arranging the exotic delicacies into abstract patterns. What little appetite Nadia had was spoiled by her daughter's irrational behavior and her own inability to cope with it. By its very definition madness was immune to reason, and she herself was incapable of applying force—hers or anyone else's, for the latter would entail an alliance with the hateful Harry against her own daughter, which might, even, God forbid, lead to his own eventual custody of the children. With a fascination tinged with horror, Nadia watched Caleb shove his food into his mouth with all the finesse of a goose being stuffed for paté. His breath labored, his immense body bulging over his belt, he interrupted his eating only long enough to emit a loud belch, which his mother greeted with a shrill burst of laughter.

"But, Nina, darling," Nadia protested. "The boy simply has to be taught some manners. It's not good for him to gobble his food like that. And if you encourage him—"

"Oh, Mummy, I fear you're much too grand for us. We're simple peasants here."

"It's not a question of being grand—"

"Yes, Granny," Elena interrupted her artistic endeavors to join her mother and brother in the attack, "we're only simple Amarriken peasants."

"Amerrikens," Caleb corrected, rolling the R's with gleeful malice. "So minny Amerrikens."

"What's the expression Granny always uses that so tickles Nikki?" Nina asked, looking from child to child with proprietary glee.

"Shipboard manners," Elena rejoined, pursing her lips. "We must all put on our best shipboard manners tonight."

They were three children playing together, and though she could not entirely hide her own hurt feelings, she was too relieved at their laughter to say or do anything to terminate it. It was only when Nina and Elena got up to clear the table that hurt gave way to dismay. The empty dinner plates were removed and five dessert plates laid, one at each setting, including Nikita's; only Harry's was left empty. It was, Nadia knew, the inauguration of a new family ritual. But when Nina placed the first piece of cake in front of the empty chair, the children once again retreated into self-absorbed silence. Almost immediately their mother seemed to realize that she had crossed an invisible boundary beyond which she would have to travel alone, that her children would go along with her so far, but only so far: a plate, yes, but an empty plate; yet she could not, without admitting the inadmissible, retrieve the plate already served. And the uneaten piece of cake weighted every fork so heavily that none of them, not even the ordinarily insatiable Caleb, could do more than pretend to nibble at their own serving.

113

*

Harry, who returned from his solitary dinner after Nadia had already retired, left so early on Christmas morning for the Caribbean that she did not have a chance to bid him goodbye. She was thus spared any discussion of her daughter's eccentric behavior and its possible adverse affect upon the children with so biased a witness, yet she could not help feeling that he had, by his precipitous departure, once again proven himself less than adequate as a man and a father.

Nina herself seemed delighted by his defection, if only because it gave her one more piece of evidence in her long-running indictment of The Father Who Failed. That she could, under the circumstances, make his desertion of the children before they had opened their packages a capital offense seemed, even in Nadia's prejudiced eyes, as much a comment upon their mother's odd sense of values as upon their father's callousness.

There was also the awkward problem of Nikita's gifts still heaped in rich profusion about the tree. Nadia's suggestion that the Salvation Army be called to distribute them among the needy and spare them all the cruel reminder their presence must afford was met with such a vehement rejection that she was made to feel she had somehow desecrated her grandson's memory. That the desecration proved not merely a matter of sensibility but of economics as well merely added to her dismay.

"How typical of you and your set," Nina snapped, "to want to lavish expensive toys upon the needy, when, as your very name for them so condescendingly indicates, they more properly *need* something to wear. Shoes, not automated robots."

"So you and your set end by giving them nothing," Nadia could not refrain from retorting.

"Certainly not what doesn't belong to us. The gift's are Nikki's. Not yours or mine. And I'm sure," she continued, speaking now with oracular authority, "he'd rather they stayed here with the rest of his things."

A brief respite from the venomous insularity came with Charles's sudden reappearance. Boyishly pleased by the enthusiasm with which his arrival was greeted, he blushed as he eased his oversize gift onto the dining room refectory table.

"I threatened your daughter with a practical gift," he said to Nadia, who had cleared a space amid the welter with a sweep of her arm, "and despite her howls of protest, that's precisely what she's getting. So nobody's to expect anything grand. Or even beautiful."

"Oh, Charles, I never howl," Nina teased. "I may bleat occasionally, but I certainly never howl."

With a shy, uneasy smile, he directed his gaze at her for the first time. Cheeks flushed, eyes shining, her protean beauty disconcertingly resplendent, she might have seemed to the unwary observer almost anything but bereaved. But only to the unwary.

Goosed by a large wet nose, Charles jumped, laughing, his scrutiny happily interrupted before it had time to become mired in bathos.

"Thor, please. You're being far too fresh." His voice determinedly hearty, he tugged at the dog's floppy ears, only to be thanked in turn by two giant paws falling like pile drivers upon his shoulders. "No," he continued, backing off as his hands clasped the forelegs. "It's far too early for dancing, and moreover, there isn't any music." But Thor's importunities were not to be denied. "Caleb, please," Charles called, "get this monster off me." And both children, rushing to the rescue, wrestled the delighted Thor onto the floor, where he lolled like a giant puppy, legs up, paws curled, begging for his belly to be scratched.

"Well, Charles," Nina peering into the open package chuckled maliciously, "for once I'm convinced you chose the gift only with me in mind." And she pulled out a half-dozen red Lucite clothes hangers.

Once again Charles directed his words to Nadia, his voice paternally indulgent: "Your daughter never seems to have trouble finding the cash whenever she falls in love with a new Kazak, but when it comes to something so prosaic as clothes hangers, the poor thing is always destitute. So all her elegant frocks are hung on throwaway wire hangers left over from the dry cleaners."

"Oh, Charles, when was the last time you saw me in anything that could remotely be described as a frock?"

"What you have on right now comes pretty close."

115

Puzzled, Nina frowned, looking first at herself and then at her reflection in the large wall mirror as if completely unaware of what she was wearing: an old Fortuny original of pleated silk, the iridescent mauve clinging to the body that had once again become fashionably slim in the last few months, a change previously hidden beneath bulky homespun sweaters and full peasant skirts. Though she could have chosen nothing more flattering to herself or her figure, the gown's seductive elegance seemed oddly inappropriate for the hour as well as the occasion, particularly alongside her mother's simple black mourning dress of such unadorned chic it must almost certainly have cost as much as the pearls that accented it.

"Oh this. Nikki made me promise I'd wear it today," she said, her pale cheeks suddenly crimson. "It's always been his favorite. How many are there?" she asked turning from the mirror back to the box of hangers.

"Four dozen," he answered, then suddenly disconcerted, he added, apologetically, "I got them months ago."

"Red, yellow, blue, and white."

"I want the blue," Elena called out.

"And I want the yellow," Caleb was quick to add.

"All right. Then Nikki can have the red and I'll keep the white for myself. A color for each of us. Isn't that lovely?" Blind to the obvious discomfort of her guest, she smiled prettily. "Charles, you are a dear."

As Nina left the room with the box of hangers, Charles answered Nadia's inquiring gaze by closing his eyes and shaking his head, to excuse his monumental gaffe.

"No, dear Charles." Speaking in whispers, she took his hand. "Don't blame yourself. You can't imagine what I've been through. And I don't know where to turn. Who to talk to." Her eyes misty, she looked at him, pleading. "I'm so frightened. For the children as well as for her."

"And just what are you two conspiring about?"

As Nina reentered the dining room, Nadia, with a sudden squeeze, dropped Charles's hand.

"Beware, Charles, of the green-eyed monster," Nina said. "I can never leave Mummy alone for a minute that she isn't up to something."

"Oh, Nina, what a thing to say to your mother."

"Oh, Mummy, what a thing to do to your daughter. Trying to vamp her friends. And in front of her very eyes."

Her smile was far too thin to cover the very real malice behind the joking words.

*

The respite was brief. As soon as Charles departed, the insularity became more stifling, the venom more toxic.

"You mustn't, dear," Nadia ventured as they prepared to retire for the night, "ever be ashamed to seek professional help, if you feel the need of it."

"Professional help?" Nina's defenses were instantaneously aroused. "And just what profession is it you had in mind?"

"There are, you must know, in almost every major hospital, counseling sessions for just such situations. I'm surprised Dr. Palmer didn't recommend one."

"Do you mean a psychiatrist? Is that what you're talking about? Because, if it is, I think that's just about the silliest suggestion you've ever made. And offensive as well."

"Well, your behavior hasn't exactly been—"

"*Comme il faut?* Is that what you're trying to say? I know you'd be much happier if I went around the house moping in black weeds. Turned grief into a fashion show, as you did for Daddy and seem prepared now to do for Nikki. But I'm not going to. To please you or anyone else. I know exactly what I'm doing. Nikki loves bright colors."

"That is not what I meant at all." Nadia's protest was virtually subliminal, so softly was it proffered.

"A psychiatrist! Really, Mummy, you've outdone yourself." Unpinning her hair so that it fell to her shoulders with a single coltish shake, Nina grabbed a brush from the vanity top and, pacing the room, brushed her hair with such vigor, the crackle of sparks seemed to charge her words. "You want me to pour out my heart to some jargon-spewing old charlatan, do you, just so he can tell me how I secretly lusted after Daddy, and when I couldn't steal him away from you, turned round and tried to seduce my own son? The Gospel According to Saint Sigmund. Really, you haven't the ghost of a notion what I'm all about. You never have. And I suppose never will. Sometimes I think it's simple jealousy. Why else would you have thrown away all my paintings? Because you couldn't bear to be reminded I might be more talented than you, that's why."

"Really, Nina, do you forget nothing?"

"How can one forget the unforgivable?"

"Those poor sad watercolors." Nadia sank with a sigh onto the edge of her bed. "What an inflated importance you do give to things! Why, if they had been so precious, didn't you take them along with the rest of your belongings? You knew very well, as your father got older and less manageable, as long as you were no longer using it, I needed your old room for myself. How else was I to get any rest? Unlike some people," she continued, her eyes scanning the long wall of mirrored closets, "we didn't live in a mansion. Space was precious. And you can't say I didn't give you ample warning."

"Which is hardly the point. They were *my* paintings. And if I had meant anything to you, you would have treasured them for that reason alone. Any proper mother would. Just imagine how I'd feel now if I hadn't kept every precious scrap of Nikki's."

"Oh, my poor baby!" She was not sure herself how much irony tinted her sudden outburst of pity, nor whether it had been inspired by her daughter's words or the sudden glimpse she had caught of herself in the mirror, her own face so withered and comfortless. An unfeeling old harridan.

It was a moot point for pity, too, Nina rejected.

"Oh, Mummy, please don't slobber."

"Well, it would do you no end of good, if you'd only let yourself go. Weep your eyes out. It's nature's way."

"Mummy, really, your banality never ceases to astound me. Nature's

way, indeed! You make it sound like a laxative. As if all I need is the
right pill to wash him out of my system. Well, I don't want him out of
my system, do you hear? Now or ever. I mean to keep him alive," she
continued, beating her breasts with the back of the brush still clutched
in her fist, her eyes fixed upon her mother with malevolent fury, as if she
might at any second transfer the physical attack from herself to Nadia.
"Here, in my heart. Always. I will not let him die! Don't you understand
that! I won't let him die! Ever!"

Such denial there was no answering—though Nadia remained convinced, despite its purported banality, normal, healthy grief was what her
daughter most needed to indulge in, but it was all Nadia could do to
maintain her balance in the face of Nina's wildly erratic changes of mood:
from the breast-beating of high tragedy to the petulance of a spoiled little
rich girl who has for the first time found herself unable to buy, charm, or
force her will upon the world; from wild virago to hapless orphan of the
storm. Nadia's very presence had become an irritant. She could do nothing to please. If she dressed with her usual care she was playing the great
lady out to put the provincials in their proper place; if she neglected her
toilet, she was playing the martyr; if she attempted to talk, she was intruding upon Nina's solitude; if she retired with a book, she was pouting. She
could not so much as straighten a flower in a vase without Nina immediately rushing to the same vase to return the flower to its original state.

And those poor lost paintings! They had first made their appearance on Nina's long, long list of grievances about the time her marriage had begun to go wrong—not that it had ever, from the first, been
right. Pleasant, imaginative, one might even call them promising—but
as works of art! Never! The pretty daubs of a dilettante. Nor must one
display every crude bit of glazed pottery her children had ever fashioned
as if it were a treasure for the ages to prove one's love. Sometimes one
could best do that by leaving the loved to their own devices. Yet she
could not, in good conscience, abandon her daughter to chance and the
vagaries of an intemperate grief without at least delegating some trust-
worthy person in her place. There seemed only one possibility.

"Bijou Byzantine." Charles moved his eyes with bemused disdain
from the two arched alcoves covered in mosaics copied from Ravenna to
the brass-plated chairs studded with oversized colored-glass jewels. "I do
apologize, but I took you at your word and chose a restaurant I'd never

been to before. Nob Hill's finest. I'd heard it described as 'sumptuous.' But I fear 'tacky' is closer to the truth."

"Positively ghastly," Nadia agreed, gleefully sharing Charles's disdain. "But just imagine how much more hideous it would all be if the lights were turned up. Can you imagine what those gilded plaster cornices look like in the daylight?"

"I shudder to think. Let's hope the chef has a more secure sense of taste than the decorator," he added, turning his attention to the oversize menu.

Warmed at last after the damp chill of the taxi ride, Nadia dropped her sables from her shoulders onto the back of the chair. Though her eyes in her quick survey of the room had fallen on no single diner, she was quite aware that their table was the object of intense curiosity—a heady reassurance that even in distant climes she could still take possession of a room merely by stepping into it.

119

The years had already begun to slip away as she had sat at her toilet, and now, like some great Bernhardt drawn out of retirement once again onto the stage, queening it for all she was worth at a decidedly grand—if admittedly ghastly—restaurant with a handsome, elegantly dressed gentleman—who might himself be anyone or anything—she felt positively young. Once again at the height of her powers. This, she knew in her blood, though she knew no one here save her escort, was her true métier: the theater of life. A heavenly respite from the grim hell of the last few days.

"But Charles," she began, "you must tell me: *what* am I to do? You've seen her, how she treats me. As if I had absolutely no feelings. When she must know hers is not the only heart that's been broken."

It was marvelous how the tears could well in her eyes, which glistened bright with tragedy, and yet never quite overstep their bounds to mar her mascara, so generously applied that it set off the marvelous pallor of her complexion with ghostly drama—a Pierrette in a mask of painted grief.

"Yes, I know." He cupped his hand reassuringly over hers. "Even she admits her behavior has been cruel. She knows you're here to help her and she's being grossly unfair. But for some reason, she can't help herself. She's been so deeply hurt—"

"Has she told you to tell me this?"

"She hasn't *told* me to tell you anything."

She found his smile disconcerting.

"I'm sure she trusts me well enough to have dinner with her mother without any fear I'll betray her in some way."

"And that's the very thing I so depend upon," she was quick to rejoin, "her trust in you."

They were interrupted by the waiter hovering anxiously nearby, fearful of intruding, yet even more fearful of a failure to serve. Once they had ordered, she handed Charles the wine list.

"I know nothing about California wines, so you must choose. I hear some of them are quite splendid."

It was a ploy she had long ago learned, that any gentleman being taken out to dine could only be flattered by the assumption of his own greater expertise and would at the same time be far too considerate to order—as she might herself feel compelled—anything grandly extravagant.

"But you still haven't told me what I'm to do," she resumed as soon as they were once again alone. "Should I return to New York, since my very presence seems to provoke her? You know as well as anyone: what does she want me to do?"

"Maybe it would be best, after all. Give her a chance to catch her bearings."

"Oh, what I wouldn't give to see her settled down! With someone secure and sensible—and, yes—white, I am not ashamed to say it. Why should I be? Someone like yourself, Charles."

She was momentarily stirred by a twang of ironic nostalgia, at the long ago memory of a time so innocent she had marked the very much younger and slimmer Charles himself as the prime fortune-hunter to be wary of. If she had only known what was to follow!

"I'm flattered." He smiled. "But I doubt very much Nina will ever again marry. Anyone."

"I suppose not. After Harry," she added, bitterly. "That last courtroom experience left an indelible imprint. But you'll promise me, won't you, if I do decide to return, you'll be here to look after her? And if there's anything at all you think I should know, or can do—anything— you'll call me. And if there's any expense involved—"

"You have my word." His interruption was peremptory without being rude. "Though I may not for an instant want to become your daughter's husband, I do, after all these years, feel an almost paternal interest in her. As brilliant and talented as she may be, on one level she's still as innocent as the day she was born. That's part of her charm: this strange mixture of extreme worldliness and absolute naïveté."

"And am I to blame for this—'innocence,' as you call it? Though I think a lack of common sense might be, if less poetic, more to the point."

"We are what we are," he answered, a sudden weariness in his voice, as he moved back his head to allow the first course to be served. "We always seem to be so busy trying to assess blame—all of us—we seldom get around to accepting what is. I'm afraid it's too late, at this point in her life, to expect her to become someone else. How is your soup?"

"Not quite as warm as it might be, but good. And your quenelles?"

"Rubbery, unfortunately, and not good."

"And you, Charles, what are your plans?"

She did not think it necessary to tell him she had already, that morning, booked a flight to New York on the Saturday before New Year's.

*

"So that's what you were up to. Repaying Charles for his many kindnesses, indeed! Plotting your escape, you mean. I thought there was something fishy, dazzling poor Charles like that with the sable-and-royal-jewels routine. Mummy, you have no shame. And at your age. He must have, poor Charles, been mush in your hands. And did he give your plan his approval? Did he commiserate? Tell you how monstrously unfair I've been?"

"But darling," Nadia protested, "you're being most unreasonable. And unfair. To me as well as to Charles. Tell me you need me and I'll happily stay. For months, if necessary."

"No, no. Don't let it ever be said I kept you away from all your friends. Naturally you want to get back in time to celebrate the New Year with them. Why should anyone want to spend it in such a sad house as this?"

"Now, Nina, you know that isn't the reason. Just tell me how my staying here can help you, when everything I say or do seems to set your nerves on fire. If there is something I can do, some purpose I can serve, even if it's just to console you, I'll cancel the reservation immediately. Just tell me."

"No, Mummy, I insist: go—if you feel you must."

"Then yes, I'm afraid I must. For both our sakes. As long as you can't bring yourself to ask your own mother to stay."

"Ask you? Why should I ask you? When in the end you know you're going to do just what you want to do anyway."

"Ah, Nina, I was hoping that for once we might part with more loving kindness than bitterness."

"For that, Mummy dearest, one must first know how to love."

Knowing full well that no answer could be the right answer, Nadia kept her peace.

*

Although she was convinced in her mind that more accidents occur on landing than on takeoff, it was only during the latter, the loud-revving of the engines, the accelerating taxi down the runway, and the sudden, breath-catching liftoff, that panic took over. So customary was the reaction, she had been prepared for everything but the sudden apparition of the dead Nikita, his delicate features yellowed like old ivory, so intense, he seemed to be concentrating, intent upon the mystery of his own passing, the funny little wig, which only he ever believed fooled anyone, slightly askew. She longed to reach out to right it, but her hands, clutching at both armrests, would not move.

She must have cried out, for suddenly there was another hand, warm with life, upon hers. The precipitous ascent leveled, the no-smoking sign blinked off, and with a sigh she settled back against her seat.

"It is a frightening moment," the owner of the hand reassured her, both his voice and his eyes filled with concern. From his fashionably narrow silk tie to his Gucci shoes there was not, she was sure, a synthetic thread on his person. Everything about him—his neatly brushed silver hair, his winter tan, his manicured nails, the simple gold-and-lapis ring—was perfect: correct, but at the same time personal, and all borne with an authority that bespoke success. Whatever his life was, he had come to terms with it.

She was reassured as much by his presence as his words. For she was reeling still from the pendulum swing of emotions that any visit to her daughter invariably set off. She was too old for such abrupt and violent changes, the terrible virago of the night before once again that morning the wide-eyed orphan of the storm, vulnerable, dazed. Oh, it had been perfect! Even the fall of hair, those two pathetic wisps curling from each temple, the twisted knot at the top at once deceptively casual and as formal as a classic Aphrodite in white marble. And as Nina offered her cheek, like a bruised lily, to be kissed, there had been a sudden flash of terror in the malachite eyes. Nadia had seen them all so often before; just after being virtually driven from her daughter's home, at the actual moment of parting, she had been confronted with honey and rosemary, the little girl lost once again abandoned to her own devices, crying out for love, for indulgence—for the world.

"I know it's foolish of me," she said. "Particularly at my age." She lifted her hand ever so slightly, as much to display her rings as to forestall her neighbor's expected protestations, the white skin as fragile as rice-paper, the blue veins beneath a constant reminder of mortality. "But one does not, strangely, become less afraid with age. Quite to the contrary. When I was just a young thing, about the time I'd say you were being born, I was taken up over Paris, in a Jenny, of all things. And though the very memory of it fills me with astonished terror, I assure you I was, at the time, absolutely fearless. Convinced, I suppose, as the young always are, of my own immortality."

She could tell from his smile and the subtle relaxation of his pose that she was already well on the way to charming him. And how restful it was to be once again among the knowing and the known! Long before they landed, she was confident, they would discover friends as well as interests in common, and the sure knowledge that her own name, discreetly withheld until the proper moment, would be greeted with a gleam of recognition, augmented the warmth of her smile.

Her long ordeal was over. She closed her eyes for a moment, sighing contentedly, for she was on her way home at last, a survivor still, flying eastward into the dawn.

On the surface everything seemed to be going well. I had brought the scotch and Zelda the wine, so there could be no question about the quality or the quantity of those essentials. Everyone had known two of the three others present at some time or other so talk never flagged. Quite to the contrary. With three such theatrical pros, the threat was never silence, but collision. As the only person present who had never voluntarily faced an audience larger or more discriminating than a class of high school seniors, I was quite content to sit back and enjoy the performance as the others careened down memory lane.

All three, I suppose, in terms of early expectations and the world's judgment, could be written off as failures. Their names have not become "household words." Even among the majority of their own profession they might at best ring a dim bell in the kitchen pantry of memory. Although Maud Islington can still occasionally be glimpsed in some geriatric part on British television, only our host, Roger Tubbs, in their parlance, still actively treads the boards. Not in the West End, of course. His current venue is the provincial blood-and-guts circuit. Agatha Christie and her ilk in such remote outposts as Blackpool and Bournemouth.

"My gawd, I've played them all." His voice, a rather fruity baritone, was far too loud for so cramped a space as his dining alcove. "Everything from the first-act victim to the last-act master-of-all-riddles. I've been poisoned, I've been garroted, I've been shot, I've been stabbed—"

"And which do you prefer?" Zelda deftly cut the catalogue short before another "I" could be articulated. "Given your druthers."

She has little patience with rehearsed set pieces—unless, of course, they happen to be her own.

"Oh, I quite fancy the garrote." Roger was too accustomed to being upstaged to lose his balance for long. "It brings out the old song-and-dance man in me."

The sweetness of his smile was quite genuine. He is one of the few actors I have met without a touch of malice in his make-up—which may in part explain his relative lack of success. Whatever claim to fame he has came from a seldom-discussed earlier career to which he had just, to my surprise, so casually alluded, perhaps on the assumption we were all in on the secret anyway.

For he began his career as a dancer with the Royal Ballet when it was still the Sadler's Wells, and though he never became a premier danseur, he did gain a certain fame doing minor solo parts, until age and the prophecy inherent in his name rang some inner warning bell. Given the chance to join a promising revue at the Lyric Hammersmith, he decided to make the grandest *jeté* of his career. Unfortunately, it was the dying days of the revue as a popular dramatic form, and though his show did transfer to Broadway, the disgruntled critic of the *New York Times* found its surrealistic charm too precious when it was not altogether baffling (a minority view, by the way), and doomed it to an early death.

Despite its premature demise the revue did have a kind of *succès d'estime* and in London considerably more than that. The British theater, however, has a caste system as rigid as that which still stratifies British society. Though Roger had had any number of lines, his success, alas, had been that of a song-and-dance man; and as far as any British director is concerned, once a song-and-dance man always a song-and-dance man. One is marked for life. If he wanted a serious career in the theater, his single hit was a credit he could never use.

But Roger has always been an optimist. He began his career on the stage and he means to end it on the stage. It is the only life he knows. When the dole ran out, he got a part-time job selling trinkets on the Portobello Road, signed up for classes at Webber-Douglas, and accepted every walk-on part he was offered; and to dispel any lingering doubts about his dancing days, he allowed his name to have its way with him. He became tubby indeed. He virtually rushed into middle age, where the best character roles can be found. At forty-five he did not look much different than he does now at sixty, with his grizzled Chekhovian beard and his Colonel Blimp waistline. Though he has learned his craft well enough, there is still about him the air of a professional amateur. One is always *aware* he is acting. Onstage and off. Thus he is good enough for Bournemouth and Blackpool, but not, he knows as well as anyone, quite good enough for the West End.

I could sense he had not taken a fancy to Zelda. All evening she had been shamelessly patronizing him, and worse, stepping on his lines; but he would never, I knew, so much as hint at his dislike to me.

It was at his insistence we were here at all. So doggedly persistent were his efforts to reunite Zelda with her old mentor at the Royal Academy, I had finally intimidated her into accepting, "if only to get it over with." She had come, most reluctantly, for my sake, to what she had been referring all day as "the waxworks show." Although I knew before the evening began it would probably prove a disaster, I could no longer put Roger off without bluntly telling him that she would not be amused—not by him, nor his place, nor his guest—and I do not choose to be rude to those who have been kind to me.

As fond as I am of Roger, I find his dank and cluttered flat near Primrose Hill so grim, I ordinarily contrive to meet him elsewhere—a little Italian restaurant on Walton Street or a colorfully noisy pub in Covent Garden—where the lunch and the drinks are on me. But honor demands he occasionally return the favor, and since he is usually too poor for even a modest fish-and-chips emporium, that means dinner at his flat. Which in turn means your basic English roast-lamb-potatoes-and-overdone-greens. And the roast tonight, I fear, was sheep in lamb's dressing.

Even a Cordon Bleu graduate would have found it virtually impossible to compete with the rummage-sale furniture—rickety tables, mismatched chairs, and sprung sofas, musty and worn and more Stygian than their original upholsterers could ever have intended. Only the pictures are remotely interesting: charming costume designs from ballets no one any longer remembers and ancient theatrical prints too badly foxed and worm-eaten to have anything more than sentimental value; and in the second of the two adjoining rooms that comprise his living quarters, a pastel portrait of a very handsome young man that few who did not know him in his glory days would ever suspect is our host himself.

It is off this second room, his bedroom, that the kitchen obtrudes. So tiny it is a wonder any meal at all can be cooked in it, it is hardly more than a glassed-in porch and the flat's sole source of natural light; for the front bay, which faces north, is so shaded by plane trees that one can scarcely distinguish night from day. The shared loo at the end of the outside hall, which is, if possible, even darker and mustier than the flat itself and lit in the evening by an amber bulb of miniscule wattage, shelters a temperamental toilet, flushed, when it chooses to oblige, by a long chain suspended from a ceiling tank.

Zelda, who had been warned about the loo so that she might regulate her drinking accordingly, would not, I knew, find the place of even sociological interest. It is at just such moments that her origins become most apparent. Ordinarily more English than the English, she has never relinquished her penchant for certain home comforts. "There are a few things we do better than anyone else," she is apt to intone. "Making commodes is one of them."

The youngest member of the party, she had just turned fifty, but for so long had she so successfully managed to look thirty-something people had long since ceased to calculate what her real age might be. With scarcely an effort she made the rest of us look like attendant lords and ladies at the queen's court. And not very grand ones at that, as for the umpteenth time I listened to her re-create what has become one of her own favorite set pieces, the saga of our Christmas journey to Paris. It is a tale that grows more elaborate with each retelling until it scarcely any longer resembles anything that actually took place. She is a master improvisator. Even I, who shared the trip with her and have heard her version many times can never be sure exactly what is to happen next. The basic framework remains the same: the two hotels, the little restaurant across from the north portal of Notre Dame, sudden attack of the vapors, the desperate lack of funds that got us back to Heathrow with scarcely enough money left over for the Underground; but it becomes in her retelling a good deal more exciting and infinitely more hilarious than the facts warranted, with just enough of the panic when we discovered the second hotel was not going to accept my credit card to sauce the drama, and none of the boredom. The only thing left out of her account is Paris itself.

It is our drama that matters. And her telling. Paris is only a painted backdrop for which almost any travel poster will serve. Nor was I, as I listened, once again enthralled, the least tempted to interrupt her to set the record straight with a few deflationary facts. No one wanted facts. They were there merely to serve as grist for her fancy. She was giving a performance. We all understood that. And something more I understood: she was staving off Maud Islington's resurrection of another past, long since dead, and one Zelda, for various and complex reasons, wanted kept properly buried.

"What a pity the revue ever died."

Maud Islington's comment, quite devoid of malice, merely verified it had indeed been a performance we had been listening to. That she herself had got her own start in a Noel Coward revue directed by the Master himself merely added poignancy.

She was the sole member of the party I had not met before. In her mid-to-late-seventies, she was spectrally thin and strikingly ugly. Her face looked as if it had been crinkled in a fit of pique, cast into a corner, and then, in desperation, retrieved and frantically reassembled for the evening's festivities. Her voice was wonderfully deep and precise, every syllable given its full weight, though her talk was frequently shattered by a cough as loud and startling as a seal's bark. She had listened with her eyes, like a coach taking mental notes for a post-curtain critique.

"It's television that did it. Soon, like the Americans, we'll all be reduced to squeezing toilet tissues. *Oooooo!*" Roger gave a credible imitation of prissy ecstasy.

"Don't knock it. At least not before you've tried it." Zelda, whose agency would long ago have sunk into bankruptcy except for the funds garnered from commercials, was not about to allow her most lucrative source of revenue to come under attack without a defense. "It's keeping me afloat. As well as a good many of my clients. So what if they have to squeeze toilet tissue? Or anything else? As long as it pays the rent while they're learning their craft, playing minor roles at the RSC or the National."

"You shouldn't be selling other people's talents, my dear." Maud Islington's oversize features assumed menacing proportions, her voice deeply portentous. "But your own. You're far too good for anything else."

Zelda turned to me with a look of accusatory anguish, as if to say: Here it comes. And remember, *you* got me into this.

"Oh, I had the talent too," Maud began, "but with this face, what choice did I have? I could have done comedy, perhaps. But that's a special talent all its own. I got my laughs, all right. They were in Mr. Coward's script and I did know how to read a script." She paused for an instant to see if anyone meant to challenge that rather modest claim. "But I knew from that very first show, I wasn't about to give Bea Lillie a run for her money, I can tell you. If she'd wanted to, she could have annihilated me with a single lift of one of those marvelous eyebrows of hers. Fortunately, she was quite the nicest person I've ever worked with. A lady in *every* sense of the word."

Once again she paused, just long enough for us to pay tribute to the inimitable Lady Peel. Even Zelda, who knew the latter only from her recordings, happily obliged.

"But I didn't want to make people laugh," Maud continued. "I wanted to make them cry. Like every other aspiring young actress, I wanted to play Juliet." And with both hands clutched, the thick blue veins embossed on the liver-dappled flesh, she crushed her withered old bosom, her eyes shut for a moment of silent reverie. "Well, let me tell you, that *would* have turned me into a comedienne. Can you imagine this face—even in its salad days, and a skimpy salad it was—up there on that Verona balcony? Even then it was a face that might have sunk the entire Grecian fleet, if I may be permitted to mix my dramatic metaphors." And she interrupted her recitation with a boisterous laugh, which was in turn interrupted by a hacking cough as we waited in breathlessly respectful silence until she was once again mistress of her own voice, and then extended the courtesy long enough for her to wet her throat with a large sip of wine and to light yet another cigarette before resuming.

"Oh, there were always bit parts, and I did my share of those." She exhaled a dragon's portion of smoke. "And still do, occasionally. But only for the telly now. This cough, you understand." She patted her chest with one frail reptilian hand ringed with a Sitwell-size amethyst. "But like anyone else with any *real* talent, I wanted to leave my mark. And I knew the only way I was ever going to do that was vicariously. I might never be a great actress, but I could become a great teacher. And," she continued with a sudden diminuendo of intensity, in a voice so matter-of-fact she might have been giving her shoe size, "I think I can safely say, I've been as good a voice coach as RADA's ever had."

She paused, looking to Zelda for verification. Roger had been forgotten. He had already served his purpose by bringing mentor and protégé together. I didn't even exist, except as the necessary audience.

A very closed world, the theater.

"No one's ever disputed that, Maud." Zelda knew a cue when she was given one.

"Well, then, having heard my credentials, I'd like to tell these people here—" With a sweep of her scrawny hand strewing ashes in its wake, she spoke as if she were addressing an audience of fifty or more, "this young lady's diploma performance as Blanche is still a legend for those of us lucky enough to have seen it. Far, far better than Miss Leigh's ever was. On stage *or* screen. Sheer magic." For an instant her ugly old face became almost beautiful, so intensely riveting were the eyes, so compelling the voice, remembered emotion rejuvenating the crinkled old flesh. "Oh, the rest of the cast were perfectly adequate. But adequate is not enough when you're sharing the stage with the likes of a Zelda Duke." She pronounced the name as though it came bathed in klieg lights. "She acted circles round them all. Particularly poor Stanley, who was certainly no Brando. So of course it failed as a production. But as a performance—well, I can tell you, it's never been bettered. She won every prize we had to offer. And deservedly so. There wasn't another girl in the class who could touch her. Why, if anyone else had got the RADA Gold there would have been a riot. So why, my dear, aren't you still out there?" She hurled her challenge like a gauntlet thrown to the stage. Proving our faith justified.

My heart froze in sympathy. Zelda seemed in control, but seeming and being were not always the same with Zelda. She had listened throughout with a placid, almost serene detachment that I found spooky. As she began to speak, her smile was sweetly benevolent, her voice steady, though her cheeks were somewhat more highly colored than her make-up warranted, and not because she had been so greatly flattered by one whose judgment she respected. She was, I knew only too well, hurting.

"You seem to forget, Maud, I was an American. And the British theater has always been a closed shop." She began calmly, her words smarting from the slightest edge of bitterness. "I couldn't very well go on playing Blanche for the rest of my life. And I was, at the time, you may recall, still young enough to do a credible Juliet of my own. Just barely. With the proper lighting. But what British director was going to cast me in Shakespeare? So Blanche it was, with an occasional Mary Tyrone thrown in for variety's sake. But that's neither here nor there." She quickly reined in any impulse to charge headlong into a defense of her past. "It's over and done with." Her voice became suddenly dismissive. "We all know luck and timing play as big a role in success as talent, and they were both against me. I have no apologies to make. To you or to anyone else."

"Nonsense!" Putting down her wine glass, which she had been sipping as if she feared it might be snatched away from her before she'd had her fill, Maud was having none of it. "Don't talk to me about time. Why, I might have mothered any or all of you. Even dear pudgy old Roger here." She smiled, patting him on the thigh without turning to look at him, her note-taking eyes still fixed on Zelda, who, despite her discomfort, could not help smiling at the thought of so formidable a mother, as unlike the dear, sweet, rattled wisp of Southern gentility as it was possible to get.

"I did say 'timing,' Maud. Not time. There is a difference. Or always used to be."

"Not really." Undaunted, Maud would not be put off. "Because that's what you're most afraid of now, isn't it? Time. Well, let me tell you, it doesn't matter how old you are. And we've all been given fingers for counting, my dear." She chuckled maliciously. "It's all an illusion, anyway, the theater. You *look* marvelous. That's what matters. Why, when I think what I might have done with that face of yours!" Flushed with wine as well as ardor, she was losing her sense of direction, her interest in Zelda's prospective career giving way to the wasted potential of her own. "Just think of all those great roles out there waiting for you. What actress worth her salt wouldn't far rather play Gertrude than simpering Ophelia?"

"But you seem not to have heard." Zelda's voice remained coolly reasonable, but unlike her interlocutor, she had clearly not had enough wine to get her through the ordeal unscathed. "I was never going to be *allowed* to play Gertrude. Surely you know what my one big success was. My single West End triumph? I even made the cover of *Theater World*. It wasn't Blanche or Mary Tyrone. It was *The Dirtiest Show in Town*." She paused to allow what could have been a surprise to no one present but Roger to register, her face lit with masochistic glee. "I made more money from that one trashy piece than from all my Blanches and Mary Tyrones lumped together. And I wasn't even asked to sell my soul. Well, perhaps one teeny corner of it. I was the single member of the cast who *didn't* take her clothes off."

She threw back her head for a raucous laugh. "But even that boon held its sting. I'm sure the audience thought I kept them on because my tits were too small. Well, after that, no serious producer would have anything to do with me. Oh, the theater is filled with ironies. I made my little nest egg, all right, and then found out the egg I'd laid wasn't about to hatch."

"Yes, that was a mistake." Maud's lips were wet with the Mouton Cadet, but her eyes remained unclouded. "I could never understand why you did it."

"Simple enough. You see, I'd quite got used to eating. It was a choice between that show and independence. Or Harry." Then with a sardonic chuckle, her eyes alight with mischief, like a naughty girl caught with her hand in the cookie jar, her mouth already smeared with jam. "So I ended up with both.

No one present had to be told who exactly Harry was.

"But you had it in you to become a *great* actress." Maud was relentless. "And I never use that word lightly."

Zelda's retort was instantaneous. "I *was* a great actress." Suddenly she seemed larger than all of us, her lovely turquoise eyes shining with conviction. "I knew it. You knew it. A few dozen others knew it. So the world wasn't given a chance to find out—well, that's the world's loss."

Only the last line failed to ring with absolute conviction.

"I don't see why it had to be London," Roger surprisingly interjected. "What was wrong with New York?"

It was a question Maud would never have asked. For her the theater began and ended in London. Broadway was one long chorus line that extended all the way to the tinsel purlieus of Las Vegas and Hollywood, cities as remote and unreal to her as Sinbad's Baghdad.

There was a flash of panic in Zelda's eyes as the attack came from a new quarter. But Roger's question was far too complex for any simple answer. Maybe if you'd grown up in some little Southern backwater in the forties you wouldn't have to ask." Her voice was curt, almost to the point of rudeness. "Besides, I wanted to play Chekhov, Ibsen, and Shakespeare, as well as the great moderns. That theater was here. In England. I had nothing personally against New York. Except for the obnoxiously sweaty hands of one particularly lecherous producer. But I was determined, if I was ever going back, I was going back a star. Or not at all."

"How true were the rumors you were going to do the Broadway revival of *Streetcar*?" Relinquishing her role as proselytizer, Maud seemed

133

genuinely curious about an old bit of theatrical gossip.

Zelda sighed with weary fatalism. "Another carrot on a stick. My life's been full of them. Harry did try—God bless his golden heart—to get the Broadway rights. Whatever else his faults may be, he does believe in my talent." She played with her empty wine glass but made no effort to fill it, her eyes falling to the dregs of pudding on the plate before her. "I wasn't a big enough name. He was willing to gamble *his* money, but no one else would go along. So they hired some balloon-busted movie star instead, then all too typically, when Harry withdrew his money, moved the whole project from the stage to television. Though why anyone would want to give Blanche boobs is beyond me. That was part of the poor dear's problem, as just about any fool of a director should know, small tits *and* pretensions to gentility. A deadly combination I'll tell you about someday."

Convinced of the inadequacy of her own, she had a positive fixation on the relationship between theatrical success and the size of one's breasts. Granted, hers did not resemble the monstrous silicone-injected horrors made fashionable by the topless craze of the sixties, when she was getting her start, but they were quite touchingly beautiful and hardly cause for such bitterness.

"But who can compete with starlight?" she continued, anger giving way to resignation. "When that fell through, I decided, once and for all, it was time to hustle my bum behind the scenes. And that's just where I mean to keep it."

*

There are failures that cut so deep they never heal. The hurt was palpable as I took her hand.

"Yes, darling, I know. It's time we left."

Her gratitude also was palpable as she responded to my squeeze.

"You do have a 9:30 appointment," I lied. She never saw anyone before ten, and not before noon, if she could help it.

"It's a ghastly life, anyway." She rose and we all rose to join her. "I'm well out of it. Beside talent and dedication, a little lunacy helps. You have to be more than just a teeny bit mad to stay in this business." Then suddenly turning soft, her great eyes moist as she rummaged through her purse for her car keys. "It almost breaks my heart to watch those poor darlings out there hustling their talents, their dreams shattered, three and four times a week, in some cases. And brave little dears, they just fall to their knees and glue the parts right back together again—time after time—as if nothing had happened. Well, do that often enough, and one day you discover the glue doesn't hold anymore."

She caught herself before she could become maudlin, and she was apt to be sentimental only about others, never herself.

"Oh, I suppose it's tolerable if you're a star. Which doesn't necessarily mean you're an actor," she added, snapping her purse shut and dangling her car keys before her as she pinioned Maud with stiletto eyes. "We've all known stars of the first magnitude who couldn't act their way across a stage without a director to take them by the hand. And worse, in films. All camera angles and cleavage. My God, it makes me sick!" She turned to me, her face beginning to register the strain as she mustered a wan smile. "Darling, why can't *you* strike it rich and take me away from all this? We could build a garden in the country. Like old what's-her-name at Sissinghurst. With only the flowers to live up to. What bliss!"

"Could you drive Maud home? It's not far along your way."

Without so much as a token protest at the break-up of his party, Roger put a cap to the evening. If he was smarting from having been used and then mostly ignored, he wasn't showing it. And Maud, grateful to be spared taxi fare, could hardly expect anyone maneuvering an ancient Jaguar through London traffic to give her full attention to anything else. All tearful sentiment, warm, alcoholic endearments, and abject apologies for having played such a "cruel old harridan," she was soon dropped off in front of a flat even more grimly uninviting than Roger's. As she bent for one last wave, her already grotesque features, ghastly in the streetlight, were suddenly contorted beyond recognition, as she was convulsed by a hacking cough, and callously, without a second glance, we were off on our own at last.

Since I had been responsible for inveigling Zelda into the ordeal, I submitted to my fate without a murmur as we tore through the narrow streets of North London as if they were ramps onto some LA freeway. And very soon my worst fears came close to proving themselves more than justified, as we braked with a neck-wrenching jar a hair's-breadth away from disaster. The change of manner was as dramatic as it was sudden. All pale docility, she accepted the loud blare of the victor's horn and a clenched fist shaken at the night as her just due.

"Well, my darling," she said, idling her heart as well as the Jaguar's engine, as frail, tiny, and defeated, she sank back against her seat, "you need no better proof of my love. I went to your bloody party."

"Yes, I know." I had difficulty mustering sufficient breath for speech. "And I'm sorry I ever put you to the test. But you needn't cripple me for life just to get your own back."

She took my hand and kissed it. "A bit clammy, duck."

"The true taste of fear," I said.

She laughed, a joyous, bubbling geyser of a laugh. "Surely you're inoculated against my driving by now. Though that was a bit close for comfort. But how sad it all is." Restoring my hand, she resumed driving, non-combatively this time, at what was for her a leisurely pace. "Those two poor old things living in their dark little holes. Like rabbits before Beatrix Potter got in there and gave them all a proper scrubbing. All that scrimping and saving and passing off mutton as lamb! If ever I needed an object lesson on the future I was determined to avoid, there it is. It chills my blood to think of it!" She screwed up her face, shuddering. "But worse, imagine playing Agatha Christie in Blackpool during the height of the season! Playing Agatha Christie *any* time is bad enough. But in Blackpool! To an audience of unwashed cretins." She pronounced the word—along with "toad" one of her favorites—as if the "e" were a long "a," craytins. "And for what? A mere pittance wouldn't keep this car in petrol."

My sympathies were all with her. We share a common taste for luxury and both indulge in extravagances we can neither of us afford, trusting in some good angel to stave off disaster. And so far the good angel has never altogether failed. Yet I could not allow her to dismiss "poor" Roger as though he were fit only for our pity.

"Oddly," I said, "I can think of few people I know who are less discontented with their lot than Roger. Granted, I couldn't bear to live like him either. But he doesn't seem to notice how grim his life is. I think he likes his dark little hole. It's his and he's proud of that. An ungentrified Peter Rabbit."

"However did you meet him?"

"I saw him onstage long before I actually met him. He was with the Royal Ballet on their first visit to San Francisco. With Fonteyn in *Sleeping Beauty*. He was quite a dish in those days. I know it's hard to believe, but trust me, he was. He danced the Bluebird, and passably well. He had quite a following, San Francisco being what it is."

"So even he's had his moment of glory."

She might have been speaking from another place at another time.

"Oh, yes. We can't take that away from him," I said, speaking to the darkened city. She seemed for once to be attending solely to her driving. "But sadly, it's one he can't even talk about for fear someone will move his card over to the song-and-dance file and turn him into Archie Rice. He was having another—and final—triumph when I finally did meet him. In 1956. He was at the Lyric Hammersmith in a wonderfully zany revue. I'd been to Greece and the Middle East, where—I know you'll be surprised to hear—I spent more money than I'd allowed for. So my host in Beirut, a mutual friend, arranged for me to stay with Roger for two weeks while his roommate was off on tour. You can't believe the people I saw that year. Gielgud. Edith Evans. Richardson. Peggy Ashcroft. Redgrave père. You name them, I saw them. Everyone except Olivier, who was probably off making a film somewhere. It was a vintage year. For me as well as the British theater. And I could never have managed it without Roger's spare bed."

"Was I really dreadful?" Her voice now tremulous with remorse.

"Not positively dreadful. But close. Anyway, Roger's such a dear he won't hold it against you. Or me."

"And you?"

"Me?" Her question startled. "I never hold anything against you. You know that."

"That's because you're good. One of the few genuinely good people I know. There aren't many in the theater, you know."

"That's the kind of remark only a drunk is allowed to get away with. And you didn't have that much to drink tonight."

She giggled. "Only because I couldn't get the bottle away from Maud. Poor thing. She'll die from pickling, if the emphysema doesn't get her first. What an evening!" She sighed as the lights of Oxford Street greeted us. "I feel as if I've just, after a long, long trial, been acquitted of murder."

"Well," I said, "acquitted is better than convicted."

"I suppose so." The pause was oddly chilling, perhaps because I knew what was coming. "But I was guilty, my darling. Guilty as sin. And nothing can change that fact. I may have fooled the jury, but I've never managed to fool myself. Not for an instant."

Such a confession there was no answering with words. So we drove on in silence, past Marble Arch and into the park. Without looking at her, I slipped my hand beneath her hair to massage the back of her neck. It was as taut as a drawn bow and she bowed her head to my touch; and just for a moment, the car swerved, once again threatening disaster. But she quickly righted it, and without further incident, we headed for South Kensington and home.

His hand trembled as he wrote out the check. He had not until the last minute remembered the sales tax, so long had it been since he had purchased anything of real value, and he could not now, to his consternation, remember whether "forty" had a "u" or not. He opted to leave it out, not that anyone would be able to tell, so bad had his handwriting become. (Illegibility, he used to tell his students, is the coward's ploy.) Seven hundred forty-five dollars and fifty cents. It would leave his account at the first of the month with a precariously low balance, but there was no helping that.

"You're not looking quite up to snuff, Mr. Ashley. Not going to be ill, I hope?" His few surviving strands of hair choreographed across his bald head, the proprietor hovered solicitously over him.

"Just a summer cold," Harold Ashley replied as he removed his glasses and, blinking at the sheen of oil on the slick pate, slipped them, uncased, into his breast pocket. Then feeling compelled to add a touch of levity to the proceedings, which had, for some peculiar reason, been far from festive, almost, in fact, funereally grim:

"Mark Twain, as you've undoubtedly heard a thousand times, is reputed to have said, 'The coldest winter I ever spent was one summer in San Francisco.'"

The proprietor's smile, as stiffly contrived as his coiffeur, veiled his concern like a transparent mask.

"No one," Harold continued, "has been able to tell me just *where* he said it. But it is the kind of thing he might have said. Of course," he added, aware suddenly that he was rambling tiresomely, like the retired pedant he was, but unable to bring himself to a sudden halt without compounding his fault, "it isn't quite summer yet, is it? So technically, I suppose, it can't be a summer cold. Not for a few weeks yet." And he capped his dissertation with a fit of coughing.

"I do think you should be at home in bed, Mr. Ashley. I really do. Can I call you a taxi? We don't, after all," he added with a deprecatory chuckle, "want to lose a customer as valuable as you."

Shaking his head, Harold Ashley rose to his feet. The sudden movement made him surprisingly giddy and he feared for a moment he might fall.

"No, no," he answered rather too forcefully for his own comfort; then checking himself, he continued more coolly: "Walk will do me good. Get the old juices flowing. Cough it all up before nightfall."

But the man—he could never remember the name; something ending in a *ski* or a *stein*—was not to be put off.

"Look, why don't you let me close shop for a minute and give you a lift? Won't take a second."

His concern seemed touchingly genuine.

"No, no," Mr. Ashley protested. "Very kind of you. But I wouldn't dream of letting you do any such thing. If you'll just bag the caddy for me, I'll be on my way. Into the wild blue yonder," he added, his facetiousness trailing off in a lugubrious drone as he tried to recall the line about the kindness of strangers. Not that anyone one has just given a check for seven hundred dollars can rightly be called a stranger or his kindness totally disinterested, yet he did feel oddly touched. Which made him all the more determined not to exploit the man's concern.

Outside on Sacramento Street the glare momentarily blinded him. His eyes had always been acutely sensitive to sudden changes of light; and he paused now to catch his bearing, so light-headed he feared people might think he'd been drinking.

"Tennessee Williams," he called out, too elated at the sudden revival of his memory to care about his breach of decorum. Another retired schoolteacher, poor Blanche—though in her case, he imagined, the suspected dipsomania would not be far from the mark. And for an instant he was overwhelmed with pity for the pathetic creature struggling so ineffectually to piece together her shattered world. Then smiling at the improbability of his tears (which of those strangers passing him could ever, given a thousand guesses, hit upon Blanche Dubois as the source?), he contemplated the bizarre unreality of other people: a Pacific-Heights matron in flat shoes and tweeds redolent of moors and money, a stalwart hike over English downs, lavender soaps and sachets and a no-nonsense briskness that spoke of breeding, private schools, and green-book listings; and in her wake a mincing male browser in his fifties, perhaps, mocking both youth and age with a wig so inept it could have fooled no one but the wearer, his smirking smile an invitation, repellently ingenuous, to share in his smug delight. Strangers both and likely to remain so though he had seen both before many times. Neighborhood regulars.

Despite the damp chill he could feel beads of perspiration sprouting on his forehead. Catlike, he had always, at the first sign of illness, crept into a solitary corner, and had not this business of the tea caddy called him out, that was precisely where he would be, hidden away from the world's gaze. For, unlike Blanche, he did not want to be ministered to by strangers—or anyone else, for that matter. Except, possibly, the indefatigable and faithful Lily, like some almond-eyed Jewish mother plying him with bowls of chicken soup. The very recollection made him grow faint with hunger. The shop windows were blurred now with the steaming memory. Or was it merely his eyes misted over with tears? Of appetite as well as affection. How long had it been since he had tasted anything quite so delectable? He would not hazard a guess. And why was he suddenly so weepy? He was not, ordinarily, given to self-pity; and the tears we shed for others, fictional or real, he was wise enough to know, are shed, finally, for ourselves.

People were looking at him, their customarily warm smiles transformed. A troubling and troubled curiosity. He could never shake himself entirely free of the childhood suspicion that the secret laughter of others was directed at him, his whippet-slimness accentuated by the old-fashioned elegance of his Chesterfield topcoat. Could he, too, like the wearer of the vulgar toupee, be legitimate game for laughter? A slightly ridiculous anachronism? Nettled, he stopped to study his reflection in a shop window. Tie straight, hair in place, but face gaunt, eyes glittering. As gray, he felt, as the day. Not so much as a trace of that other face he had, only a few days before—and with what a heart-wrenching pang!—come across. A snapshot fallen from a book. A mere child he had been, thirty perhaps, tan and slender, an hibiscus rakishly tucked behind one ear, on a street in Rhodes, a thousand years ago, and so achingly beau-

141

tiful, he could not link that other reality, the person he had once been, with the person he now was. So much of him had already died he was followed by a legion of other selves, a ghostly retinue of memories that would not stay buried. And as yet another face, spectral in the window shadows, superimposed upon his own reflection, smiled back at him, his heart grew chill at the apparition. His forehead was rimmed with ice, a terror so real he could taste it, like the stench of his own putrefaction, until he realized with a frown, terror suddenly dissipated in embarrassment, the specter was merely an anonymous salesman, his presence initially obscured by the window's glare. Disconcerted, he nodded curtly and moved on. He could not bear to be observed contemplating his own reflection; to have the mirror itself turn into another face was to be exposed with all defenses down, naked in some private shame. Though he did not himself know what it was he would have kept hidden. From himself, probably, as well as the world.

At the corner of Walnut he moved up to Clay, away from the shoppers. The slight incline seemed a veritable precipice. He had to pause at the top, catching hold of the lamppost to keep from falling. Just for an instant he toyed with the prospect of turning back and making his way to the misnamed Children's Hospital; he carried his health card with him always. But the thought of some chill, impersonal room painted an antiseptic green was more than he could bear. It would only spread the infection to his soul as well. A quiet night between the cool sheets of his own bed was all he needed. It was, anyway, only a summer cold. Though after a certain age, he knew, the "only" ceased any longer to comfort. How many, he wondered, were each year laid away with that "only" frozen on their lips? Not that he was ever going to be laid away. About death he was not the least sentimental. Or frightened. (Dying was another matter altogether.) This gentleman was for burning. The fastest, cheapest incineration was all he'd require. A solitary sprinkle of ash on the chilled and murky sea. And then eternity. No fanfares. No orotund obsequies. It was life that interested him, not death with its cumbersome monuments and dreary rituals. The only heaven he had ever truly longed for was this city—even at its grayest—and his house, which seemed now almost as ephemeral as that other promised heaven. Well beyond his reach.

The caddy, he remembered, looking at the bag clutched in his hand.

For he could not for a moment think why on such a day in such a state he was out on the street in his shopping best. Again his eyes filled with tears. Happily there was no one now to witness them as he cursed whatever bug it was that had come to spoil what should have been a day of celebration. So long had it been from that bright January to this gray June.

He took out his handkerchief and wiped his eyes, moving it to his mouth as he broke into another fit of coughing. Which was unusual, as his colds ordinarily followed a pattern that ended, rather than began, with a cough.

Only six blocks and he would be home. His legs pained him now. It was the fever. He had, perhaps unwisely, passed up his annual flu shot, though flu season was long over. Like some wound-up toy he moved with a peculiarly stiff, staccato rhythm. He had a horror of ever becoming ridiculous, an object of fun. A doddering old dodo mumbling to himself. Like age and penury, disease too was a cruel joke played by the gods on our defenseless bodies. One more assault upon the spirit. Well, he was not about to give in to a few measly germs any more than he had given in to age or inflation, those twin curses of the seventies. His as well as the century's.

In the brown study at last he sank onto his leather sofa. Poor Pirandella! He had had to have her put away soon after its purchase, his last cat with her lethal claws, and he seldom sat on the sofa without a sigh for her loss, for she too had once been beautiful, a chinchilla Persian with malachite eyes outlined, like those of some Egyptian princess, in black and soulfully trusting. Exhausted now, he sat looking at nothing, his mind gone empty. Momentarily at peace with himself and the world, he did not want to move. Here was home and everything that loaded word implied. His own holy of holies. Here alone he could simply *be*—without pretense or strain or shame, without humility or pride, without guilt or fear.

The bag in his hand fell to the floor. Stirred by the noise he picked it up, stared at it absently for a moment, then removed the tortoiseshell tea caddy from its tissue wrappings. For the first time since January, he held the precious object in his hands. The markings were marvelously intricate. A rich, warm brown that seemed worlds removed from any prehistoric hangover breasting the southern seas with all the grace of an armored tank, its most splendid ornament hidden beneath lay-

143

ers of grime, the patina of a dull and plodding life. Why, he wondered, should anything so ponderously ugly, so stultifyingly clumsy, with little to commend it but its own power to endure, be granted a lifespan in centuries, while man must count himself lucky with three score and ten and blessed with each blessed hour beyond?

Rising, he placed the caddy on the table beside the ox-blood lamp; then stepping back, he once again sank, almost fell, onto the sofa. A sudden inexplicable depression overwhelmed him, weighting him with its lethargy. Some poison of the mind as well as the body. Once again experience had failed to live up to expectation.

But deflation was the fate of all lovers, and he could not, certainly, at his age, have expected the heavens to open, the trumpets to sound. The color was perfect, but the scale was wrong. Something more was needed to give it bulk. With a groan, he rose, catching hold of the small gate-leg table to steady himself, and for a minute the caddy and everything else was banished from his thoughts. He could think of nothing but the disease that was fast taking possession of him and he was seized with a brief, gut-twisting panic.

No, he would not indulge in self-dramatization; he would not give in to the usual hypochondria of age. He would work his way up to bed soon and sleep it off. The best remedies were still the simplest. Starve a cold, his mother used to say. Feed something—he could not remember what—but starve a cold; that much he remembered. And the stern woman with her clipped commands for whom he, her second and last son, had been not even an afterthought, merely an *un*thought, a pre-menopausal child twenty years younger than her other well-loved, ruthlessly ambitious, diabolically successful firstborn; and though he, Harold, had never truly known his father, he had, having known his mother all too well, never been able to believe there had been any more joy in his conception than in his upbringing, a grim task grimly performed, his mother's wisdom meted out like oracles carried fresh from Sinai: Starve a cold! Not that there could, in the present instance, be much choice in the matter. And perhaps rest would be the best medicine.

But duty first. (His mother's own son he was.) And after so long a wait he did owe a duty to his latest purchase. He must find something to fit the caddy into its new home and give it as well the security of belonging. In the kitchen he removed a small bronze vase from one of the cupboards. A classical Japanese urn. Then stepping out to the enclosed garden, he was once again dazzled by the glare. The damp chill revived him momentarily as he stooped to pick three white hydrangea blooms and a collar of leaves. He wanted to weep for their beauty. No artist had ever come close to capturing a white of such staggering purity, each four-petaled blossom centered with a speck of robin's-egg blue heartbreakingly delicate, a tiny blue eye pulsating with life. He could scarcely, for some reason, bear to look at them, though it seemed equally difficult to tear his eyes away.

Once again inside, he sank onto the sofa and studied the caddy, given bulk and character by the background of white hydrangeas. Yes, precisely, he thought. Perfect—as he had known it would be. Smug in the security of his taste, he smiled; it was the only thing about himself he had never doubted. He had always had an "eye." Only where his own work was concerned did it ever falter—in the face of those furtive, meticulous still lifes which he had worked and reworked, constantly refining, revising, and then, ultimately, secreting out of sight in the upstairs studio closet. Still by his own definition a Sunday painter, though at periodic intervals throughout his life he had painted seven days a week, he had always been far too modest ever to think of himself as an artist, yet when the time for judgment came, as it soon did, his only measuring rod was the best. Another legacy from his mother, perhaps, who had always measured his ever childishly inadequate promise against his older brother's fulsomely manly reality. Mere prettiness was never enough. Until he could some day paint an apple fit to hang unashamedly alongside one of Cézanne's, they must all be banished to the attic cupboard. Once or twice he had, he thought, come close to fashioning an apple that one could not merely feel, but taste—oh, so close—if only he had been able to take the leap beyond refinement, into that raw area of crude genius. But there was a timidity in his touch he could never quite overcome, a modesty so deeply engrained he had never been able to worship with any assurance at the altar of his own divinity. He was, he knew, even in his moments of wildest excess, indisputably earthbound. All too finite. What his pictures most lacked, aside from genius, was passion. Though what it was that drove him, year after year, failure after failure, to persist, if not a kind of passion, he could not surmise. A dogged obstinacy, perhaps—the capacity to take infi-

145

nite pains that the shallowest of misguided critics always confuses with genius, when it is the very nature of genius to create without any pain at all, blooming as the flower blooms in answer to the sun.

For infinite pains he had always been able to take. It was precisely there lay the comfort of his collages—or paste-ups as he preferred to call them—in the ability to lose himself for hours and days even, cutting out the photographs, reproductions, etchings that took his fancy and then recomposing them with wit and taste and humor, and, yes, here, even a kind of genius, but one he never himself took seriously. An artistic joke. His masterpiece was a six-panel screen of strange, dreamlike images, uninhibitedly erotic, that spanned one wall of his upstairs study and hid the few surviving canvasses that had, he thought, revealed the greatest promise and might yet *someday,* he hoped, be worked into something of merit: That one perfect apple to hang alongside Cézanne's.

But here too, of late, there had been a kind of retrenchment, a ruthless weeding out and paring down until an entire lifetime of work had been reduced, after the resulting immolation, to some dozen pictures in varying stages of completion. In his fragile state the dreadful challenge of an unfinished canvas exposed more than he could any longer bear with equanimity. What had once been a joy was now a chore. Gods can with impunity be stripped naked. Apollo on his pedestal wins our adulation, but mere man with his knock-knees and less than ivory flesh, with his sagging breasts and fallen hams, with his discreet pot, be it ever so humble, was best, he decided, left clothed. And art stripped one naked. The mystery of the apple must therefore follow him to his grave, unresolved: how to extract with mere brush and pigment the soul of anything so simple that it becomes not a reproduction but a re-creation, a living, growing being.

And with each fresh failure he turned once again to his house. A more modest challenge—there were no Cézannes among decorators—he met it with a sureness of touch with which he had never been able to confront a blank canvas: the model, only, for a work of art which he could for hours sit contemplating—though never capturing—the changing light, the transitory sheen of carved mahogany, the luster of old velvet, letting his eye alone compose the pictures that would never be painted with any pigment more permanent than his own imagination.

From the time he had first seen the caddy he had not been able to enter his study without his eyes falling involuntarily onto the empty tabletop. The entire room had called out to him—which was, he knew, the pathetic fallacy; but he couldn't any longer be altogether sure it was a fallacy, that things as well as people did not have souls. What else was it that Cézanne had caught but the very soul of things? Whatever has been made must partake of the soul of the maker as the creation of the creator, as man of God; as all these precious things about him partook of his soul and better expressed his inner being than he had ever managed with words. If he must sit in the judgment seat, it was they that would speak for him—the Chippendale side table that had been the greatest "find" of his life, or the tiny, third-century Roman bust he had liberated immediately after the war from the floor of a dingy little shop on the Via del Babuino—so many years ago. His life, it seemed to him, had been measured out in shops. His own soul, such as it was, forged in the marketplace.

*

"If you don't mind my saying so, Mr. Ashley," the proprietor of the Sacramento Street shop he had been browsing, remarked, "it's such a pleasure to see a man of your years so well turned out. So many seem to stop trying the minute they reach retirement."

Since he had, because of his slenderness, eschewed the wide lapels in vogue at the time of its purchase, his suit was perhaps more fashionable now than when had had first acquired it, its knife-edge creases still cuttingly sharp. Its subtle stripes gave him, he fancied and not altogether without cause, for he had always *looked* the part destiny had given to his brother, the air of a retired ambassador whose waiting Rolls might be just around the corner, its motor idling beneath the well-slippered foot of a liveried chauffeur. That at least was the role he chose to assume and he had always entered into the drama of his public appearances with the relish of an old trouper who knows his audience well enough to give it precisely what it wants.

For there was, in his manner as much as his person, the startling good looks of an aging matinee idol—some quality that sparked the fancy of others and made one feel that anyone of his years and bearing, so imperiously slim, so meticulously groomed, so coolly self-assured, must at the very least have been touched by romance. And the admiring glances gave an added bounce to his step, a fresh lift to his walk. If all the world is truly a stage, why should not one then respond to the

147

applause? And since beautiful septuagenarians are rare enough to warrant anyone's second look, the glances that he had always battened upon
had, if anything, increased with his increasing age.

"Living well, they say, is the best revenge." With a polite nod that
was surprisingly awkward in one so imbued with grace, for he wanted
the admiration of others to be, if obvious, never expressed in any form
so blatant as words, he acknowledged the compliment, then once again
perused the tortoiseshell caddy in his hands.

"And living well is one art you do seem to have mastered."

"Yes." He met the proprietor's eyes with a cool modesty that in no
way reflected the turmoil of emotions he was about to subject himself
to. "I do my best. Eight hundred, did you say?"

"That's right. Eight hundred. Of course, with the usual discount
that comes to seven-twenty. Let's say an even seven and we won't argue
over pennies."

A cloud momentarily darkened Harold Ashley's face. He never
argued over pennies. Or dollars, for that matter. He either bought or he
did not buy, but he certainly did not stoop to bargaining.

"It may seem somewhat high," the proprietor continued, the tone of
apology just short of obsequious, "but with the current ban on importa-
tion, the available tortoiseshell is fast drying up. I'm afraid it's that old
law of supply and demand at work again."

"Yes, I quite understand. Thank you," he said, and without further
comment he handed the caddy back to the proprietor, who knew his
customer well enough to know that silence did not necessarily portend
a lost sale.

"It's Regency," he added as he placed the caddy back on its glass shelf.
"But then I needn't tell *you* that."

No, Mr. Ashley agreed, he did not have to be told its period, and
with another nod and a smile more gracious than warm, he stepped out
onto the street.

In the magical winter light the city might have been painted by a
seventeenth-century Dutch master with stunning clarity. His heart leapt
at the sight of it. No longer did he dream of Paris, London, Rome.
Though he had loved them all in his time, he was quite content now,
for those years left to him, never to step foot beyond San Francisco's
boundary. The world—his world—was of necessity shrinking, its bor-

ders retrenching, and he, concentrating his powers, focused what light was left upon the scenes about him. He did not any longer even venture to Marin or the peninsula. The eucalyptus forests of the Presidio or the wilds of Lands End were all he needed of the country. From the well-mansioned crest of Pacific Heights or the cypress-lined vistas of Lincoln Park, he could catch comforting glimpses of Tamalpais brooding over the bay like some guardian deity. It was enough to know it was there—he did not have to climb its slopes—and occasionally, sometimes when he least expected it, to be surprised by its grandeur, the beauty of the scene so palpable, its embrace left him momentarily spent with wonder.

The mild westerly breeze obligingly swept waste fumes in the direction of Oakland, a city whose reality he had never been quite able to take seriously, leaving San Francisco's air so dazzling in its clarity he could savor the walk home that would save him the five-cent carfare and form the ceremonial cornerstone of his seven-hundred-dollar purchase. Though it had taken him a year past his sixty-fifth birthday before he could bring himself to accept the hateful, patronizing phrase and show off his senior-citizen's card to take advantage of the reduced fare, he had ultimately resigned himself to the indignity—as he now resigned himself to the walk, which would, anyway, help keep him fit, down Sacramento Street to Baker and the last of the shops, then over to Clay toward the Alta Plaza and the small Victorian he had bought more than thirty years before for a price so ridiculously low it made him positively giddy to be told now what it was worth in the current inflated market. Although there was a kind of smug satisfaction in knowing that his original modest investment had proved providential beyond his wildest expectations, it made him rather more uneasy than not, as if he were standing on a cloud that might at any moment prove itself just that, mere vapors, and send him plummeting to the earth. For the inflation of the seventies had very nearly dealt the final blow, turning his once adequate state pension into the barest prescription for survival.

The means of succor were there, of course, but they could not be employed without some sacrifice of style and he chose not to sacrifice. The Picasso drypoint—one of forty—for which he had years before paid less than four hundred must easily be worth at least four thousand now—though four thousand was inversely worth what four hundred used to be, so where did that get one? In an instant it would all be

149

gone and he would be left where he had begun, before the sale, but one Picasso the poorer. It seemed hardly worth the effort, let alone the sacrifice. So he made neither.

No, he had long ago decided, he would not trudge to the grave like some pauper, cup in hand for the ready handout. And what other notable ports-of-call did a man in his seventies have to look forward to? He meant to walk there with head high, and despite the newspaper cutouts lining his smart Bally loafers, with all the style he could muster. An anachronism, perhaps, but an elegant anachronism. The last Edwardian gentleman. And when he was forced to bow—well, there would be an end to it: a quick and tasteful exit.

Fortunately his mortgage had long been paid off, and thanks to Proposition 13 the property taxes were relatively insignificant. What was not insignificant was the cost of upkeep on an old house. Just a few months before he had been presented with a staggering bill to have the sidewalk acacias pruned, though he himself kept the boxwood and Eugenia neatly trimmed, there was no way, short of cutting them down to the ground altogether, he could manage the trees. For one or possibly two more years, the house could get by without another paint job. How he would then contrive to repaint it he did not dare to think. Of course, at his age, time itself might bring its own solution, radical, but neat. And there were moments when his prospective death did loom up almost with relief, as the most honorable out, for he had, making a rather poor joke of it, long ago decided, as with poor Butterfly, it would be death before dishonor. And his honor—a Victorian concept clung to with Victorian tenacity—resided in the same Victorian house as he.

It was not until one entered the front door that the real treasure was revealed in the hush of serenity. The stained-glass overdoor speckled the entrance hall with muted colors. A pot of yellow chrysanthemums sat in a white porcelain cachepot on what had in the eighteenth century been a sewing table. Beyond it a narrow stairway led to the garnet-colored dressing room. Before changing, he stepped through the French doors onto the adjoining sundeck. In better times he would have been greeted by a host of golden daffodils mocking the winter chill with their sunny faces, but for the last few years all flowers that could not be started from filched seeds or slips had been foregone. Aside from water and his own ministrations, the garden, he had decided, must prove self-sufficient. Yet there was nowhere a sense of frugality. So lush was the growth, so prodigal the camellias and azaleas in the garden below, there was, despite the economies, a richness of abundance, of growth crowding in upon growth.

Back in the dressing room he stowed his suit in a zippered bag and his shoes, their newspaper soles still in place, in felt slipcases. As a young man he had been rather careless with his possessions. Necessity, not character, had made him fastidious. The loud groans which accompanied his disrobing were good-naturedly self-mocking, for he bore the physical indignities of aging with bemused detachment. What other choice did he have? The alternatives were few. His ankles in the morning, on his first shuffling walk to the bathroom, seemed at times made of glass too fragile to support his weight, slight as it was; and his left hipbone joint was apt at unexpected moments to give way, sending him precipitately to his knees like an importunate lover, but on the whole he had been surprised at how gradual the process of disintegration was: it seemed to him he had pretty much looked and felt the same for at least the last ten years. Then, too, time proved kind in other ways, obscuring distant prospects in hazy mists so that one lived now from day to day pretty much as if the supply of tomorrows were unlimited. In his health as in his life—having so timed his birth as to be too young for the First World War and just too old for the Second—he had been remarkably lucky, suffering nothing more serious than an annual cold, and though he felt the strain as he bent to untie his shoes, he had felt much the same strain at sixty. His hands, moreover, were still surprisingly free of liver spots and steady, without so much as hint of tremor. Even the hunger pangs he had come to accept as a matter of course.

Dressed in frayed black turtleneck, worn corduroys, and an ancient pair of Hush Puppies, he descended the stairs like a scruffy mendicant who has wandered by chance into princely quarters. Only now did he seem out of place, but he had become with age resolutely invisible to himself, moving like a ghost among his possessions. Only on his public excursions was he ever aware of his person, of a role being played, and for that role he always dressed with the greatest care. If the eyes of others gave his physical being a sharper reality, he felt compelled in return to give the camera-eyes their due and make of that reality a fitting drama of suggested mysteries and high possibilities. But once again alone, even when he looked into the high mirror over the dining room fireplace, he saw, instead of his own reflection, arrangements of blue and white porcelains on the pearl-gray walls or the Boston fern cascading from the brass chain in the bay of the summer parlor, the white slats of the half-open louvered shutters luminous in the afternoon light.

The pot of chrysanthemums on the round Empire table beneath the fern had virtually bloomed itself out; the white heads with brown centers bowed, the foliage drooping. That the five dollars it would take tomorrow to replace it might better be spent on a dozen eggs and makings for the week's salads he would not let himself dwell upon. That way lay defeat, if not madness. The pots of chrysanthemums that always adorned the entrance hall and the parlor bay were as integral a part of the decor as the tables upon which they sat, and though he was prepared to make all manner of allowances where his own person was concerned, wearing shoes that he would only a few years before have blushed to be seen dropping into a Salvation Army bin and skipping lunch altogether, he was determined not to lower the standards of his house.

The kitchen alone ever gave him the least uneasiness, so well stocked was it with china and cooking utensils, most of which would most certainly never again be put into service—place settings for eight and elaborate crockeries for elaborate casseroles arranged on the open shelves in Chardin-like still lifes. Three years before when it had seemed likely his cavalier disregard for budgeting might cause him to lose his house, he had been forced, finally, at a very late date, to take stock of himself and his future prospects as he had never really done before. The shock came close to killing him. But he soon recovered, a better and a wiser man with his priorities firmly established. For once in his life he knew precisely who and what he was. And more important, perhaps, who and what he was not—that retired ambassador with the waiting Rolls with whom he might bluff the world, but never himself.

Except for an occasional afternoon tea, he gave up entertaining. He also gave up being entertained, not because he had developed any latent aversion to people or discovered late in life any particular talent for monasticism, but because pride would not allow him to accept what he could not return. He had always, perhaps merely as the gratuitous reflection of his brother's accomplishments, exuded such an aura of wealth and well-being, his friends had never been able to believe in the reality of his poverty and attributed his retreat from society to simple misanthropy, which they were in their turn determined to honor. On rare occasions a former student or colleague stopped by to take him out to dinner. For these invitations he felt he had already "paid" in his way. Otherwise he dined alone, if so grand a word can be used to describe so austere a practice. He *ate* alone, rather; one does not "dine" on plain rice and salad.

Alcohol had been the easiest of his major household expenses to liquidate. Although he had always enjoyed a good wine with his meals, he had never been a heavy drinker. He had not, anyway, a "head" for drinking. There was a streak of timidity in his nature that had always acted as a rein upon his behavior, a reticence that had never allowed him, even as a handsome and healthy youth, to abandon himself to drunkenness. Ecstasy was a word he had always shied from. He was an Apollonian, not a Dionysiac. His greatest pleasures had always come from refinement, not excess, so that his current abstinence proved, if not an easy, at least a tolerable, sacrifice and one from which he could claim to draw much benefit. As he could also claim at first from the stringent changes in his eating habits. He would have liked some philosophical basis more ennobling than mere need upon which to justify his economies, so he clung to the fiction that they were taken for the benefit of his health. There were other compensations besides a robust liver and a low cholesterol attendant upon his hunger: an acuity of vision he had never before attained to. It seemed to him that he had at last in his newfound asceticism begun to fathom the mystery of the apple—or orange or whatever else it was his hungry eye fixed itself upon—if only he had now the energy left to extract its soul and fashion it on canvas. But since it was the vision itself and not the translation of that vision which truly mattered, now that he had finally, and probably forever, abandoned the brush, he knew himself to be a better painter than ever.

The greatest blow had been the necessity to let his housekeeper of more than two decades go. Though Lily had never learned to speak English, they had somehow, she with her shrill Cantonese and he with his English-accented sign language, always managed to communicate. More important, she had seemed to share his love for his house. Almost aggressively efficient, she was, for a southern Chinese, exceptionally tall and large-boned. She knew all about "face," both his and hers, and a good deal about quality, particularly where porcelain was concerned, dismissing his Japanese imitations of Chinese originals with a back-

153

hand contempt he had always found endearing. She was strong, loyal, proud, intelligent—everything, short of beautiful, he most admired in a woman—and he had always thought of her more as his collaborator than his servant. They had both wept unashamedly when he gave her notice, yet she, more than any of his friends, sympathized with his dilemma: confronted with the choice of selling his house along with his treasures and buying a small apartment in some high-rise monument to senility or drastically curtailing his standard of living and holding onto his house, literally for dear life, he had not for a moment hesitated. He had seen enough of retirement homes with their palsied inmates, drooling mumblers shuffling their aimless way through cheerless halls, to freeze his blood at any such Swiftean prospect and welcome sudden death as a savior.

She still had her key, which made him think of their parting as a separation rather than a divorce. Bearing gifts of Chinese delicacies, she made periodic forays to see that he had not fallen too far behind with his dusting. Though she was a good ten years younger than he, there had always been something maternal in her ministrations, as if he—and possibly all Caucasian males—were helpless, slightly comic figures powerless to cope with the ordinary routines of everyday life.

He could see from the package left on the maple counter she had been in during his absence. There were two gifts: a kind of Chinese tamale wrapped in a tai leaf and stuffed with rice, pork, and all manner of delectable spices, and traditional New Year's almond cookies. It would be his last feast before the long fast he was about to set out on, and to complete his celebration of the Lunar New Year, he would open the last of his Christmas gifts—from his two nieces, daughters of his now deceased brother (and his own near contemporaries) with whom he maintained a discreetly formal acquaintance that was on both sides more dutiful than affectionate—a precious bottle of cabernet sauvignon.

As he carried the weak tea brewed from the leftover breakfast tea leaves, a ritual known as the second pressing, into the brown study, he noticed with an affectionate smile Lily had washed the windows of the French doors leading out to the garden and the white camellia that was always the first to bloom. He lit the light on the painting over the leather sofa. So much did the picture resemble a Vuillard, a typical patterned interior with a woman sewing at a table while a child at her feet beats a toy drum, he could easily have passed it off as a work of the master himself, rather than the quite competent but considerably less famous follower who had actually done the painting, a minor Nabi in a major moment of inspiration. Like everything else in the room, it had arrived there partly through luck, partly through connections (which had once, before death began to hew down their ranks, been extensive), and partly through an unfailing eye for quality matched with an equally discerning nose for a bargain.

Like his collages, the room was a triumph of startling juxtapositions of disparate styles and cultures joined together in happy, but unconventional, wedlock. One could not change anything without changing everything. Since every piece of furniture, every picture, every object, was the reflection of some deeply personal need or fancy, they were all, having been filtered through a single unifying sensibility, subtly related. It was love, if nothing else, that linked them. Nor did they simply belong to him; they had become, over the years, a part of him, his family, he might have said, for they were dearer by far than mere friends, and their loss or injury would have been felt as deeply personal as his own illness. Indeed, given the choice between, say, the loss of a finger or the loss of his Roman bust, he would not for an instant have hesitated to lay his finger on the sacrificial block.

The crisp New Year's cookie added spice to the bland tea. Constant fasting had so refined his sense of taste, on the rare occasions when he did indulge himself he felt positively debauched, and he savored every last crumb, licking his fingers with the shivering, close-lidded titillation of an inebriate. Then placing the empty cup back on its saucer, he let his eye fall with arch reluctance to the long, low Parsons table beside the easy chair. It had been designed originally, with its long, low shape to hold a small television, but so offensively jarring had he found the set, it had almost immediately been banished to the closet of the upstairs study, from which it could, when needed—which was almost never—be wheeled out for viewing. It was here beside the ox-blood lamp where the exiled television had once sat that he had immediately known the tortoiseshell caddy belonged.

He had been struck not merely by the high degree of craftsmanship or the subtle intricacies of shape, but by the particular beauty of the shell markings themselves, and the color, like burnt caramel, the whole perched on four tiny ivory feet. Even the inside caddy lids, each with its ivory knob and its ivory rim, were in mint condition, so perfect it might

155

have come, unused, direct from the maker's hand.

That it would form the perfect complement to the room, the final stroke in his yet incomplete masterpiece, he had recognized at once. And now that he had found it, he knew that his eyes would never rest content until they rested upon it, brought home at last—for it was thus that he thought of his purchases: as homecomings. He was merely the intermediary in the ultimate realization of the Platonic ideal that was his house: the fleshing out of a soul that had always existed from the beginning of time. The Chippendale table, for example, had undoubtedly been made for some grand country house, probably Irish, yet despite its palatial scale, it had also, from its inception, he never doubted, belonged as well to this particular room. That it might later "belong" to some future room to be built in some other century and treasured by eyes as yet unborn, he did not doubt, but the chances of those particular eyes and that particular room focusing upon this particular table with both the will and the way—to say nothing of the means—were so remote as to make its present realization virtually miraculous.

Here in his brown study was the quiet center of his life. And if the world chose to call these representations of tranquility, order, and beauty with which he surrounded himself luxuries rather than necessities, that was more rightly a comment upon the world than upon him. For the core of his religion also was sacrifice, not indulgence. Even during the days of his greatest affluence he had never been able to make a major purchase without a long period of deprivation; he had always had to starve his body to feed his soul. He had never learned to drive, never so much as considered owning a car, never married, fathered no family, and for months on end, after each new acquisition, he had gone into virtual seclusion, a kind of voluntary purdah, to recoup his depleted resources.

And always until now with a joyful heart. But necessity had transformed him from creator into mere conservator. And that was a crueler blow by far than age. His upstairs canvases, he knew, would remain forever unfinished. All of his depleted resources, all of his failing energies, must be directed now toward one end alone: keeping what he had already created from deterioration. Even to toy with the notion of a seven-hundred-dollar purchase in his present economic plight was a form of madness. The spirit, unfortunately, could not subsist without the flesh; unless the latter were fed, the former must also starve, and the idling motor of that waiting Rolls be forever stilled. No, the tea caddy would have to be forgotten, his room left unfinished. The crucial question was survival. There could be no other.

*

But resignation did not come easily. A sullen discontent soon inhibited all action. Inertia bound him to his chair, the pages of the book in his hand left unturned, his mind unable to register the words his eyes followed with plodding incomprehension. Cobwebs were spied in corners it seemed scarcely worth the effort to reach with the feather duster; plants drooped for lack of water; dishes were left unwashed, his bed unmade, his face unshaven. A stultifying lassitude weighed down every muscle. It was weeks before he could bring himself to don his shopping best for another stroll up Sacramento Street, and though he did not dare enter the shop, he did pause with studied casualness to peer through what seemed in the afternoon glare more mirror than window to reassure himself that the object of his lust was still safely stowed behind the locked doors of the vitrine.

He confined his visits at first to one a week. Every Wednesday he would saunter past the shop, pausing at the window to verify the caddy remained safely in place. But each fresh reassurance merely intensified the subsequent apprehension. So keen was the sense of impending loss, Monday was soon added to Wednesday, and before long Friday as well became a routine part of his daily constitutional. His emotions, however, were as ambivalent as they were intense; the only consistency was the obsession itself. Thus there were times when he hoped, even prayed, he might find the caddy gone, the burden of responsibility lifted by some unavoidable and irrevocable chance from his shoulders. Once, with a sudden irrepressible start of panic, he thought his prayers had indeed been answered, for instead of the tea caddy, a blue-and-white Imari bowl sat on the glass shelf of the vitrine; but his anxious eyes soon spied the caddy against the far wall, sitting on a small, undistinguished commode like some proud Europa atop a scruffy barnyard bull.

The discovery brought such a rush of blood to his head, he feared for a moment he might faint and he had to reach out to brace himself on the brass door handle to keep from falling, his forehead pressed against the cold plate glass. Panic gave way to relief, relief to anger. The proprietor was toying with him, the practiced old harlot was teasing him,

157

luring him on. The choreographed strands of plastered hair, just visible through the glass door, became suddenly more diabolic than comic, the invariable welcoming smile unctuously avaricious.

Well, that was a game two could play. Scowling, Harold quickly righted himself and with an icy stare that froze all welcomes, he moved away from the door with fierce dignity. For a full week he avoided all contact with the shop. He did once pass the store on the opposite side of the street, but without so much as a glance in its direction he strode briskly past with eyes fixed intently upon nothing more distinguished than the corner fireplug. It was, however, a short-lived boycott. For such heroism proved, ultimately, even more exhausting than temptation, and a week later, once again humbled by that great leveler, desire, he was back for yet another tantalizing glimpse of his precious caddy.

Bouts of the profoundest melancholy now alternated with periods of equally overwhelming discontent. For hours he would sit in his unlit sanctuary staring in utter silence at nothing in particular with a kind of dull stupor, the blood in his veins as heavy as mercury, until a subtle and insinuating ire roused him once again to sullen life. Was he to be reduced at last to a demeaning struggle for mere animal survival? Were his entire life and energy to be directed now solely to feeding a frail and failing body while his soul languished for lack of nourishment, condemned to die before him? At such moments it seemed to him if what was left of dignity and manhood were to survive, some grand gesture was called for, a final marshaling of his powers to strike heaven on the face for this the body's ultimate insult.

As the months wore on and the caddy remained unsold, he knew what that gesture must be. The caddy, anyway, he had long been convinced, was destined to be his. Fate had obviously ordained it. Resistance, he should have known from long experience, was not merely futile, but self-defeating: it first destroyed what it must ultimately surrender. There would be no escape, he knew now, as well as he knew himself. Madness or not, he must have it. And wisdom be damned.

*

"Ah, Mr. Ashley, come for your revenge, have you?"

The proprietor's greeting had baffled him, but interrupting his thoughts as it did, he had left it unremarked.

"Yes. Yes, the caddy—I think I will, after all, have to have it."

"Then yours it shall most certainly be."

As he closed his eyes to savor the joy of fulfillment, his thoughts sank like some heavy, armor-plated amphibian, diving deep through the warm and dappled sea, and when he opened them again, he had, it seemed sunk well beyond the reach of light. The room was dark.

"Not looking quite up to snuff, Mr. Ashley." The blood in his ears pulsed. "Not going to be sick, I hope."

Troubled, he looked about. "Only—" he began, but something was clearly out of joint.

Why was it suddenly so dark? Black shadows against a dark ground began slowly to assume familiar shapes: the flawless, coldly sensual curves of the unlit ox-blood lamp. He was at home. In the downstairs study. The brown room. He must have dozed off without knowing it. But for hours? He did not, certainly, feel refreshed. His tongue stuck to the roof of his mouth, dry and heavy, and as he rose, his legs seemed made of aspen leaves. His whole body ached, the back of his eyes, his chest, his arms. The pain resided in bone as well as muscle. The least movement required effort, each lift of his foot a ponderous engineering feat. With no more than a cursory glance at the caddy, only a black shadow now snug beneath its umbrella of hydrangeas, he left the room, and without turning on the lights, he made his way through the darkened hall. The streetlight outside illuminated the wings of the stained-glass butterfly in the overdoor, its flight frozen forever in stillness. The sharp, beveled edges of the body glistened with ghostly luminescence. Mounting the stairs, he paused every few steps to catch his breath and steel himself for the next ascent. When he had bought the house, he recalled with a sudden stab of grim humor, he had jokingly checked out the stairway to see that a coffin could be maneuvered down its narrow landing and passage, for he had meant the move, even then, while still young enough for such macabre jokes to lack all sting, to be his last, and this house his final resting place. The temple of his spirit as well as his body.

But that look down so long a passage of time increased his vertigo. He seemed to be sinking so fast time itself became a meaningless jumble: that first joke, its latest recollection, and its final realization overlapping transparencies of but a single picture. It was the fever. Prospero's every third thought—the plague of all old men. And it struck him for the first time, like a mortal blow, that he was indeed an old man. The con-

159

cept seemed to him who had only yesterday been so young so patently absurd he could scarcely credit it. Yet if he sat down before he undressed, he knew he would be lost, his body and soul both mired in an inertia from which he would never again be able to extricate himself. He left his shoes where he kicked them off, his trousers crumpled where he had stepped out of them, and coughing violently, rubbing a dry cloth across his fevered brow, he made his way to bed. As he sank onto the cool sheets, a sudden euphoria enveloped him and he lost consciousness.

When he woke, he was sopping from neck to toe. Had he, he wondered for one startled instant, suddenly become incontinent? An old man's failing. Soon there would be nothing left of dignity or pride. But, no, he was merely swimming in his own sweat. The chill from the wet pajamas must have wakened him. He stepped dizzily out of bed, and shivering, he took off his pajamas, letting them fall in a damp heap at his feet, his teeth chattering as he donned a dry pair. In the bathroom medicine cabinet he found the thermometer. Sitting on the edge of the immense, lion-clawed bathtub, he waited for his temperature to register, his exhaustion so great he feared his head might fall and by sheer weight snap off the mercury tip of the thermometer.

He could not read the results without his glasses. Where had he left them? He could not remember. He could not remember anything. Something about revenge the man had said. What could he have had in mind? Against whom or what would he want to revenge himself? It didn't matter. Communication was at best a difficult art. The eye, he had for years been convinced, heard better than the ear. Those sweeter, soundless melodies composed of color and form. Rummaging through his discarded clothes he found the glasses finally in the breast pocket of the jacket dropped onto the dressing room chair. They steamed when he put them on and he had to move them down to the tip of his nose before, squinting, he could decipher the startling message: 104.

A fever! He remembered suddenly, and with a sinking sense of foreboding a tremor swept over him, a chilling wave of terror. It was: feed a fever. Starve a cold, but feed a fever. Why had he forgotten it, he wondered, as though the forgetting had been the fever's cause. There were no accidents; all was ordained. He wanted to cry, to give way upon the instant to every weakness, physical as well as spiritual. A weeping mass of disintegrating flesh, he was not an old man afraid of death but a child afraid of the dark. He was a child again, his mother in the background, too severe for softness, a desert prophetess dispensing her outworn wisdom as well as her bitter medicine—a gritty throat roughly swabbed with iodine. Though the memory was far from delectable, he ached for the comforting reassurance of a female voice. Someone to illuminate the dark with her warm, engulfing maternity.

Lily!

At his study desk he fumbled through his address book. Everything a blur. She was, he knew, somewhere at the beginning of the L's. Like everyone else she too had a last name, but she had always been simply Lily to him. Stars did not require two names. Strong. Capable. Efficient. At the sound of her voice, high-pitched and defensive as always whenever she answered the telephone, her shield against the English language, which alone ever seemed to daunt her, his spirits soared and the tears ran down his cheeks.

"Lily," he said, it was not a question so much as a tribute.

"Hari?" It was her own familiar version of Harold, the only nickname he could remember ever being given. Even as a child, more at home with things than with people, he had always been Harold, to his mother and brother as well as his classmates.

"I sick, Lily," he said and did not even attempt to listen to more than the comforting sound of her answer, his own voice swept away on a flood of tears. Without understanding a word she spoke, he knew she would stop whatever she was doing to come to him.

"Yes, yes, come, Lily. Come."

He had only to wait. An hour at most. She had her key. All would yet be well.

Like fasting, illness also had its attendant compensations. Along with his anxiety the years too fell as he returned to bed, moving as one does in a dream, without any sense of touching earth. The old man had regained his youth. Time, anyway, was a mirror trick. An illusion. That imaginary point upon which two unrealities are pivoted.

What was it? Scarlet fever. How old had he been? Eight or nine, perhaps. He smiled. There was snug security in the memory of the drawn shades and the dim light of the sickroom. A kind of bliss it had been to be helpless, watched over by ministering angels. The cool sponge on his hot body. Soups siphoned into his parched mouth. All sound softened to a whisper.

He did not even notice the dampness of the sheet as he sank with a sigh onto the soft mattress. He was a small child again waiting placidly for the mother he knows will mount the stairs to kiss him goodnight. A duty seen is a duty performed. And love, too, was a duty. As he waited, the world behind his closed lids, a sugared brown as warm and rich as melted caramel, became streaked gradually with darker, tortoiseshell markings closer to fudge. Once again he seemed to be sinking, a prehistoric hangover diving deep into unknown seas. The darkness spread, the tropic waters grew chill—though he was himself past registering it. Or anything else.

She was a tiny woman made even smaller by age. In the last decade of her life she shrank five inches—as she was the first to tell anyone. And with a pride in the force and number of her afflictions that dared one to snatch the cup from her own arthritic fingers. But as the body waned, the will waxed, until it seemed impossible anything so small could contain so large a store of anger. Age she accepted as a personal affront. It was, she knew, a struggle to the death against unequal odds, but she was never one to shirk a fight and every fresh assault was met with fierce resistance.

Until that fateful Saturday there had always been something grand about her anger, directed as it was against so formidable an enemy. Though one might wish she could have borne her afflictions with a little more Christian forbearance and been somewhat less voluble in the enumeration of her symptoms, there was a kind of Homeric dignity to the catalogue of her complaints. Her battle then was epic, and one was forced to grant it, at the very least, a grudging respect. But when that anger was turned, instead, upon her husband, all grandeur was forfeited, and what should have been her tragedy became his as well.

*

Perhaps there is no such thing as separate tragedies for those wedded in mind and spirit as well as in law. And no one who knew them had ever, until their final months, doubted that Louise and Henry Ramos, still, after nearly sixty years, were that. The force and durability of their love touched even their children as something fine and rare. True, they had spent a lifetime together vociferously quarreling, but almost always about small things—which tree to prune how much, which shrub to plant where, which turning to take off which ramp of the freeway. But these deceptively acrimonious disputes were merely a sign that things still mattered enough to raise one's voice in defense of one's convictions. They were part of the ritual mating dance and as such a form of love-making. The bored and the indifferent merely shrug their shoulders; only the deeply committed storm the barricades. And they were both committed—to life as well as each other.

Though he was by the calendar somewhat older than she, he seemed in every other respect far younger. His leonine shock of white hair capped a surprisingly youthful face. The large nose and the Buddha-ears added an ageless serenity that belied the often turbulent emotions they masked. He complained constantly that "the place" was getting to be too much for him to handle, that he would not, next year, attempt to plant any more tomatoes or garlic or corn; yet once the sowing season arrived, he was invariably out in the field with his cane and his hoe, and with a vigor that might have been the envy of a man a good decade younger, plant-ing his tomatoes and his garlic, and seeding his corn—and just for good measure, adding a row of eggplant and another of bell pepper. Then com-pelled to defend himself for having gone back on his word, he would, with an apologetic tone, as if his most laudable exhibition of strength had been, instead, a shameful weakness, once again promulgate his catalogue of first principles: that the only tomato worth eating was one ripened on the vine; that corn must never be picked before the water has been put on to boil; that modern planters have sacrificed taste to size; and as long as *he* could still distinguish between one of his own slender, home-grown asparagus and some wilted store-bought monstrosity, he meant to indulge this most enduring of man's sensual delights.

At the age of eighty-three he was still, with wry cynicism, nursing camellia seedlings he knew he might never see bloom. He even took a kind of perverse pleasure, when showing off the garden he and his wife had spent over half a century creating, in reminding the awed viewers that the prospect before them must all very soon fall before the inevitable bull-dozer. The ugliest aspects of this terminal disease called life he accepted with calm, unruffled dignity. Only one prospect dismayed him: that his wife, who gave every evidence of doing just that, might die before him. It was not the grave that dismayed him, but the solitary trek to it.

Oddly, he had spent a considerable portion of his married life in search of the very solitude he now so feared: some retreat from the encroachment of children, in-laws, family, and friends upon his most private person. From the first the need "to get away" had been almost as strong as that other need—to share—one's thoughts as well as one's body. He was far from being a misanthrope; he needed others, but his appetite for companionship was decidedly limited. He all too quickly reached the point of satiety, and just as his wife was going strong, he would feel the even stronger need to retreat—to his model ships, his books, his garden—a need that was usually satisfied so unobtrusively that visitors seldom noticed his absence until long after he had given them the slip.

All his married life his wife had acted as a buffer between him and the world. Since her own garrulity made few demands upon his attention and seldom required a serious response, he had come to find in her presence so happy and enduring a compromise as to give him the best of both worlds. They could be alone and together at the same time. She had her sounding board and he had his solitude and they both had each other.

Habit creates its own necessities, and he soon discovered that without her he was not simply alone, but lonely. As he grew older, he found himself, more and more, during her absences, not merely awaiting her return, but anticipating all manner of disasters—head-on collisions, strokes, muggings, heart attacks. And as she grew yearly frailer, he grew ever more solicitous of her comfort and her welfare. He was forever fluffing pillows to support her back, serving her her evening cocktail, helping out in the kitchen with tasks he had always before disdained. It was an attitude she herself was quick to foster. So familiar had she made him with every erratic beat of her notoriously poor heart, he lived in neurotic dread that he must wake one morning to find her lifeless form beside him, and his first thought of the day was always for her: to reassure himself that she was still there beside him breathing.

With the rest of the world his impatience not only endured, but increased. In crowds he was always looking for escape hatches. It was, in fact, this very need to get away that precipitated the accident.

*

"I suppose in her eyes I've been designated to play the villain," he told each of his children in turn and then paid little heed to their reassurances. Everything he said seemed to he part of a rehearsed speech and he did not like to be interrupted—partly because his poor hearing, with the telephone pressed against the aid he could not manage without but could scarcely bear to live with, left him unsure precisely what had been said unless he had it repeated, which was a bore for him as well as for everyone else, so he just kept right on talking; and partly because everything he said now *was* rehearsed, so often had he gone over every detail in his mind, he had given permanent form to every defense as well as every accusation: his angry impatience, her confusion, the break—

"There's no mistaking the sound of breaking bones," he said, speaking into the mouthpiece with that strained impersonal voice one usually reserves for a microphone. "Not a pretty sound, I can tell you. I knew the moment she went down, this time it was different. And she'd broken something. If that colored girl hadn't been there to give us a hand, why, I don't know what we would've done. When we tried to get her up, it was clear that wasn't going to work. So she called an ambulance and waited with me till it came. Tried to give her something for her trouble, but she wouldn't take it. Fine looking gal, too," he added, then trailed on ruminatively: "Don't know why any of them should stop to help one of us, after the way we've treated them all these years. But she did, and I'm damn grateful for it."

And his interlocutor on the other end of the line could only bide his time and let the story come out in its own fashion to find out exactly which bone it was that had been broken.

"We were on our way to a reception in Oakland. One of your mother's friends having on anniversary party. Don't know why anyone bothers to celebrate a fortieth anniversary, anyway," he interjected with all the churlish disdain of one about to celebrate his own sixtieth in a few months and without a lot of public fuss. "I tried my darndest to talk her out of it, but she was determined to go, and when your mother sets her mind on something, you know as well as I do, she usually gets her way."

Yes, they all reassured him, there was no disputing that. But why hadn't someone given them a ride? At their ages . . .

"Well," he went on before they could launch into another tiresome dissertation on the hazards of modern freeways, "they did, as a matter of fact, offer to have someone drive us. I will give them credit for that. And your mother was willing enough. But dammit! You know how I hate to get stuck at one of those affairs. If I can't get away on my own, I always feel trapped. Drives me up the wall. Your mother'd be happy enough to stay on till they close up shop, but I always seem to get cornered

166

by some damnfool reactionary, who doesn't know beans about history, mind you, but feels he has the right to tell *me* just how all those tired old liberals left over from the New Deal—meaning me, naturally, though they're always too polite to come right out and say it—are still out there doing their damndest to bring America to its knees.

"Yes, yes, I know we probably shouldn't be out on the freeway alone at night, but dammit, a man can't be his own master in somebody else's car. And everything would've been all right if your mother hadn't forgotten the directions. Couldn't even remember the name of the restaurant. Left the invitation in her other purse. Seems everything she ever needs nowadays is always in that other purse. And no one had bothered to tell us the damn square we were looking for was *underground*. All she could remember was it began with a B. The restaurant—Bartalini's, or something like that. Blake's, it turned out to be, so she was right on that score. And I suppose I *was* egging her on. She'll tell you I was, anyway, so I might as well admit it. When I heard her fall. And that splintering noise. Not a pretty sound, I can tell you . . ."

And finally directed back to the crucial point he had been circling but seemed incapable on his own of ever touching:

"Oh, her hip," he answered the by now insistent question. "The left one. Shattered, it seems. Won't be operated on till Monday. And naturally, with her heart, it has us all pretty worried, I can tell you."

*

Her heart, however, proved far stronger than anyone had been led to expect. Misled, perhaps, would be more accurate. Everything, in fact, seemed to go well at first. She greeted each new visitor with a self-mocking, "Well, I've really done it this time," and though she quickly let it be known who was truly to blame, her resentment seemed almost light-hearted, as if she had gained a minor advantage she did not mean to let go of, but one that she did not mean to exploit either. She was clearly the victim, but a villain at this stage could only have acted as a distraction and she did not mean to share the limelight with anyone.

By Sunday afternoon she might have been enjoying herself. She hadn't had so much attention in years, with more visitors and flowers than her tiny, shared room could accommodate. The operation the next day went off "without a hitch," the doctor told her anxious husband. "I don't know what you were all so worried about," he added, with a single

167

sentence blowing up a family myth that had kept them all intimidated for years. "Considering her age, her heart's quite remarkable."

She was frailer than ever, with a mass of ugly bruises so dark they looked like birthmarks, but her spirit remained undaunted. She was still feisty enough to demand her room be changed three different times in five days for sundry, mostly petty, reasons. And before the week was out she seemed well on the way to taking over the administration of the entire hospital, keeping the staff so busily "on their toes" her family half suspected—and not without a good measure of sympathy—that she was sent home four days earlier than had previously been announced simply to get rid of her and give her doctors and nurses a well-earned rest.

Whatever the reason for her early discharge, it proved disastrously premature. She was home only for one night when everything suddenly went wrong, and her husband, whose fear and guilt seemed well on the way to early alleviation, was once again plunged into despair. The following day she returned to the hospital with pneumonia in one lung and an embolism in the other, both of which, separately and together, seemed determined to choke what little remained of life out of her. Her decline, was rapid, but she stubbornly refused to die. Her much maligned heart would not give in. It was her mind that proved most vulnerable.

*

They were not to worry, the doctor said. It was standard, in such cases, with patients her age. A combination of drugs and trauma. They should be prepared for symptoms of acute paranoia, until she regains her strength—if ever, he might have added, but didn't. It was left for everyone else to think.

For days she lay in the intensive care unit like a cadaver, the skin stretched over her mouth in a bitter skeletal grimace, her eyes brewing dark and ugly suspicions. It would have been easier for all had she not recognized her family. Like the solicitous nursemaid of an ailing child, her husband hovered over her whispering encouragement and endearments. It was care she did not mean to reward, and he was now made to pay in full for his part in her accident. Her few lucid comments were spat out in barbed whispers:

"Maybe next time you'll listen to me! If there is a next time."

"Oh, Loo! Loo!" he pled. "Don't make it any worse for me than it already is."

But pain had made her immune to pity.

"And why should I make it easy for you? I wouldn't be in this mess if you had done as I wanted."

Nor was it merely her husband she seemed intent upon hurting. When her children visited, her customary welcome was a rebuke:

"Well, it's about time you came to see me."

"But Mother," they might protest. "I was here yesterday. And the day before that." To no avail. With cold, unforgiving eyes she would insist:

"No one's been to see me for days. No one. Not even your father." And when they challenged her with the log of daily visits, she would hurl at them the ultimate silencer: "Are you calling me a liar?"

She did not mean to be contradicted. With facts or with anything else.

Then for one night, already more dead than alive, she seemed once again happy. She was on a cruise ship. She had, she boasted with considerable hauteur, already had her picture taken with the Queen. What did they think of that? And a bishop had come to give her communion. She was sure it wasn't the Pope—though it just might have been—but it was certainly a bishop. With crosier and miter. And when her daughter Teri, happy for once to leave her mother in such august company, leaned over to kiss her goodnight, the old woman dismissed her like a mere party crasher.

"Yes, you'd better leave. After all, *you* weren't invited."

All of which seemed most peculiar since she had never before evinced the least interest in a cruise of any sort, and though she had always had a weakness for bishops, she had never revealed a secret hankering after royalty.

*

Her daughter Teri was again, the next day, the last to see her. Cool and level-headed, a woman of infinite patience with gentle features and a soft voice, she seemed to have inherited nothing but her mother's looks, the oval face and the olive complexion; in every other way her father's child, she was also his staunchest champion.

"Tony and Linda have taken him out to dinner," she offered now to mitigate his marked absence.

"Ah, he's having himself a holiday, isn't he?" The bitterness of the retort was not the least diminished by its frailty, the words so faint Teri had to bend over the bed to catch them:

169

"Well, you can tell him I want to see him, once he's through gallivanting about. Tonight. And why hasn't Tony been here to see me?"

"He was here this morning. And so was Dad. For at least three hours. What more can you expect from him?"

She looked skeptical. "Then why didn't they wake me?"

"They all talked to you, Mother. So you obviously must have been awake."

"But the nurses give me things so I don't know who's here. They don't want me awake when he's around." She looked about to reassure herself they were not being overheard. "They know I'd make him take me out of here. You wouldn't believe the things go on in this place," she added with an intensity not to be denied. "When I get out of here I'm going to blow the whole thing sky-high. That's what they're afraid of. Oh, there'll be a scandal, I can tell you. Heads will roll. They'll all be made to pay for what they've done. Every last one of them."

"Oh Mother," Teri strove to bolster her words with a note of cheerful reassurance, "they're only trying to help you."

"Help!" The contempt was flagrant. "I thought you were smart. I thought all my children were smart. But you don't know anything, do you? Well," she continued without waiting for on answer, "I want you to stay with me until your father comes. Do you hear? And don't let them give me anything. I want to be awake when he arrives. Because I'm not going to spend another night here if I can help it."

Though irrational, the fears were too distressingly real to ignore and the habit of obedience to that imperious tone still, in middle age, too deeply engrained to contravene without a pang of guilt. Hoping to divert her, Teri tried to coax her mother back onto the cruise ship, where she had at least been happy.

"How did you enjoy the rest of your cruise?" she asked in a bantering tone so falsely light-hearted she had to wince at her own words. And then winced again at the look of disgust that greeted the question. For an uneasy second she wondered whether the fears might not, after all, have some basis in fact, so sinister did all the monitoring machines appear, blinking or bubbling away, so glumly efficient the nurses, like some mad doctor's automatons, more robots than women, she half expected to see Vincent Price leering down at her in an outrageous caricature of every child's nightmare of medical mayhem. As she looked into the other uncurtained rooms of the unit filled with their ghostly wraiths, scarcely identifiable as human beings, let alone individual personalities, lying with skeletal mouths agape, gasping for one last breath with the aid of enough scientific equipment to run a small nation, madness seemed compounded. A higher form of madness that she was not willing then to explore.

"How would *you* like to sail up the coast strapped to this bed? With all these tubes stuck in you?"

Teri greeted the confirmation of her mother's madness almost with a sigh of relief; the irrational she was better equipped to cope with than the sinister.

"But last night you seemed to be enjoying yourself. You even bragged about seeing the Queen."

The old women looked troubled.

"Well, she wasn't around when the nurse—the one who's here in the morning—the one with all that hair—tied me to the stool in my room. It took me all day to free myself."

And she seemed once again struggling to free herself from her imaginary binds, her eyes brimming with panic.

Only with difficulty could Teri recognize even the ghost of her mother in this virtually impersonal, sexless skeleton before her, the face so haggard it had lost all identity. The woman she had once known and loved was already dead and this mockery had come to take her place. To prolong so fruitless a discussion could only torture both of them. Whatever her filial obligations might be, she had to escape, or she too would soon be babbling away. And with eyes half blinded by tears, she leaned over to kiss her mother goodnight for what she assumed must be the last time.

There was no goodbye in the look her mother returned. Fear and accusation alone smoldered in the dark craters that were her eyes.

"So you won't stay till he comes."

"I can't, Mother. I've my own family to care for. And you need some rest," she added as a sop to her conscience. "I'll see if I can get them to give you something to put you to sleep."

"Well," she sighed, "it doesn't matter." And she turned her head into the pillow. "Nothing matters anymore."

And with that terrible negative her mother's life seemed destined to end. Surely nothing short of a miracle could snatch her now from a death that had become, for everyone, except her loyal and too-loving husband, desirable. There is a time to die, when death comes not like a thief, but a welcome guest. And that time, Teri was convinced, had arrived for her mother.

*

But she did not die. Even the doctor, irreverently referring to his patient as "one tough old dame," could not altogether repress his admiration and wonder.

Her mind returned, if not quite to normal, at least to a speckled normality, filled with as much shadow as light. The dappled world of the aged. She was no longer irrational, but she was decidedly different. She had come out of the fire forged into something new and strange, a woman at times they scarcely recognized.

She still had difficulty remembering who had been to see her the day before, or indeed, an hour before, but she knew now that the forgetting was due to her own faulty memory and not to some failure of love, that what she did not remember had not necessarily not happened. And that was a great advance.

Certain things remained as fixed and lucid as ever: she could, for instance, have reeled off the number and names of every stock in her portfolio. Not a single interest coupon was forgotten, not a rise in the prime rate overlooked. But she spoke now about *her* money as distinct from *theirs*—something she had always before been too solicitous of her husband's feelings to draw attention to, as if she meant now to take charge of that portion of their estate inherited from her own mother and use it to buy her future independence.

She could very well afford private nurses, if she needed them, she assured her doctors—and anyone also who might sabotage her campaign to gain on early release. She wasn't a charity case. And she had had enough of hospitals for any one lifetime. She wanted to go home. And she would go home, she threatened, if she had to call her lawyer to get her out. So what if the blood clot were not entirely dissipated, her temperature less than normal. They must all die sometime and she was as ready now as she would ever be. In the meantime, for as long as it continued, it was her life and she meant once again to take charge of it.

No longer did she believe in plots and conspiracies. Just bullheadedness and incompetence. The nurses now were sometimes efficient, sometimes indifferent, but hardly sinister; yet they all, for some reason, persisted in treating her as if she were a girl of sixty instead of a woman of eighty-one; and she would not be teased or threatened into doing more than she knew she was up to. And who, pray tell, could know that better than she? She would get up in her own sweet time. She would walk again when it came time to walk, and not one second sooner, and it was she who would determine when that time would be. But never again would she risk another fall if she had to spend the rest of her life hobbling about with an aluminum walker caging her in. A little old lady. And she laughed at the grim reality that had caught her so unaware.

Well, she did not altogether mind being waited upon and fussed over, just so long as she got what she wanted when she wanted it and not, as was all too usual, an hour later. Such services as the hospital offered she could just as well have at home. Better, even, for she would not there have to wait that extra hour, or there would then be hell to pay.

Yet her family, ringed protectively round their father—oh, how he loved playing the grand old patriarch!—seemed as reluctant as the doctors to join her in her fight for freedom, which only further fueled the resentment harbored against them, They had all, in the hour of her greatest need—though she could not pinpoint precisely how—failed her. So strong was the feeling she needed no bill of particulars. Abandoning her, her children clung now to their father, whose very vigor seemed an affront to her newly crippled state. Though she shied away from ever talking about it, except for an occasional cryptic aside, she could remember every detail of her cruise up the coast with all the clarity of some crucial childhood crisis: the feel of the rough knot of rope binding her hands to the cabin stool, the panicked struggle to free herself, the bishop—or had it indeed been the Pope?—bending forward to offer her the Sacrament, and the Queen—every inch of her bespeaking her royal heritage and yet at the same time a woman like any other, so ordinary, they might have been sitting opposite each other at a bridge table, exchanging pleasantries.

She had only to close her eyes to feel the roll of the sea. But she would not, could not, for some reason, discuss the voyage with anyone. Least of all her husband, who had, she was sure, been on the ship with her—she would, after all, hardly have taken a trip without him; she was not that kind of woman—though why he had not then come to her aid

173

when she had so desperately needed him, she could not for the life of her imagine. For better or for worse, they had promised each other; in sickness and in health. Words only. Too busy he must have been having himself a holiday to keep a thought for her.

> *While the cat's away,*
> *The mice will play.*

An old ditty she had once known. Well, this cat would not be away for long. And she chuckled at the timeliness of her slang; the world had not altogether passed her by. Not by a long shot. She might be eighty-one, she might be bedridden, but she would not be used.

174

And as frail and weak as she was, she out-willed them all. Yes, they finally agreed, she could go home. On one condition: that she first learn to use the portable toilet—the potty, she called it—on her own. And she agreed. So great a victory was worth one small concession. And home again she went.

*

That some tragic change had taken place became clear first to Teri, who, as the only child still living in San Oriel, was the most frequent witness. She could never talk to her mother now without quarreling. Her father was the usual subject; for the more difficult she found the one parent to deal with, the more protective she became of the other.

There had always been a close bond between them, but her father grew dearer as he grew older. The quiet dignity with which he went about the troublesome business of living never ceased to impress her. There was something both splendid and touching in the picture of him out in the field stooping with cane in hand to check the progress of his tomatoes or his corn. In loving communication, he seemed, with silent friends. The only friends that any longer gave him pleasure.

Yet there was something almost unnatural—and for her, at least, almost as infuriating as it was praiseworthy—in the meekness with which he submitted to his wife's inordinate demands. He never complained, and in face of the provocation given him, that alone seemed to warrant canonization. As close as he ever came to criticism was to reflect upon how like her own father she had become with age, and because his children all knew how much he had despised the old tyrant, his father-in-law, he always felt moved to defend the indefensible by adding:

"I know you get impatient with your mother sometimes. But you must remember, she's never had a thought that wasn't for one of her children or her grandchildren."

Well, if he needed to believe that, his daughter was not about to disabuse him.

But she had begun to wonder of late if her mother had ever truly had a thought for anyone other than herself. For the last twenty years, certainly, the virtually exclusive, one might say, obsessive, topic of conversation was her own health. Never once in all that time, when asked how she was, had she ever had the grace to answer, "Fine," and leave it at that. And when Teri listened now to the shrill rebukes directed at her own granddaughters ministering to their invalid grandmother, she remembered most how as a child she had burned with shame at the public scenes created to right some wrong, real or imagined. Her mother seemed, in the remembered past, always to be screaming about something, as much an object of fun as of dread in her terrible rages. But to those more personal rebukes directed against one of her own children, there had always been such a biting edge, that Teri, even now, in middle age, seethed with both hurt and resentment as she rushed to the defense of her daughters.

"They've never been trained as nurses, Mother. And you might show a little more gratitude for what they're doing."

"Gratitude?" Louise huffed. "They're being paid, aren't they?"

"Not enough to be yelled at like that."

The retort was scarcely more than a provocative whisper, but it did provoke.

"Well, it hardly seems too much to ask they show a little more consideration when they move their old grandmother, is it?" she asked, with a curt smile patting the hand of the granddaughter nearest her. Then turning once again to her daughter:

"I want your father in here. He's the only one knows how to do it properly."

"He's out in the garden. And I'm not calling him." Though softly uttered, the defiance was unmistakable.

"Then I'll send the girls out after him."

And both girls, bored and lanky, with the smooth, slender bodies of swimmers, looked from grandmother to mother.

"And I'll tell them to stay right where they are."

And without altering their expressions of bored neutrality they did just that.

"He needs some recreation," Teri continued, determined to win her father a slight respite. "You're killing him with your insistent demands."

"Nonsense." Spectral-thin the face was that of a predatory hawk, the fragility of her person belied by the ferocity of her manner. "He's as strong as an ox. Far stronger than I've ever been."

"If you haven't noticed how tired he looks lately, you're the only one hasn't. I still don't see why you refuse to have professional help. You can easily afford it."

"It isn't a question of money. There's enough of that. And mine to do with as I please. But I won't have strangers in the house. And that's that."

"They'd hardly be strangers after they were here a few days." She laughed before adding: "If they can last that long."

"I fail to see the joke." Even at her best Louise Ramos had never been noted for a sense of humor, least of all when the joke was on her. "It's your father's fault I'm in this condition, so I guess he can cope as best he can."

"Oh, Mother, it's no one's fault, and I do wish you'd stop making him feel guilty. It was bound to happen sooner or later. You've fallen at least once a week for the last five years. You've just been lucky, until now, you haven't broken anything more serious than an ankle. He didn't push you."

"He might just as well have. If he'd listened to me in the first place and let the Andersons drive us, I wouldn't be lying here."

"Oh, Lord!" With a loud sigh Teri rolled her eyes across the ceiling. "If! If! If! I don't know how God has managed all these years to run heaven without you up there telling Him how to go about it."

Her exasperation was leavened by her daughters' giggles. Since they nursed no childhood resentments, they were more amused than intimidated by their plucky grandmother.

"Don't be irreverent."

"All right, Mother, I'm not going to argue with you any longer."

"Good. Because you're just wasting my time as well as yours. Now go get your father."

"No." Though her voice remained quietly under control, there was just enough inflexibility in her manner to prove her her mother's own daughter. "You go get him. The doctor says you should he walking. And don't think I don't know what you're up to. You're turning yourself into an invalid out of spite. That's all—spite! So if you want him, go get him yourself. I'm sure he'd be pleased to see you."

*

But she resolutely refused to walk. Except, as promised, from her bed to the portable toilet anchored with a rope to the bureau opposite. And even that perilous journey she seldom attempted without assistance.

She was a demanding patient, and since the person most often there to answer her demands was her husband, he became, in effect, her private nurse. His entire life had come to center about her bed. He was patient, he was gentle, he was cheerful. With a desperation born of futility he strove to lift her sagging spirits with his own patently false optimism. Though it did not work, failure did not daunt him, and in her presence his face came to wear a fixed smile, as stylized as that on some archaic sculpture, a mere convention, and yet for all its artificiality it exuded a beauty of its own. Only when she woke him at night from some deep slumber did he, disgruntled by the shook, ever voice so much as the suggestion of a complaint.

Nor did she reward his devotion with anything like gratitude. Or affection. She received his every kiss with passive indifference, her eyes closed, her own lips set in what seemed more grimace than smile. It might have been her corpse he bid farewell to each night. She took what he offered and then demanded more. She had continually to be turned and powdered and massaged. She was never comfortable. Pain was constant and moved like an itinerant preacher across the entire map of her body with its hellfire and damnation.

Even her nagging criticism he took with placid good humor, attempting with it to coax her into some interest outside herself.

"You need a haircut," she said to him one morning, inspecting his face as though she had not seen it for days. "You're getting to look like one of my father's hired hands."

Her allusions now almost always had their point of reference in a far earlier age.

"I'll get the scissors and you can trim it." He was quick to exploit her opening. "It's been a long time since the last one."

"Through no fault of my own. But you certainly don't think I can continue cutting your hair any longer."

177

"I don't see why not."

"Well, if you don't see that, you must be blind."

And she would not be coaxed.

Only with her medications did he ever contravene her demands. In this matter alone his will proved quite as strong as hers. Her painkillers were meted out, according to the letter of the doctor's instructions, every three hours on the hour and never a minute earlier or in a dosage larger than that prescribed. She lived from pill to pill with her eyes upon the clock. He never argued with her. Where her medicine was concerned he simply ignored her demands, and though she never won her point, she never ceased to berate him.

"What do I care, at this stage, whether I become a dope addict or not? I want the pain to stop. And I want it to stop now. Not an hour from now."

It was the fixed point about which all else orbited. The world beyond her room held no further interest for her. She did not read so much as the morning headlines. She did not watch television or listen to the radio. When visitors came, she was the sole topic of conversation, and when they tried to divert her away from herself, she quickly brought them back. So much was any one like every other, she seldom even attended to the days of the week. Sunday alone had its distinctive ritual, but she received the Sacred Host from their visiting pastor as impassively as she received her husband's kisses.

Their sixtieth anniversary came and went with scarcely more than a token recognition of its passing, so little was the day any longer a reminder of joy. It would, everyone seemed to know, be their last. Death was so insistently present as to make a mockery of any celebration of life. The death of love infinitely sadder than the body's death.

Henry lived now for the brief respites offered by her naps. The instant she dozed off, he fled into the garden. It was the sole pleasure left to him. Under the open sky, the hydrangeas seemed more flagrantly pink then ever, their proud and prodigal beauty almost an affront. Pleasure and pain had melded. The lush beauty a mocking reminder of the mutability of all things. At every turning he could hear the bulldozer, waiting in the shadows, its motor warming. Stunted by hordes of aphids, the roses were a truer measure of the garden's own invalid state. And since his only helper, an aging, pony-tailed flower child, refused to touch chemical sprays, he would somehow have to find the time and energy to spray them himself.

But aphids were an enemy he could well understand and knew how to fight. The same could not be said of the depression that weighted his every step and blackened his every thought. Ordinarily too tired even to dwell upon it, it was there, nevertheless, feeding upon his exhaustion, a heaviness in the chest that would not be leavened, that sapped his vigor and bowed his shoulders. Each morning, like old Sisyphus, he faced the task before him without even the smallest measure of hope that that day's labor might lead to anything more than its own expenditure. Even the brief moments of respite in his garden had to be paid for. The longer his wife slept during the day, the less she slept at night, so that his own sleep was constantly interrupted—to massage a cramped leg or help her to the toilet or turn her on her side. Had it been a concerted plan to wear him down to her own measure, she could not have been more thorough.

179

*

Teri met with her two brothers. Their private quarrels were put aside for the crisis, each deferring to the other two with such exquisite politeness, they might have been members of the same club rather than blood brothers and sister. Something, they all agreed, must be done to spare their father, or he too would be dead before the year was out. A convalescent home for her seemed the obvious solution, and a part-time housekeeper for him, but when they broached the subject to their father, he refused even to listen.

"The doctor says there's no reason she can't walk. She's simply given up. That's all. And because she has you here to wait on her every minute of the day, she hasn't even made the effort."

They all spoke now with one voice, he scarcely attended to who was saying what.

"The only thing keeping her from getting out of that bed and walking is her own unreasonable fear of falling again."

"Why, the move might even frighten her into making an effort. It could save her life. As well as yours."

But, no, he was not about to frighten her into anything. As long as he had any say in the matter, she would stay right where she was. In her own bed, in her own house.

"You don't just throw people out when you're through with them. Like an empty milk carton. She's taken care of me for sixty years. Why shouldn't I now turn around and care for her?"

And since they suspected he had, with his discarded milk carton, himself in mind as much as his wife, they could think of no adequate reply.

Instead of relieving him, their distress compounded his. If they really wanted to help, he told them, they could visit their mother more often. For despite everything she was still their mother. And there would never be any changing that.

But their visits now were to him, not their mother. Dutifully they called first at the sick bed, but their mother seemed little happier to see them than they to see her, and they were pleased enough to be through with that part as quickly as possible; yet the moment they adjourned to the living room to sit down with their father, he would he called by her insistent demands, away from them, back to his bedroom post, and they marveled anew at his patient resources, at the unflagging sweetness with which he accepted her most abusive complaints.

"I don't remember her ever giving any of *us* that kind of attention when we were sick," one of them would say and the other two would smile knowingly and then with a chuckling, "I remember," resurrect some ancient and now comically transformed memory of neglect.

For memory had already filtered out all that they had most loved about her. Forgotten now was the way a smile could mock away her own pretensions and in an instant transform all that was harsh and strident into something soft and beguiling. Forgotten too was the protective warmth of her caresses—her generosity, her loans, her gifts, her pride in their least accomplishment. It was her slaps they remembered best—her gibes, her strictures, her obloquy, which had always, with a single devastating phrase, been able to reduce the self-esteem of any one of them to cinders. Certainly there was little left to love in the whining, bitter, vindictive creature she had become. She did not even look like the same woman. Her face had grown hard and oddly masculine. A desiccated caricature of her own father.

As they had once prayed for her recovery, they prayed now for her quick demise so that their well-loved father might be granted a few last peaceful years on his own. If only, just once, she could bring herself to thank him, to kiss him or smile at him, or in some small way show that she appreciated his extraordinary devotion, they might have forgiven her all. But she could not. Or would not, which was worse.

Curiously, he himself never seemed to expect any such show of gratitude or affection. He simply took both for granted. A few months could not wipe away the habit of decades. And if need is any measure of love, she did, certainly, then still love him; for though she berated him constantly for being too rough or too clumsy, too fast or too slow, or too something or other—it was *his* assistance she wanted and no one else's—not her daughter's nor her sons' nor her grandchildren's. Though he never seemed to do anything right, no one else could ever get anything wrong in quite the right way.

They took turns, whenever they could, sitting with their mother to relieve him, but they all had their own lives to live, and except for Teri, miles away in opposite directions. Nor did their visits after a while seem to please him any more than they pleased her. Their obvious disaffection with their mother hurt him far more than it hurt her, who seemed as indifferent to that as to everything else that did not concern her own comfort. They could not love him without also loving her. They must understand that or they did not know what love was. All the rest was mere sentiment, the dregs of love.

Yet he could not manage alone. He was, he found, in more ways than he cared to recognize, as dependent upon them as his wife was upon him. He was helpless in the kitchen—and in many other places every bit as much a part of modern life. He had never, his eldest son discovered, both to his surprise and amusement, made a bank deposit on his own. Making the money was, the poor old man apologized, abjectly, as though some secret inadequacy had been exposed for the world to mock, his job, managing it their mother's, and he had now to be led through the most basic of daily rituals. He was, moreover, terrified of ever being accused of taking liberties with "her" money and would touch no funds but his own pension and what remained of their joint account. But finances were the least of his problems.

It was the ordinary routine of living that presented him with the greatest difficulties. He could fry an egg but little else. So his children saw to it that the refrigerator was always well stocked with baked hams, cold meat loaves, fancy casseroles ready for warming, and the rich caramel custards that were his favorite desserts. On weekends there was always someone there to prepare hot meals. But he could enjoy neither his meal nor the company. He sat throughout, listening, not to his guests, but for her call, and when, as rarely, she failed to interrupt his dinner, more frightened by her silences than put out by her demands, he would leave the table unsolicited to check upon her as if she were a candle in the wind that might upon the instant go out and he must shelter her from every breeze.

He was the only one who did not pray for her death. He did, however, pray. For nothing in particular except the strength to endure, for there remained now not the slightest hope that she might ever recover. Or even wanted to recover. As her own faith gave every evidence of waning, his grew firmer. The tenacity with which he held to his nightly rosary at her bedside was fed by her own lack of response, his voice firm and resonant as she lay staring at him through sunken eyes, dark with brooding wonder. Though she never joined his prayers, she never interrupted them. Nor did she ever interfere with his attendance at Mass. There was never then any need for his ministrations.

Each Sunday, while some member of his family waited upon her, he sat alone in his customary pew with sad, impressive dignity, his eyes fixed unwaveringly on the altar before him, both hands crossed over his ivory-topped cane with its carved horse's head. And later, after the final benediction, as he moved through the vestibule and down the front stairs, he would pause along the way to answer all inquiries with a perfunctory, "Oh, she's coming along," but he did not linger, as he would have once, to talk. With his head unbowed, his shoulders high, his back erect, he would trudge the short distance home in proud solitude, with his every movement fending off unwanted pity.

It was effort wasted. Like everything else, pity also has its limits. Friends had long since ceased to call. Nor did he encourage them. Once he discovered they were as powerless as he to tease her back to health, their visits became burdensome. Nor did his fellow parishioners wish to probe any deeper then his perfunctory replies to their perfunctory questions. They could read the answers to their unasked questions in his face, which, despite its resolute and forbidding dignity, said all there was to say—and that was more than any patronizing "Poor old Henry" could wish away. Time, they all knew, must be the ultimate resolver.

*

The resolution came far sooner than most expected and in a fashion they had all, at one time or another, considered, but never seriously anticipated.

It was Teri who discovered him.

Her mother's voice on the telephone had been shrill with injury. "I want you to find your father. He's been out in the garden for hours." There was not a suggestion of panic in her demand as she concluded with a self-pitying: "It's way past time for my pill."

"Well, he's entitled to a few hours on his own."

Teri's defense was automatic. But so unlike him was it to overlook a single medication, that even allowing for her mother's undoubted exaggeration, reducing the "hours" to probably somewhat less than one, she felt enough unease to stop what she was doing, and without even bothering to remove her apron, she drove to her parents'.

She found him lying face down among the corn. And for an instant her own heart stopped. She did not have to touch him to know he was dead. He had not even had warning enough to break his fall. A fly crawled over his ear and another on his right hand, already puffed and disconcertingly gray. She thought for a moment she might be sick, but anger drove out nausea. Covering his head with her apron, she returned to the house. A hot wind blew. The hydrangeas in the September sun were drying on their stalks, lavender and maroon.

183

In the bedroom her mother lay waiting, a rebuke trembling on her haggard lips. "Well?" she said.

The anger swelled. "You've killed him." The words seemed to be torn out of her in a voice she did not recognize as her own, hysterically high-pitched and scarcely human. "Are you satisfied now? You killed him." And the first tears to streak her face scalded rather than relieved.

Perplexed by the force of her daughter's words, Louise seemed at first not to comprehend.

"He's dead. Do you understand? He's dead. And you killed him."

The smile that greeted this second outburst was more terrible than any words. Just for an instant a young girl danced in the old eyes. Then the smile died, and turning her head into her pillow, she shut out the world.

She never spoke again. She took no more pills, and without so much as a glance in their direction, she refused all food and medication from the strangers who came now to care for her; and in the early hours of the morning following his burial, having already granted her husband his fondest wish, she too died.

They get off the train at Leeds. Pausing to catch their bearings, they scarcely notice the vast and sooty canopy sheltering them from the thick gray mist that softened the bleakness of the approaching city in an Impressionistic blur. It is mid-August, but the chill is decidedly wintry. Burying her hands deep into her fur-collared camel's-hair coat, she shivers. He puts an arm about her, pressing her to him, as much to reassure her as to warm her.

"There is a sweet little train that goes very near to Haworth," she says, looking straight ahead as she speaks, rather than at him. She seems to be bracing herself for the long trek and only half attends to what she is saying. "With a perfectly darling little toy engine. But if you don't mind, I think we'll take a taxi instead. We can catch the train on the way back. If we're up to it."

"Whatever you think best," he answers. "The point is to get there. How scarcely matters. Not to me, anyway."

"But we must settle upon a price before we get in." For the first time since disembarking, she looks at him, smiling. Gratefully, he assumes. "No endlessly running meters, or we're apt to find ourselves in a real fix."

His own smile is so sweetly passive it is virtually impersonal, concentrated upon something inward, rather than her, like one deep in meditation. "I leave the arrangements entirely in your hands." Since they have very carefully packed all of their belongings into a single bag, one of his arms remains free to support her. She clings to it, lovingly, leaning her body into his as they move in silence and slowly toward the taxi stand. There is something vaguely dance-like in their synchronized progress, but it is clearly she who sets the tempo.

Though not young, they are a handsome couple. He looks fifty, but is, in fact, too close to sixty for serious dancing. Just short of six feet tall, he has abundant but fine hair the color of tarnished silver, glistening here and there with a polished sheen. His mustache is both coarser and darker. Though scarcely lithe, he is still slender enough to pass from a distance for a fairly athletic forty. He keeps his Burberry buckled tight as a reminder to hold in what little gut he does have, less out of vanity than a desire to complement his companion's cool elegance.

The instant he speaks he declares his American origins, but his vowels are too soft, his diction too careful to place him more precisely. Over the past six years his accent has become, unconsciously (for he himself is unaware of the change) ever closer to some mid-Atlantic compromise. Except for the long summers and the Christmas holidays, California is his home. Northern, he would hastily add, for Los Angeles is as foreign to him as New York, and both are far more foreign than London, which has become a second home.

She is small, no more than five foot three in her heels. It is impossible at first glance and not particularly easy even upon closer inspection to fix her age with any assurance. What immediately strikes one is her beauty. Nor is it merely the ruin of some former glory, but very much a present reality. Her eyes are immense, their color varying according to the light and the time from turquoise to robin's-egg blue; her cheeks and jaw are finely sculptured, the skin taut. The hair, which is real, but not her own, is reddish gold and luxuriously abundant, like some pre-Raphaelite heroine, the Lady of Shalott. Too full for so small a figure, it is possibly the single flaw, a minor one, in her make-up.

Her origins, however, are far more problematical than his. After more than twenty years in the country her idiom is flawlessly British. Her talk is filled with lorries and lifts; she always goes to hospital without a definite article; she caters for, not to others; and she never takes a vacation but invariably goes on holiday. Yet no Englishman would for an instant mistake her for a native. Her accent is so peculiarly her own, most are completely at a loss what to make of her. Only when she is tired, as she clearly is now, do certain key words (in this instance "little" and "darling," the final "g" of which she has swallowed whole) expose the transplanted Southerner and a soft current wafted all the way from Anniston, Alabama, warms the damp and chilly Yorkshire summer.

Indifferent to the misty prospect, she huddles next to him in the taxi, her head pillowed against his arm. What little he has noticed of the passing scene is too lacking in distinction to command his attention for long, more suburbia than country, and not a particularly affluent or picturesque suburbia. Mean little houses cheered by bravely ineffectual gardens walled in stone. Whatever welcome the roses offer the walls proscribe and his gaze remains intent upon her rather than the view outside. Not until they reach the outskirts of Haworth and begin the steep ascent does either of them speak.

"Now you mustn't be put off by the hordes of tourists," she cautions, as passing a carpark filled with buses, they wend their slow way through the crowds and over the slippery cobblestones. Viewed through veils of mist, the town is as funereal in aspect as the wet slate roofs, which have become, in the near-rain, slickly black. Even the sky is slate-colored so that they seem to be moving through some covered mine shaft, brightened here and there by an occasional flower basket, giddy with cascades of impatiens, or the electrically colored jackets and spandex trousers of the tourists, their vibrant hues swimming past the taxi windows like so many tropical fish caught by some diver's intrusive light.

"Or the horrid little shops built to cater for them," she adds with a dismissive gesture of her hand. "The real Haworth has nothing to do with this. Or with them." Her gaze is more impassive than disdainful. "Past the Bull's Head," she instructs the driver. "As far up as you can go. To the top of the hill. On the right. That," she adds, turning once again to her companion as they pass the Bull's Head, "is where poor Branwell wasted away his young life."

He turns to look but does not answer. It is the ghost of Emily he is after, not Branwell or his other siblings. As he reaches for his wallet, she places a gloved hand on his. "No, my darling. I told you, this is my treat. The entire weekend. A sadly belated birthday present."

"But that," he protests, "was so long ago I've already conveniently forgotten which it was."

"I know, darling. But circumstances, as you well remember, were not under my control at the time."

He acquiesces without further ado. It doesn't truly matter who pays. Whatever money they have is shared; and when there is none left, its lack is also shared. The inn is a startling, nonconforming white, a welcome relief from the ubiquitous gray. It is a converted house, Victorian, he surmises, though its foundations he soon discovers are older. Their room is as bright as the weather allows and considering the dour landscape, surprisingly cheerful, the walls papered with cornflowers. Bachelor buttons he calls them.

"I don't suppose you remembered to bring an umbrella," he calls, for she has secreted herself in the bathroom. Leaning against the wall of blue cornflowers, he peers out the window. Though doggedly persistent, the mist seems unable to commit itself to an honest-to-God rainfall.

"No, darling," she calls back.

"Nor did I. And in this benighted country we should both know better than to allow ourselves to be seduced by conventional images of August. It's closer to January out there than anything I remember of summer. Even a San Francisco summer. I wish—" he begins, but lets his voice die on the extended sibilant. He has long ago promised himself there is to be no wishing. The present moment is to be sufficient unto itself, each one savored without any thought left over for the next.

"Well, we can always buy a new one," he says, turning as he hears the bathroom door open. A silk turban wound about her now bald head, she is wearing a smart negligee and in her right hand carries her wig on its styrofoam stand. She looks so comically like a miniature Statue of Liberty about to thrust her welcoming torch into New York Harbor, he cannot help smiling. Thrown off guard by his levity, he allows his eye to fall to the small lump in the hollow of her neck formed by the clavicle and his smile quickly freezes. It is always carefully concealed in public. Though she conscientiously spares him so much as a glimpse of her bald head, she makes no effort to keep her neck covered when they are alone.

"A new what?" she asks.

"Umbrella," he answers. The word falls from a dry mouth. Possibly because of the unfamiliar setting, he is suddenly struck by how frail she has become in the last two months.

"Yes, do that." She sets the wig stand on the oak chest and picking up a copy of *The Tatler*, she climbs into her bed, not very gracefully since it is an unusually high one. He helps her brace her back with a bank of pillows. "Thank you, darling," she says, settling into the pillows. "I'm going to look at my magazine and rest awhile. Why don't you go have a look at the moor. But do save the parsonage for tomorrow. I want to show it to you myself."

As soon as he leaves, she lays aside the magazine she has never intended to read and closes her eyes. She does not so much sleep as submit to the weariness that seems now to lie upon her like a dentist's lead blanket, and it is instantly apparent how much a matter of will her beauty has been. Gloved and scarfed, he stands beneath his new umbrella. It is black because for him a gentleman's umbrella is always black. His head is dry, but the damp is already seeping through his unrubbered shoes to stocking his feet in an icy chill. The cemetery that separates the church from the parsonage and blocks the approach to the moor is appallingly, grimly bleak. A city of the dead paved in a dull gray granite, roughly hewn. There is scarcely earth enough for a blade of grass to grow, let alone a flower. Each cramped grave impinging upon its neighbor, shoulder to shoulder, the scene is as overcrowded as some jostling, rush-hour train depot, the stone entablatures all askew, as if even in death the bodies beneath were still struggling to escape to some warmer, drier clime. And who can blame them, he thinks, curiously detached, even slightly amused at the macabre excessiveness of the scene, so grotesque the effect is more comical than portentous. It is a stage set that has simply gone too far, a good idea vitiated by the designer's overwhelming lack of temperance, taste, and good sense. A Victorian caricature of a graveyard set up to frighten young children into trembling subservience. A Rocky Horror Show in which the only rocks are gray, hard, and damp.

Like a plane flying on automatic pilot, he traverses the graveyard. It is a sensation he has had for weeks: that his will has been subjected to some higher force and thought been replaced with a kind of numb acceptance. It is a benign state, and though he knows it cannot, will not, last, he means, for both their sakes, to indulge it for as long as he can. Beyond the graveyard there is a gray stone wall; a few gray, stone houses down another walled lane, each boxed off from its neighbor by its own stone wall, formidably uninviting; a not very prosperous looking farm; and then suddenly, there it is—the moor.

It is vast and magnificent in its bleakness; but more austere than rugged, it is not remotely what he expected. Momentarily disconcerted, he folds up his umbrella, which seems suddenly effete in the face of so primordial a scene. The always timid rain has, anyway, once again become a thick mist and he finds the chilled mask it forms on his face refreshingly invigorating. As far as he can see, the irregular, rolling emptiness, covered by dank brown stubble and intersected here and there by ancient stone walls, like the foundations of some ruined Valhalla, stretches out before him. It is a little like standing on the edge of the world. One step further and he might be transported anywhere.

So where, he wonders, for he cannot spy a single building in that vast emptiness, is Wuthering Heights? No name from his childhood ever conjured more magic. The book was not so much read as devoured and when he had finished he was left for ever after a changed person.

It is the movie, he suddenly realizes, that has interjected itself between the book and the reality. Though he had always known the cinematic backgrounds were an all too familiar California disguised by painted drops, the vision of Cathy and Heathcliff in their wild joy gathering up great armfuls of heather remains as sharp as any image in the book itself. He smiles now at his disappointment, for the heather gathered here would hardly fill an infant's arms. Fit for a nosegay rather than a bouquet, it is a scrub heather, a pale-to-dark lavender glossed by the mist, more like a ground cover than a shrub. One would be at pains to find a single branch six inches long.

He squats to pick a few branches, using his umbrella to brace himself as he does so, for he is not so limber as he imagines. The stems are like leather and surprisingly resistant to tearing. Nevertheless he persists and eventually gathers a miniature bouquet. Fearful he may have broken some local law, he tucks his trophies into the pockets of his Burberry and returns to the town. Making his way back through the graveyard surrounding the parsonage, he is struck by a detail he had not previously noticed. Many of the stone entablatures are raised on twin supports above the graves beneath. To what purpose, he cannot imagine, unless, perhaps, for easier egress on Judgment Day, he thinks, smiling again as he moves on, for he can view the scene only as some monstrous joke.

At a novelty shop in the town he stops to buy two pieces of ribbon, one red, one blue, and forming a tiny nosegay of his booty, he binds it with a bicolored bow and, still on automatic pilot, he returns to the inn. As still as a stone effigy of herself, she has with closed eyes been half listening for his return. As soon as she hears the outside door open, she picks up her magazine and miraculously revitalizes her face. The stone effigy is once again flesh and blood.

Fearful of waking her, he opens the door to their room gently, and peering in, meets her welcoming turquoise eyes.

"You look, my dear, like Lillian Gish in *Orphans of the Storm*," he says as he hands her the tiny bouquet. "A present for you."

"Thank you, darling. At the moment I feel fit only for the silents." She lifts the heather to her nose. "It doesn't smell," she says, clearly disappointed. "I'll have to drench it in my White Linen. Did you gather it on the moors? Like Heathcliff?" Their voices are soft and gentle, almost conspiratorial, like two children sharing secrets.

"God, how I loved that book!" He sits on the edge of her bed and lays his hand on hers. "But the only character I ever identified with was Cathy, torn between the call of the wild and the lure of luxury. Now that's a dilemma I can sympathize with. But I don't see you in the book at all," he adds, studying her carefully. "Your face was always far too filled with freckles and sunshine for these damp Yorkshire moors."

191

The choice of the past tense is unfortunate, but she seems not to notice.

"I'm afraid I had a bit more sunshine than I should have," she says, wistfully, though as a throwaway line not to be dwelled upon. "You saved the parsonage for me, I hope. I love thinking about them all pacing around that tiny room, like wild creatures in a storm." She shivers for the dead sisters. And if the emotion seems misdirected, there is a kind of unreality to their own lives now that makes them confreres of the doomed siblings. They too seem to be playing roles assigned to them, bit parts in some large, inexplicably complex plot, whose end can be guessed at but must never be anticipated. As they walk through the town later, people step aside, intrigued and deferential, pausing with a flicker of bafflement as if they should know who the couple are and might, if they just put their minds to it, come up with an answer. It is conceivable, but highly unlikely, that some few recognize her from an old television drama or one of the few film roles she has played, but the latter were so minor and the former so long ago, it would have been a different face they saw.

They are dressed for a stroll through Knightsbridge, not a country outing, her cruelly high heels never intended for the rigors of sightseeing. But the interest their presence excites is due not simply to their beauty or their dress. She has always walked through the world as if it were her own private theater and everyone else her audience. Her every public venture is a performance, and once outside, all sign of weakness disappears. Half smothered in her fur collar, her beauty still has the power to move. Even her recent loss of weight serves to accentuate the marvelous bone structure and make the large eyes even larger.

But more than her manner or her beauty it is their mutual absorption in each other, to the exclusion of everyone else, that draws all eyes to them. Like old dance partners who can anticipate each other's every move long before it is made, they seem attentive only to some secret music no one else can hear, and wherever they go the music follows. Even their age adds to the aura of glamour and romance.

It is not until they are in the parsonage the next morning that he is given any inkling why, despite her exhaustion, she has been so insistent upon bringing him to Haworth. As they move from one tiny, box-like room to the next, every window seems to look out upon the vast clutter of graves outside. There is no escaping them. Even the light seems tinged by their presence.

He pauses to peer out the dining room window. She joins him, taking his arm, and they both stare at the surrounding necropolis.

"How terrible," she says, "to spend eternity in any place so crowded. The very thought gives me the shivers." As he feels the very real shiver course through her, he realizes this is the message she has brought him here to impart.

"I mean to go out in a blaze of glory," he says, and without looking at her, he puts his arm about her and draws her closer to him. "At least it'll be warm." Her answer confirms his suspicions.

"Amen to that," she says, then quickly, defiantly adds: "But we aren't either of us going anywhere. Not for some time yet." Silence is the only answer he can offer.

"Can't you just see them all sitting there." She turns to look at the table about which the three remarkable sisters did their writing. "Scribbling away. Taking turns to pace about the room to keep their feet warm."

"It's like a birdcage." He joins her in her fantasy. "Hardly large enough for humans at all. Even wee creatures would feel caged in such quarters."

"Yes, exactly. Caged birds. The poor dears!" Her emotion is quite genuine. For them, the long departed, tears are permitted.

"Oh, but we mustn't pity them," he says. "After all, they accomplished enough in their short lives to bring us here to pay homage."

"Yes, but they didn't know that. The poor things. Shivering in this cramped little room. And with such a view outside. I can't understand how they didn't all go mad." And she turns to him huge eyes luminous with tears.

"Probably because they were so busy scribbling. Now let's go get something to warm ourselves. A steaming bowl of hot soup might do the trick."

"Oh, yes, let's. I am cold. And surprisingly hungry, for a change. It's the damp. It chills the marrow." Her eyes are dry now. She even manages a smile as she adds, "And that view certainly doesn't warm the cockles. Or anything else."

"How dare they call it August?" he says, lifting his head to drink in the mist as arm in arm they head for the village. "It's a libel against summer."

She presses his arm but doesn't answer. All that needed saying has already been said. Snuggling against him, she is content now with the promise of warm soup.

KIMI

The war made all of us hostages to history. Even sweet Kimi, who had turned babysitting into so fine an art that any party my parents attended became also a party for us, and if truth were known, I loved her far more than I loved my mother or my father. She was younger and prettier and never never raised her voice or hand in anger, so gentle, in fact, that not even the terrible Tony, my older and more bellicose brother, ever had the heart to put her marvelous and patient tolerance to the full test.

It was Monday, December 8, 1941. I was on my afternoon paper route, my poor old balloon tires straining under the weight of more news than they had ever before had to bear. The awnings of the Yamoto shop windows were mysteriously down, but the door was open. Inside, in the muted light fragrant with the odor of carnations, I could see one of the windows was broken, the faded striped canvas awning blocking the wind. At the sound of the counter bell a tiny, shriveled head peeked through the door leading into the living quarters. No sooner did it appear than it was gone. The door closed and a moment later opened again and Kimi entered.

It had always been her manner more than her features, a flower-like delicacy in all her actions, that set her apart from her neighbors and made her unique. She moved now soundlessly, with a soft, sliding, motion that seemed the embodiment of grace. She was now smaller than I. Almost a child herself she seemed without her shoes as she shuffled before the counter in white stockings, the big toe separated from the rest in its own snug glove. Her hands gently folded in front of her apron, she seemed more foreign than I had ever before noticed, more Japanese, as if she longed with an obsequious bow, to back away from me and slip quietly into the inscrutable cliché.

"My, how tall you've grown!" she said.

"Kimi," I answered and stumbled toward her with more feeling than grace.

Without altering her expression, she backed away. Then picking up a piece of a carnation stem from the counter, she ran the curled leaf across her knuckles.

"I don't get to see you so often anymore. Now you're big enough to look after yourself."

"I stopped by last week," I defended myself against the implied rebuke, "but you were at the university. Didn't your mother tell you?"

"Why, soon," she continued, speaking as if she had not heard my reply, "before you know it, you'll be a man yourself. With a family of your own."

A shadow crossed her face, for who, at such a time, would welcome anyone into manhood?

"But today," I stammered, struggling, as the shadow on her face grew darker, to find the right words, "I was afraid you might be at school again."

"Today?"

Her eyes moved from my face to the broken window to the counter spread of floral pieces that had not been called for.

"Who did it?"

She shrugged. "Do you think you should be here? Does your family know?"

I winced. And as for my family, I would have disowned them all if they dared disown her.

"Yes. Of course." Then as if hurling a challenge: "Why not?"

She made no attempt to answer the obvious.

"Then come inside."

Without enthusiasm she led me into the unpainted, scrubbed-wood living room, as bare of ornament as a monk's cell. A rustic table was surrounded by four unpainted chairs. The only color came from an oleograph calendar, a view of a Kyoto temple. Her father, sitting at the table, and her mother, standing with hands clutched before her, both bowed their heads at my entrance and never fully lifted them until I left.

"To say goodbye?" she asked, as though continuing an interrupted conversation.

"Goodbye? Where are you going?"

Again she shrugged.

"Who knows? They'll send us away now."

There was no rancor in her voice, which was so coldly impersonal it sent a chill shivering through me. Her father's head bowed deeper in assent.

"*They?* Send you where?"

"The authorities. Prison. A concentration camp. Who knows?"

"But you're American. You were *born* here."

Her comment angered me. It might have been she who was betraying her country's most sacred trust and not her country that was about to betray her. Concentration camps indeed! This was not, after all, Germany. Not even Japan. For there was the Constitution, almost as sacred as the Bible itself, to protect her

"Ah, yes, and the War?"

"The War! But *you* didn't start it. No one thinks that, The Muellers are German and no one's suggested they be put in any camps. You're just as American as they are. A natural-born-citizen," I added, giving each word equal emphasis.

"But you see," she continued, the infuriating docility of her voice finally sharpened by an edge of irony, "I may blow up the bridges. And Mrs. Mueller would never do a thing like that, now, would she? And there's the radio. The shortwave. Oh, don't bother to look for it. We've already hidden it. Very cleverly. We keep it buried beneath the floor and wait until dark to send our messages."

"*What* messages?"

For a moment, I fear, I didn't know what to believe, and my confusion, read as doubt, must have been written in my eyes.

"Please, Kimi. Don't talk like that, no one's going to send you anywhere. There are laws. You've committed no crime. No one's going to put you in prison. They *can't.* Even if they wanted to. They simply can't. Until you've done something wrong. And even then you have to have a trial."

So disturbed was I that she took pity on me.

"Perhaps you're right."

"Of course I'm right."

That she should at such a time impugn her country's honor seemed to me inexcusable, for certainly the virtue of its cause was beyond dispute: If ever there had been a just war—

197

Her pity was bounded by the same narrow limits as my patience.

"And my parents?" The challenge was in her eyes rather than her voice, which became once again flatly impersonal. "What of them? They've no claim of citizenship to protect them. What's to become of them?"

Again her mother and father dropped their heads in profound bows.

I was defeated, mostly by the oppressive atmosphere, and longed suddenly to escape.

"My grandfather says the war'll be over in six months," I blurted out without thinking, and then blushed for what I had failed to add, what my grandfather had also said:

"Put every last one of them behind barbed wire, I say. Every last one of them. There won't any of us'll be safe until every last one of them's locked away."

"Let's hope so," she said.

And then I blushed again as I wondered if her allegiance were not, perhaps, divided, but a crash of glass and a screech of brakes brought my momentary disloyalty to an abrupt end. It was with a sense of relief as well as drama that I ran back into the shop. The hole in the display window was larger. Pierced by a spear of glass, the awning flapped noisily.

Kimi followed. With no more than a glance at the damage, she lifted a bunch of peppermint-striped carnations from their green tin vase and held them in the air to let the water drip to the floor. With a final brisk shake, deftly professional, she moved to the counter and wrapped them in a sheet of crinkled, oil-slick green tissue. He face revealed no emotion as she handed the flowers to me.

"Give these to your mother. With my love."

I held the carnations like a torch from one extended arm.

"Aren't you going to call the sheriff?"

She shook her head.

"Then *I* will."

Again she shook her head.

"I can't get over how much you've grown." Her smile was timid and affectionate again. "And so handsome. Why, it seems only yesterday. Remember? My riddle books? What's black and white and red all over?"

"A newspaper," I whispered, blushing so violently I could feel the tears welling. I wanted to kiss her, but I felt, now that I was taller than she, much too clumsy and shy. And a kiss, moreover, would be an acknowledgment on my part that our goodbye was truly a farewell.

"I'll stop by next week," I said, standing already in the doorway.

She, however, knew me better than I knew myself.

"No." She made no attempt to follow me out. "You won't, if only because you'll be ashamed."

Almost angrily I turned to face her. She was standing in the shadows of the shop, lovely and composed in the debris, her straw slippers and the edges of her white tabbies wet. Her eyes were as bright as the slivers of glass that lay scattered at her feet.

"Ashamed? Of *you*?"

"No. Not of me. Never that, I hope."

"What then?"

"Ah," she answered, her smile ineffably sad, "time will have to tell you that."

And time soon did.

I saw her only once again, some years after the war. She was walking along the gravel siding of the street that ran before our house. We spoke briefly. I don't remember what we said. Too much had happened to both of us and we met as virtual strangers—to our old selves as well as to each other.

The fierce valley heat was oppressive but hardly unexpected. My brother's children have a talent for selecting the hottest weekend of the year for their weddings. "One hundred and five," I heard someone intone in a voice prickling with contempt for those of us who had all too obviously driven in from the cool coastal fogs and still reeled, as though bludgeoned, from the contrast. For my part, it might just as well have been 120, for once the thermometer breaks into the three-digit range I become catatonic. Hell is hell; whether it is turned onto high, medium, or low, is almost irrelevant. The damned are still the damned, beyond all reach of salvation.

The discomfort—too weak a word for misery—was compounded by the coat and tie so formal an occasion demanded. Such serious vows would be mocked by a gathering of tanktops and bare midriffs. Far more sensible in their battle with the elements, women have always cleverly contrived to wed comfort to elegance. Though there were no exposed navels, bare arms and décolletage were everywhere the order of the day. Airy chiffon prints and featherweight organza hats.

A disgruntled lot straining civility with forced banalities, we were waiting in the shade of a gigantic elm, a noble survivor of the Dutch plague that had only recently decimated the town's trees, for the arrival of my parents, who were being driven in from the temperate East Bay by my sister. My father, I knew, would be in a vile temper—not because of the heat, which he bore far better than my mother or I made any pretense to, but because he had allowed himself to be intimidated into being driven.

It is not easy to remind a man a few months short of eighty-five that he may, on so long a journey, be a danger, not merely to himself and his passenger, but to innocent motorists as well, without offending his *amour-propre*. My father's sense of his own dignity and independence have always been as fierce—and sometimes as oppressive—as the heat.

He made few concessions to age. To his own, that is; his wife, two years his junior but far more frail and forgetful, was another matter. Although one felt her increasing frailty was caused as much by some new marital game-plan as by the natural ravages of time, he treated her with a gentleness and deference that were both new and touching in their solicitude. His manner toward her had become of late more that of a courting novice than a sixty-two-year veteran of close combat. Only in the evening, when she was safely seated in her pillow-propped corner of the leather sofa, drink in hand, did he ever in public renew their old battles, and the words would once again, for a brief hour, fly, harsh and sharp, rousing the tired blood and stirring old juices.

Though the acerbity of their quarrels sometimes, in the old days, frightened the youngest of their grandchildren, it never fooled any of us. Acrimonious as they appeared, their quarrels were invariably about trifles. Blood was seldom drawn and over a long lifetime few scars were visible, and those few long since lost in the sagging flesh. Quarreling had always been their way of saying they still cared, about things as well as each other, and their new harmony was the clearest sign that both were finally coming to terms with mortality.

Their approaches, however, could not have been more different. My father viewed the miracles of modern medicine more as a threat than a promise. For him, doctors were the enemy, white-coated charlatans and fast-talking conmen to be avoided at all cost. My mother, on the other hand, pursued them with a passion that was shameless in its ardor. For her they represented the new priesthood, the names of the latest drugs falling from her lips with a reverence once reserved for the old Latin liturgy. And each of us was, at every visit, invariably cornered by each of them in turn, proselytizing for their different points of view.

"I'm worried about your mother," my father would begin in his most confidential whisper, though no one else but his interlocutor was within shouting distance. "She can't seem to remember a thing anymore. The day or the hour, let alone the year. I'm afraid one of these nights she's going to forget herself and take so many of those damn pills she's forever swallowing. And that'll be that—the final cure. . . . The drugs only seem to make her more confused, anyway," the indictment continued. "Becoming a proper junky in her old age. Wish you'd have a talk with her. She won't listen to a word I have to say. Thinks it's the cost I begrudge her, when I'd happily see her spend twice the money to give them all up. Flush every last one of them down the drain and she might be her old self again."

"Your father's not at all well, you know," was my mother's opening gambit. "Oh, I know he seems strong enough to you. But you don't see him every day. It's all bluster and showmanship, when the truth is, he may very well go before I do." And her very failure at this juncture to allow herself to be distracted by a catalogue of her own numerous ills was proof sufficient how seriously she took the matter. "His heart's been acting up and he won't do a thing about it. See a doctor or cut back on his work about the place. If only to set my own mind at rest. But he won't listen to a thing *I* have to say. I might as well be talking to a stone wall. So you children are going to have to get after him."

And then as a final inducement, she would add in the plaintive voice usually reserved for her own cherished ailments: "I don't much relish the idea of being a widow I can tell you." Which had the unpleasant effect of turning the entire exercise into a concern as selfish as it was loving.

*

And health, *her* health, to no one's surprise, was the chief topic of conversation the moment they arrived. For despite her diminished size—a mere five feet with her dowager's hump and the gnarled hand clutching a surprisingly inelegant aluminum cane—she still exhibited enough force of will to command center stage at almost any gathering.

In the background my father nurtured his silent resentment, the indignity of having been driven exacerbated by all the helping hands anxious to set him safely on his feet. He could not bear to be treated as an invalid, to be helped in or out of cars, or guided up a steep flight of stairs. So he now hid his unsociable emotions, as he had always done, behind his wife's distracting volubility.

Even in her salad days she had never been able to respond to the conventional, "How are you?" with the single word, phrase, or sentence the question at best deserves. Since her health had for years been of such overwhelming interest to herself, she lacked the imagination to conceive a world that might not be equally fascinated. No one truly attended to

203

her complaints—they were far too numerous and familiar for real sympathy—yet few besides myself ever dared interrupt her. And since her memory was at present even more deficient than her imagination, any new arrival brash enough to greet her with the same time-honored question was apt to set off a rerun of the pre-programmed tape.

"All right, Mother," I interrupted the second recital before she had time to work her way higher than the killing pain in her left knee, "this is supposed to be a jolly occasion. So we don't want you hopping onto the autopsy table any sooner than it's absolutely necessary. Besides, we'll *all* be ready for a hospital if we don't soon get into that air-conditioned church."

Though a sense of humor has never been one of her strong points, she usually responded to my gentle mockery with an uneasy laugh, set off, I don't doubt, more by the tone of my voice than the actual words. And we all entered the cool silence of the church.

204

*

The wedding went off without a hitch. The bride was beautiful, and the groom, if a good inch shorter than his well-heeled mate, certainly handsome, by far the best looking of my brother's three sons—though none of them could come close to equaling their father's own once-spectacular good looks. The nuptial couple were, in fact, almost too perfect, so blithely self-assured they might have been two models sent by some advertising agency. They seemed air-conditioned like the church, altogether too cool for so momentous an occasion and completely unaware of the enormity of the commitment they were about to make. The heat outside had clearly not yet touched them.

The daughter of a retired army colonel, the bride exhibited neither virginal timidity (which one, I suppose, should hardly any longer expect) nor the least suggestion of passionate anticipation—or even, for that matter, passionate attachment, as if there were, as one assumed, little left to anticipate. Nor did the groom—a rookie policeman with a bantam strut undoubtedly enhanced by a silver-studded black leather belt and holster—reveal sweaty palms or the excited befuddlement one usually associates with his traditionally comic role. With his white coat and white carnation, he might have been a floor walker at a Macy's White Flower Day Sale being groomed for executive advancement. One felt they had not yet earned the right to be so pleased with themselves and longed for an unruly cowlick or a wrinkled bodice to reveal a redeeming touch of human fallibility.

*

As the bride came from New England, the few of her relatives to attend the wedding were strangers to the rest of us.

"A fat lot of prosperous Republicans they look," my father mumbled to me in a treacherous aside, since I am the only one of his sons to share his politics.

The observation, I agreed, seemed justified; but if far from fat, my father himself looked every bit as prosperous, although he wore his prosperity with a Democratic flamboyance that banished his counterparts to the dimmest shadows.

To my shame, I must admit I was well into my forties before I could set aside the jealousies and resentments of childhood to arrive at a proper appreciation of my father's worth. The process has been gradual, but I have changed over the years from mama's boy to papa's pet. Good stoics both, we struggle manfully to hide our affection for each other behind the most formal of façades.

205

The very proclivities I once found annoying, even embarrassing, are those I today find most endearing, most notably his enduring sense of style. The affectations of a dandy, my intolerant youth was apt to sneer. But what else is style if not affectation that has become so integral a part of one's nature, it ceases any longer to be affectation? And practice has brought perfection. If my father was still the dandy, he was the dandy par excellence. Evidence the blue-and-white polka-dot bow tie, the miniature pink camellia boutonniere, the snug vest (which not even the heat could intimidate him into relinquishing), as well as the leonine mass of white hair a mite too long for conventional taste. There was flare even in the way he carried his ivory-headed cane, as if he might use it at any moment to point out some peculiar configuration on a nearby wall map. But like most poets and performers he was subject to vagrant moods and he had chosen at his grandson's wedding to keep his formidable charm cloaked under a mordant melancholy.

*

The melancholy persisted as the party moved from air-conditioned church to air-conditioned restaurant, where the reception luncheon was to be served. Rows of tables were already set up with modest bouquets, white cloths, stainless flatware, and—I could not help noting with a sigh—plastic champagne glasses; but the last would, I was willing to wager—with an even heavier sigh—be altogether suitable to the quality of the beverage they would soon hold.

Since there were no place cards, the party once again—as at the church—divided itself along family lines—his and hers—without any effort to mingle. The lunch—frozen Cornish game hen, rice, and peas, all heated to bland innocuousness in microwave ovens—did not add measurably to anyone's good cheer. Nor did the speeches that accompanied the cake. My brother, acting as host, since the bicoastal wedding was irregularly being held on the groom's turf, began the proceedings; the bride's father soon followed. Neither was a novice in such matters and neither disgraced himself. They were speeches one might have heard at any Lion's Club in America, filled with well-intentioned clichés and good-natured jokes as bland as the food. It was not until the bride's grandfather rose to pay a few patronizing compliments (from Eastern WASPs to Western Catholics) to the groom's family (Spanish and Portuguese) and country (California's Central Valley) that my father came to life, and as soon as the well-intentioned old gentleman resumed his seat, my father rose, artfully arranging his cane on his chair and the camellia in his lapel before uttering a word. And my heart sank with misgivings.

*

Not since I was a child in short pants sitting in one of his college classrooms had I had the opportunity to watch the old pro manipulate an audience. For some forty years his lectures, I knew, had been as popular as any at every college where he ever taught. I was constantly running into former students loud in their praises of a man I scarcely seemed to recognize. It was a side of him his family seldom got to see. At home he usually left the charm to my mother, who, despite her many shortcomings, could still, with a radiantly girlish smile, melt hard hearts whenever she set her own heart to it.

"You'll have to excuse me," he began, his still magnificent voice reaching every ear without the aid of the microphone the other speakers had depended upon, "I had no intention of making a speech. Nor," he added, with a sly smile directed at his son the host, "was I asked to make one. And I was quite content to keep my peace as long as all the speechifying was left to the parents concerned. But when we got to the bride's grandfather, I decided there was no other way out. The groom's honor demanded someone on his side to show our Eastern friends here we aren't all clods and cow-boys."

The transformation was wondrous. It was as if he had cast off his chains, a previously handcuffed Mozart seated suddenly at the piano and prepared to dazzle his listeners. He was in his element and he clearly meant to make the most of it.

"Since I didn't prepare a speech, I'm going to recite a poem for you."

He paused for a moment to let the promise, proffered almost as a threat, sink in before continuing.

"When I was a college student a good many years ago, I was given pages upon pages of poetry to memorize. I think they considered it at the time a kind of mental exercise. Intellectual calisthenics. If you could put a hundred lines of Shakespeare to memory, you'd then be able to breeze through calculus. I'm not sure it worked quite like that, put I took to the practice for its own sake, and continued it long after gradu-ation, simply because I enjoyed the feel of it.

"My favorite poet was always Robert Burns. *Robbie Burns,* as I call him," he added with a commendable Scots burr. "And since I've commit-ted so many of his lines to memory, I feel I'm entitled to the familiarity.

"But don't be afraid." He lifted his right hand to forestall the non-existent opposition. "The word poetry seems to frighten a good many people today. But I assure you there's nothing frightening about Robbie Burns. He was a simple man, much like you or me. A farmer with an eye for the ladies. But unlike the rest of us, he had a touch of genius. A good many of his poems were love poems. And a good many of these," he added with a knowing chuckle, "probably not suitable for so solemn an occasion as a wedding. But one of them is.

"The true test of a marriage," he continued, the ease with which he had taken over more dazzling by far than anything he had to say, "doesn't come on the wedding night, but all those other nights that follow. The long succession of days and years that sometimes make us forget why we ever began the experiment in the first place. The young and the beautiful—and the bride and the groom are both of those—too often think love is the exclusive prerogative of youth and beauty. But Robbie Burns—who unfortunately never lived to be as old as I am—knew better. The only love worthy of the name is the love that endures. He wrote a poem about that love I'd like to recite for you now.

"There are *a* few strange words of Scots dialect"—the pedagogical manner was apologetic—"but they shouldn't throw you off. Most of them I think you'll be able to understand in context. Only one of them is essential. *Jo*—without an 'e'—is the Scots word for *sweetheart*. My Jo is my darling. And if you don't mind, I'm going to attempt something approximating a Scots accent—even if no true Scotsman would acknowledge it as such. The poem is called 'John Anderson, my Jo, John.'"

It was a poem I had myself memorized in the same public-speaking course my father once took, a course taught, incidentally, by the same teacher he had had, a dear old Christian Brother with a large bit of ham about him who loved nothing so much as a tremolo accompanied by what he called "significant gestures." Fortunately my father eschewed both, but since I could not myself at the moment recall more than the first four lines, I was fearful he had, at eighty-five, bitten off considerably more than he could chew. And I so wanted him to have his triumph. We all did. The entire room was rooting for him.

"I'd like to dedicate it, if I may, to the bride and groom. And also my own wife of sixty-two years," he added, turning with a courtly bow to my mother, who until that moment had been paying far more attention to her cake than her husband. Suddenly alert to the attention directed at her, she seemed more baffled than pleased, and my fear now was not that my father might forget his lines, but that my mother might do or say something to spoil his performance.

And, yes, it was just that—a performance. But real emotions can be staged. Giving form to our feelings in no way diminishes them. Quite the opposite, in fact.

Far more apprehensive than he, I mouthed the first four lines along with him like a silent prompter:

John Anderson, my Jo, John,
When we were first acquent;
Your locks were like the raven,
Your bonny brow was brent . . .

From there on he was on his own; there was no way I could help him if he had wanted me to. But he had little need of any assistance from me, as he turned from the bridal company once again to his wife sitting across the table from him. And my heart stood still. No longer toying with her cake, she fixed him with a smile that could have meant almost anything—except, I knew, what everyone would have liked it to mean.

But men before my father have fallen in love with surface glitter, and he continued, undaunted by her incomprehension of the great compliment he was paying her, to sing, slowly and sonorously, without a single stumble, her praises in another man's voice:

John Anderson, my Jo, John.
We clamb the hill thegither;
And mony a cantie day, John,
We've had wi ane anither:

Now we maun totter down, John,
And hand in hand we'll go,
And sleep thegither at the foot
John Anderson, my Jo.

It was a magical moment. There was scarcely a dry eye in the room, except for his own and his wife's. The old trouper had pulled it off. There was a second of absolute silence as we all peered with him into the gaping grave, a general sigh, and then for once that day, genuine applause. All the romance that had been missing from the wedding suddenly came to life. Even the bride and groom cast off their slick banality and seemed suddenly truly lovers rather than glossy cardboard representations. Only my mother remained unmoved.

"What was *that* all about?" she asked under cover of the applause.

"Nothing," I answered, determined she would not, for once, as was her all too familiar custom, turn the spotlight from him to herself. "Just smile and look pleased."

In a trice my father was surrounded by all the bride's distaff relatives, who seemed now, in their adulation, neither so fat nor so objectionably Republican as they once had. Even I would have liked to hug the old boy, but that would simply have embarrassed the both of us. The bride was the first to ask him to dance, and despite a game leg, there was no

My mother seemed at first amused, and then, as he moved from partner to partner, letting her fend for herself, ever more querulous. For she had resolutely refused the groom's invitation. She could not very well dance and claim at the same time the sympathy she thrived upon. It was clearly a dilemma, but without a moment's hesitation she chose to play the pouting invalid. And for my father's sake, I chose to keep her company.

"I hope your father isn't making a fool of himself." She fixed me with a quizzical look fairly smoldering with resentment.

"No, Mother," I answered. "He's quite the man of the hour." Then hoping to tease her into a somewhat better humor: "But I'd be a little worried, if I were you. There isn't a woman in the place—except maybe the bride—who wouldn't like to run off with him."

A loud snort preceded her chuckle. "Worried?" She accompanied the word with the smile of a woman who knows full well she's got her man, and just for an instant it was possible to glimpse the proud beauty that had once enslaved him. "Your father may not always be the easiest person in the world to live with, but about *that*—I thank my lucky stars—he's never given me a second's uneasiness. Oh, he likes his little flirt, now and then. But in the end he always comes home to roost."

"Your Jo?" I ventured

"Joe?" She looked baffled. "Whyever would you call him Joe?"

"No reason, really. It's just an old Scots word for sweetheart," I answered, sighing, as I turned to watch my father still riding high on his triumph. He was in the midst of charming a strange woman young enough to be *my* daughter and seemed quite prepared to dance on until the music stopped.

JULIAN SILVA

Like most of our neighbors throughout the thirties we raised chickens in backyard pens. They guaranteed us a daily supply of eggs and the traditional Sunday dinner, a stuffed, roasted chicken large enough to feed a family of five, and later, after the birth of my sister, six. Every Saturday my older brother and I were assigned the unpleasant task of slaughtering and preparing the next day's main course.

Chickens are a particularly unlovely animal, at least the ones we raised were, and I never felt the least bit sentimental about them. They were dirty, ugly, and mean-spirited, always pecking at one another, so that the last one in the chain of command went around with a feather-less neck, mercilessly pecked by the entire brood and left to feed on the meager dregs of the scraps we fed them. But this sad, brutalized, and underfed creature had a kind of revenge every Saturday, for she was never the one chosen for our Sunday dinner, and though her life may have been a constant torment, it was invariably long.

Because I did not like the creatures does not mean I enjoyed kill-ing them. This Saturday afternoon ritual was, in fact, the most onerous of all my childhood tasks. My older brother, who was ten, two years older than I, was the one who actually swung the ax. And he *did* enjoy his role, as I, trying not to see any more than was absolutely neces-sary, held the chicken by the legs with its neck laid on the chopping block. My squeamishness merely added zest to my brother's swing of the ax, as I then let the decapitated thing go, watching, transfixed by the grotesque flapping of its outstretched wings over the dry clods of the apricot orchard, blood spurting from its neck, for what seemed to me an interminable length of time. Even more disgusting than this ghoulish display of the body's residual life after death was the head itself, lying beside the block, its one visible eyelid closing ever so slowly over its startled gaze.

In France, I knew, such things were done to people, once even to a queen; and though I was a great admirer of Norma Shearer and an incurable addict of the Sunday afternoon movie, I stayed home the Sunday she played Marie Antoinette, because I already knew the ending and could not bear even to imagine her lovely head being chopped off.

Once the execution was over we had then to pluck the chicken, a process that produced for me the most defining odor of my childhood, my *madeleine,* if you will, that peculiar and unmistakable stench emanating from the feathers of a recently slaughtered fowl dipped into boiling water. It is a peculiarly cloying odor, repellent and unmistakably unique and one that I would recognize anywhere at any time, and once recognized, I would once again be feathered with all the insecurities and fears of a peculiarly fearful childhood.

The second most memorable odor (and odors are important because our sense of smell is the most primitive of our senses, and thus, in a way, the truest measure of our being) is the smell of a red-hot iron horseshoe being pressed onto one of my maternal grandfather's horses' hooves, an act which seemed not to disturb the horse at all, but invariably made me want to vomit. The only other animals my grandfather tolerated, for he disdained pets, were the feral cats that kept the rat population of his barns in check. Each morning they were given a bowl of stale bread soaked in milk, just enough to keep them alive but not so complacent that they would willingly pass up any rodents lurking in the shadows. Feral cats are apt to breed almost as prolifically as rabbits, and the population was kept under control by one of the farmhands gathering all the excess kittens into a gunnysack and drowning them with a stunning lack of emotion from everyone but me. For the kittens were the only cats I was ever able to get close enough to touch and I found them irresistibly appealing.

Our own mice and rats were kept under control by a series of traps, large and small, set throughout our shed and basement, since it was considered too dangerous to have a cat with young children around. For cats scratched and infants were particularly vulnerable to their sharp claws. No one in San Lorenzo in the thirties ever considered that a tame cat might possibly become a pet. If you wanted a pet, you got a dog.

And that was what we got when my father one day brought home a Boston bulldog. Why anyone would choose a pet so ugly as a bulldog, I could not understand. I would much have preferred a cocker spaniel, or a golden retriever, but a pug is what we got. Why was never explained.

The rather unimaginatively named Pug did not last long. Not only was he ugly, but ill-tempered and bellicose, particularly where chickens were concerned. We soon trained him not to kill our chickens. But our nearest neighbor's chickens were not so lucky.

Joe Freitas was one of my grandfather's foremen and as part of his salary was allowed to live in the dilapidated old house behind ours in which my grandfather himself had been born. Joe was a tiny man, five foot two at the most, and built like a jockey, wiry and tough without an ounce of spare flesh on him. His wife Mary, who came from Hawaii and obviously had Polynesian as well as Portuguese blood in her, was a good head taller than her husband, robust and not particularly good-tempered. They had two children, Ernie, a boy my brother's age, and Lydia, a girl my age, but because the driveway to their house opened onto Ashland Avenue, they went to Ashland Grammar School, rather than the San Lorenzo school my brothers and I attended. It was from their mother I learned the few Portuguese phrases I knew: *Vai p'ra casa*, foremost among them.

She was beholden to my Grandfather Smith (of the Pico Smiths, for, despite his name, both of his parents had been born on that tiny island) for her husband's inadequate salary; she was even beholden to him for the rickety old house they lived in, with indoor plumbing but nothing resembling central heating, not even a fireplace, but she was damned if she was going to be beholden to any of the Smith princelings for anything, and though few women in San Lorenzo were strong enough to resist my efforts to charm them, Mary Freitas was certainly one of them. She refused to be seduced by my best efforts and was always shooing me on my way.

The Freitases also raised chickens, which they let run free in the daytime, which proved a temptation Pug was unable to resist, and after he killed the third Freitas chicken, Pug, my father decided, had to go, and he disappeared as mysteriously and as suddenly as he had appeared, with no great sadness on the part of any of us.

My Grandfather Silva raised rabbits for my grandmother's famous recipe of marinated rabbit stew. It was my favorite of all her dishes—at

213

least until I discovered what had to be done before the rabbit reached my plate. Unlike chickens, rabbits, with their startled ears, like exclamation points, their furry coats and pink eyes, were things of beauty, yet my grandfather, otherwise the gentlest of men, would take one out of its hutch, holding it by the ears, and within thirty seconds turn this lovely breathing creature into a piece of raw meat, with a swift chop of the side of his hand to the back of the rabbit's neck, followed by an even swifter slit with a sharp knife, like pulling down a zipper, and the fur coat was peeled off as easily as a winter mitten. I was both fascinated and repelled and invariably squealed, to my grandfather's initial delight. What made this staunch, unsentimental brutality even more inexplicable to me was that my grandfather knew what it was like to love an animal, for he had a Chesapeake Bay retriever he was devoted to. Like his master, Skipper was large and gentle and I rode him like a pony when I was very young.

After my third squeal, every bit as horror-stricken as the first, my grandfather ceased to be amused and decided I needed a lesson in the facts of animal life. So he took me, aged eight, to what was to be my most memorable and shocking view of death until his own death a year later: the annual slaughter of the Mouras's hog.

My two grandfathers could not have been more unlike each other. Most people paid my Grandfather Smith, at the very least, a grudging respect, as power and wealth are universally respected; a few people feared him, since work of any kind was hard to come by and he had the power to hire and to fire; and more than a few hated him for the way he sometimes exercised that power, with a brutality that was almost sadistic. Certainly no one outside of his immediate family loved him.

My Grandfather Silva, on the other hand, was almost universally loved, by virtually everyone in town (with the notable exception of my Grandfather Smith). One of the sources of his popularity was that he never recognized anything that could be called social distinctions. He spoke to the lowliest farmhand as he would speak to a bank manager or a doctor, with neither condescension nor arrogance. When his drayage business flourished, he spent the money—on fine cars, large parties, and jewels for my grandmother—and he expected everyone else to share in his happiness. Which they usually did, so ingenuous was his joy in his good fortune. Then when his business failed, as it did after the San Francisco Waterfront Strike of 1934, he sacrificed his own well-being to keep his drivers on the payroll as long as he could. The extent of the affection he had earned, even by the men he had eventually to let go, was best demonstrated by the size of his funeral two years after the strike that broke him, when he died from a ruptured appendix at the age of fifty-six. It was the largest funeral the town had ever seen. Every seat of St. John the Baptist was filled and both outside aisles were lined with standing men in their Sunday-best black suits, holding crushed hats in their calloused hands, their Old World faces as grim and careworn as their suits.

That the Mouras raised pigs was inescapably obvious to us whenever the wind blew from the east, as it often did in the autumn, but until my grandfather had me accompany him at a time when he was looking for every and any diversion life offered him, I had never been inside their yard. They were a large family who lived behind a long driveway off Ashland Avenue. There was a daughter younger than I was and one that was already married. Just how many others there were in between I was never sure of, though there were at least two sons, one, Melvin, close to my age, whom I occasionally met at Saturday catechism class. But until my grandfather took me, I would never have presumed to enter their yard.

Nor did we take the usual route to their place. Since the back of the Moura property joined the back of my grandfather's land, we simply walked through the fields and entered the Moura farm through the back door, as it were, where the sty was kept. It seemed that half the Portuguese community of St. John's parish was already there, women as well as men, so that the afternoon had the air of a fiesta about it. Around the sty itself, there were only men, three of whom, younger and stronger than most of the others, were wrestling with the largest hog I'd ever seen, easily three or four times my weight. The animal protested vociferously with a mix of squeals and grunts as he struggled valiantly against the odds. Despite the overwhelming stench, you could not have dragged me away from the spectacle as the hog's back feet were tied and the animal eventually hoisted with pulley and tackle out of the sty and onto a large tripod and left to hang there, head down.

Before the slaughter began, the hog had first to be hosed off and scrubbed with a rough long-handled brush, for the animal in its terror had fouled itself. Once it was clean and its skin shone pink, disconcertingly like human skin, a large galvanized pan two feet in diameter, was placed under its head and Mr. Moura himself, acting every bit like a high priest at some sacrificial offering, slit its throat. There was one horrendous cry, a shriek rather than a grunt, a sound that might have come from almost any large animal, including a man, in similar circumstances. But its agony was brief, fortunately, for the blood gushed from the slit throat, rapidly at first, then slowed, finally, to a mere dribble. Every last drop was caught and saved, to be made into *morcela*, a blood sausage, what the English call black pudding, a dish my father relished, but I, convinced that eating blood was fit only for cannibals and other such wild creatures, could never be tempted to taste.

The butchering began with a disembowelment and the women for the first time became involved, picking and choosing with their bare hands from the massive gooey mess all the bits worth saving, particularly long sections of intestines to be cleaned and used to make their sausages. What fascinated me most that afternoon was to watch the women making *linguiça*, a sausage I did love, stuffing the cleaned intestines with bits of meat and chopped fat and spices. It was a jolly communal effort (the hog's final shriek long since forgotten), with the women chattering away, mostly in Portuguese, about everyone and everything. And though I could not follow their conversation, I was sure from the salacious voices and their often bawdy laughs that not a single peccadillo, committed by the least of the town's citizens escaped a thorough analysis and their judgments were passed without mercy. They accepted (maybe "tolerated" would be a more precise word) my presence as the grandson of my paternal grandfather, and graciously, for the afternoon, at least, overlooked my Smith blood. Even Mary Freitas was for once sociable, explaining each of the ingredients being stuffed into the foot-long length of sausage as if she herself had invented the ancient recipe they were following.

Nothing was wasted. The hams and slabs of bacon were hung in the smokehouse; the feet and knuckles were saved for pickling. And since there were no freezers at the time, most of those involved being dependent upon iceboxes, rather than refrigerators, which were pretty much still reserved for the rich, what could not be smoked or pickled had to be eaten soon, so that fair amounts of the meat were divided among those participating in the ritual, and sure to be returned when the time came for *their* pigs to be slaughtered.

Of all my childhood experiences it is the one that most made me

feel as though I too belonged to an Old World Portuguese community, stretching back to a time long before the dreary Depression of the
thirties had settled over San Lorenzo and the entire country like a dark
cloud; that I was here taking part in joyful, sunny rituals that had the
sanction of centuries; and without that shared past I would have been
a lesser person.

217

It's the women who capture the imagination. For the men, the long and dangerous voyage around the Horn was their door to a New World waiting to be conquered and claimed. My great-grandfather Silva was fifteen when he made that crossing, little more than a boy, and whether the deciding factor to emigrate came from the cruel exigencies of life on his island home, the poverty, the starvation, the lack of employment prospects, or simply the lure of adventure, the choice was still his to make and the long journey, even at its most tempestuous, was, once the terrible fact was over, merely the first test of his manhood. For his second wife, as for most women at the time, it was something else entirely and with nothing of the heroic about it.

Though my step-great-grandmother is not strictly speaking one of my ancestors, since no blood of hers runs in my veins, it is the drama inherent in her story that has for decades most fascinated me. The men came first, to acquire land and to cultivate it. Only later, once they had established themselves, did they feel the need for wives to people their new kingdoms, modest though they might sometimes be. There were for these early settlers few local women of their own culture and religion to choose from; but there were some and my great-grandfather was one of the lucky few to woo and marry a real woman, American born and bred, rather than the figment of some clever broker's imagination whose stock in trade is a seemingly endless supply of marriageable virgins from the Islands.

My great-grandfather's luck was great, but not enduring. His wife was handsome and literate in two languages; but she had also in her upbringing acquired certain notions of independence alien to her new husband.

She did not willing submit, as most of the Old World brides did, to becoming simply the household's chief cook and breeding mill. When at the age of twenty-three, already encumbered with three children under the age of four, two daughters and a son, my own grandfather among them, she found herself once again carrying another child, she decided to take desperate measures to rid herself of this unwanted burden—and she paid dearly for her drastic declaration of independence. Still a young man, my great-grandfather was left a widower with three small children to raise as best he might. And raise them he somehow did.

Not until his first family reached adulthood did he feel himself entitled to a second wife and this time he had no choice but to resort to the waterfront marriage brokers. He must from the first have known the risks involved, for they had to be general knowledge to even the most gullible of recent immigrants. To exaggerate the virtues of whatever product is on offer has always been a prime rule of salesmanship, and no exception when marriage is the commodity under consideration. The crux lay in the extent of the exaggeration. And what my great-grandfather had bargained for was clearly so different from what he actually got that it set in motion a family drama that would dominate the rest of his life. Though it was a family drama too common to dignify with the word tragedy, it must, for the woman involved, have produced its share of shame and suffering.

"For the woman involved." That phrase too is a measure of the shame inflicted upon her. I never knew her name and was, apparently, never curious enough to ask. She had to be, like my own grandmother, Mrs. Thomas Silva, because she was married to my great-grandfather, but she always seemed to me more like a serving woman than a wife. I was never formerly introduced to her, never touched by her and certainly never, on any of my rare visits, greeted with a kiss. I was sometimes taken to my great-grandfather's Decoto ranch in the company of my grandfather or father. It was in the early thirties a simple, run-down wooden farmhouse with sash windows and shingled dormers and scarcely a flake of its original paint left on the bare boards. With its nearby windmill-topped tank house, it was like any other less than prosperous farmhouse seen up and down the length of California. There was no garden, at least nothing resembling a flower garden. There was in the backyard a skimpy patch of greenery that passed for a kitchen garden, a wild growth of mint burgeoning near a dripping faucet, and a few, sad rows of kale. Otherwise the place was all dust and dry grass, with a wire-enclosed pen for chickens, and a sad, dilapidated automobile of some unknown make.

She always came to the door when she heard a car enter the premises, but she never in my presence moved beyond the doorway itself. Nor did anyone, either my grandfather or my great-grandfather, ever explain to me who the sad woman in the doorway was. My grandfather may have nodded to her, but never greeted her in any way more affectionate. I knew she was the mother of my great-grandfather's nine subsequent children, all those great uncles and aunts who seemed far closer to my father's generation than to my grandfather's. I knew the names of only the two youngest, George and Dudley, the last scarcely a decade older than I, because they sometimes acted as my grandfather's hired hands.

Although they might have been treated with more deference than the other workers, they were certainly never treated as my grandfather's brothers and invited into the house. Never were any of them included in family feasts such as Christmas or Thanksgiving, though they were faithful attendants at all family funerals, and the last time I ever saw or heard of any of them was at my parents' fiftieth wedding anniversary, when I was introduced to two women—spinsters, I assumed—who were my father's aunts and seemed to revere him as if he were royalty, though he himself had difficulty recalling *their* names.

It was only later, long after it was too late to do anything about it, that I began to dwell upon the plight of this woman married to my great-grandfather as she must once have been on that long, long passage around the Horn, coming to *her* New World. A small, almost tiny young woman, awkward, with coarse hands, placid sheep eyes and heavy brows, she must have lain for months on the miserable bunk of that tossing ship, all the time knowing full well that she did not even come close to resembling the woman her future husband had bargained for, that she was merely the pawn in a timeworn confidence trick. More than anything she must have feared that she would be rejected at first sight and returned unwed to a solitary life of virtual slavery and endless shame. Because she could not articulate her fears made them no less real. She knew little more than the name and age, a generation older than herself, of the man who was to become her husband—a word at the time, for her, at least, hardly distinguishable from that of master—and that her future marriage would more than likely, at best, be a kind of indentured slavery.

And my great-grandfather—how did he greet his prospective bride? When they met for that first time on the docks of San Francisco, there were undoubtedly such centuries of peasantry engrained in her mute placidity, he had to know instantly that all his pretensions to gentility must now be forever forfeited. With the help of his dead wife's family, his first three children had all completed the twelfth grade, had all three then married well, and he now, the *paterfamilias*, stuck with this woman, scarcely older than his daughters, but so transparently an illiterate peasant, almost more brute than woman, would forever bar him from that other world, the world of his first well-born family. And he did what most men of the time would have done, retreated ever deeper into a fierce, defensive pride as a shield against his recent degradation. Being poor, he had no choice but to keep her, and for form's sake, to go through a kind of marriage, blessed by both Church and State. He was a healthy, normal man with a healthy normal man's needs and nine children were to follow in regular sequence. But when he drove her and her burgeoning family to Sunday Mass at All Saints in Hayward, he, as a proper bourgeois, took his rightful place in the front pews, while his second family remained behind, where they too had their place, in the back pews. He spoke to his wife only in Portuguese and as far as possible kept his two families apart, as if the new one might somehow vitiate the great strides made by the first.

What the woman in the doorway made of all this in her innermost heart we can only surmise. Her traditional role had been set centuries before: A peasant woman's duty was first and foremost to obey her father and later her husband, and both without question. My great-grandfather was a proud and severe man, but he was not a monster. One cannot make love to the same person for decades without occasionally allowing a moment of tenderness to slip by, and she herself must at the very least have found comfort in the children who were hers as well as his, if not in the making of them, at least in the nursing of them. For they all gave evidence of fearing as well as respecting the martinet who was their father and of loving the illiterate woman who was their mother. And she did outlive him.

But we know no more about how she received the news of his death than how she received his first embrace. It was a widow's duty to mourn her husband and mourn him she did, if only for the sake of their children, but whether she mourned him with a secret relief at her liberation or with true grief we will never know. We have all heard about those who grow to love their chains, but whether or not she did, she needs a great novelist, a latter-day Flaubert, to tell her side of the story. And a fine story it might prove to be—though, sadly, no writer of the period would anymore have considered her worthy of his attention than the young boy I once was watching her stand in that bleak doorway.

223